To the readers who asked for more books in the Bad Boys Undercover series—this one's for you!

1

CARA LAYNE woke on a scream. The noise rumbled to life inside her chest but choked off as her eyes snapped open. Her muscles jerked. Without thinking, she grabbed for the inside stuffing of her narrow down sleeping bag, digging her fingernails deep into the slippery material. Bunching it in closed fists, she pulled the bag even tighter around her and tried to cocoon her body for protection. From what, she didn't know.

The weather had turned without warning. The wind built to a sick wail then faded, only to roar back to life again. It echoed around her like a child's cry as it whipped through the campsite. To block the screeching, she pulled the bag up and against her ears.

She could still see that black night surrounded the tent. The chilling cold signaled early morning, but nowhere near dawn. She tried to focus, to figure out what was happening.

Her tent mate shifted and kicked beside her. A zipper screeched. The material of his bag rustled and he said

something she couldn't quite hear over the crescendo of sounds muffled through her clogged ears. The ground shook and the air almost vibrated.

Nothing made sense. They'd ventured out on an overnight trip to collect samples. The usual work and not dangerous. They'd set down outside of avalanche and flood zones. This was the right season. The right place. Yet, dread hovered all around her. The sleepy haze dragging her down refused to lift. She tried to shake off the clouding in her brain and focus on the clicking sound. A steady tapping.

What the hell was that?

Then it hit her . . . her teeth. Chattering.

The tent shook as a new blast of air caught the canopy, the material flapping above her head. She pulled her body tighter into a ball. Fear rocketed through her as the nylon that promised to stay sturdy even during the most punishing high mountain expedition ripped around her.

The howling sound finally registered. Not weather. Not animal. Human.

She lifted her head only high enough to see a dark figure pulling at the material above her. At first she thought her tent mate held their failing shelter together with his bare hands . . . then the blade flashed. She screamed, but the sound disappeared into the cacophony of banging and shredding.

The pain came next. Blinding pressure drilled against

the sides of her head. She felt as if her skull had compressed. Had started to collapse and shatter. Stray thoughts bombarded her brain. Paranoia drowned out common sense as the top of her tent split open and more cold air poured inside.

She struggled to get to her knees then slipped and fell flat on her stomach again. Her skin flashed from cold to hot. Footsteps thundered around her. The crashing of equipment. Yelling. Still, her head pounded. Not with a headache or migraine. This pushing made her eyes ache as wave after wave of dizziness crashed over her.

Someone or something tugged hard at the seam of her sleeping bag. She grabbed, tried to hold on but her fingers slipped in the slick material. The tugging became dragging as the down slid over rocks and her hip thumped against the unforgiving ground.

She fought to force out a scream but no sound came. The bag trapped her, making it impossible to move more than a few inches. Vulnerability sent her racing headfirst into panic. Her teeth ground together as she struggled to move, to fight back, and despite the screaming in her head, a strange lethargy she couldn't kick weighed her muscles down. It hurt to lift her arm. Her thigh rolled up underneath her as she was dragged along, crushed against her stomach and stealing her breath.

She couldn't suffer through one more minute. Losing

the physical battle, she looked for mental escape and tucked her head as her mind floated away. Music filled her scattered thoughts. A familiar melody her father used to play. One she struggled to remember whenever she needed comfort. The humming swam through her mind, mixed with the pain.

She heard a crack and felt a hard *thwap* like a punch to the back of her head. Then the world around her blinked into a tunnel of darkness.

2

Two days later

REID ARMSTRONG knew the silence wouldn't last.

They'd been on the road for thirty-six straight hours with little sleep. Gone from town to town before hitting the open and now had been hiking for what felt like forever through brush and tramping over grass grown wild and tangling around his knees. Across fields and around protruding boulders.

Thirty minutes earlier they'd left the rocky trail and started free climbing, working their way toward Otorten Mountain with nothing but the march of their sturdy boots slamming against the ground now and then as background noise. Tree-lined hills and snow-capped mountains filled the distance. The scenery in this untamed and mostly unoccupied part of Russia

qualified as impressive. Not that Reid cared or even noticed. Not with the anxiety pounding through him.

The original plan for his mandatory vacation time from the office had been to grab his best friend, jump on motorcycles, and ride across the U.S. Refuse to answer their phones, and turn off the GPS that could track them down anywhere. Get away. Clear their heads. Leave work and death and danger behind for a few days.

All of those informal vacation ideas went sideways when Cara failed to check in. Hell, she refused to check in with him sixteen months ago and every day since, but she usually checked in with her brother. Not this time. Not on this expedition, which resulted in a call to Reid and an alternate trip here. No sleep as they headed to a region he had no interest in visiting.

Parker Scott swung his long knife in an arc, cutting a path through the mass of overgrown grass and weeds. He stopped and rubbed his arm over the hint of sweat on his forehead, seemingly unaffected by daytime temperatures that didn't even reach fifty degrees.

"Tell me one more time," he said. "What exactly are we doing here?"

"Hiking."

"Yeah, you already gave me that much." Parker exhaled in a sound clearly meant to telegraph a cut-the-shit message. "I mean in the Ural Mountains." He glanced around. "Basically, why am I not on a motorcycle right now?"

Looked like the time for talk finally had arrived. Reid was impressed Parker stayed quiet this long. That he went along with every change to their itinerary from the switch to a private plane to hiding in the back of a truck as it bumped over rough terrain and finally to crawling on their stomachs around a border checkpoint. Parker being Parker, he didn't complain about any of it.

As two of the U.S. members of the Alliance—a top secret, off-the-books joint task force made up of former CIA and MI6 officers—Reid and Parker hung out together, though neither man was inclined to talk or even think about their lethal pasts. They supported two different teams within the Alliance, but the shit show of cases they'd had over the last few months had thrown them together conducting surveillance and recon.

So did the stark reality of recently losing one of their own. A man who'd dedicated his life to serving in British intelligence in different capacities. On his final assignment, just weeks before, he'd been shot by a team member in an attempt to prevent a larger nightmare airport bombing. The speeches from the memorial service still rang in Reid's brain.

But death was still death, and this one touched every member of the Alliance in a profound way. Being the leader he was, Harlan Ross had bargained his own life, and they were all reeling from the sacrifice he'd made.

That was the reason for their mandatory time off. Those in charge insisted on a break while the group

reorganized. Everyone had to head out and grab some normal air, air not poisoned by danger for a change. Reid thought the idea sounded good in theory but in reality amounted to a load of bullshit. It was not as if the people they hunted ever took a break.

Still, being out on a mandatory good time allowed him to sneak away on a side trip and take Parker with him. Now they just had to make sure this exercise stayed danger-free. Not exactly their specialty.

Reid continued to scan the area, looking for the clearing he knew they should soon see. They were coming up on the coordinates. The ones that matched Cara's last-known location.

The closer they got, the more something interfered with the signal to his watch. The red dot indicating her location flickered in and out. That made him twitchy. He'd spent most of his time in the field depending on his instincts and his men rather than any so-called technical expertise for exactly this reason. Technology failed.

He squinted as the light bounced off something in the distance along the line of trees. Tried to keep the conversation mundane even as his mind constantly assessed and reassessed. "We have some time off. It was just as easy to catch a flight from DC to here as to head out West on the bikes."

Parker still hadn't moved. "You're saying you replaced Montana with Russia just because?"

Admittedly, that had been a big left turn from the motorcycle plans. A turn Parker hadn't questioned except to say "Huh?" as they caught a series of under-the-radar flights, made secret payments, and illegally purchased weapons.

Reid admired his friend's restraint, but now it appeared to have ended. "Sure."

Parker held up the older model Bizon, a lightweight submachine gun that had been modified and improved over the years. Not that they had one of the newer versions. "Don't be a dumbass."

"Meaning?"

"We're here without the required visas but with guns that may or may not work."

Suddenly Parker was a detail man. Reid didn't love that change. "Technicalities."

Parker frowned. "Are you familiar with the concept of 'international incident'?"

Since they likely stood within inches of causing one, Reid was all too clear on the potential problem. Not that he would let that slow down this extraction—or whatever it was—one bit. "It won't come to that."

"What about the part where we snuck into the country and could be convicted as spies if we're caught?"

Okay, that was probably enough talking about the details. Reid shrugged. "Then don't get caught."

Parker swore under his breath as he lowered his weapon to his side. "That's my general life plan, yeah."

Reid gestured for them to get moving again and was half stunned when Parker complied without argument. "Then we're good."

Parker snorted. "Define 'good' for me."

Reid shifted, tried to get a better view over the crest of the small hill in front of him. She should be right there. Her, her team. He hoped whatever messed with his signal also interfered with hers and she'd be standing there, pissed off and swearing at the sight of him. Right now he'd take a negative response. Hell, any response.

First, he had to clue Parker in so he understood the importance of this rescue. The guy had little ego, but Reid tried to appeal to it anyway. "It's an adventure. I thought you'd like the challenge."

"Why?"

Fair question, but Reid had an answer. "You appreciate the unknown. What with your whole Yeti, aliens, we're-not-alone thing."

He didn't understand that side of Parker. It all sounded like crazy bullshit to him, but Parker believed something roamed around out there with them. Might as well use that.

"Okay," Parker said as he stopped again. This time he turned and glared at Reid. "I'm not sure what you're trying to say here, but Yetis live in places like Nepal, not here."

Yeah, because that was his point. "And then there's the part where they're mythological."

"And for your information, out here we'd be talking about an Almas." Parker nodded. "Walk on two feet. Covered with reddish-brown hair."

"If you say so. I don't even know what that—they?—is, but do not tell me." Cutting the conversation off struck Reid as the easiest way to keep them mentally on track.

Parker was the youngest member of the Alliance and possibly the most lethal. No one knew why or how he got out of the Army early. But no one doubted his sniper abilities or dead-clear loyalty to the team. Reid recognized a fellow survivor when he saw one.

They started moving again. Less causal this time. More focused. Without issuing a warning, they both snapped to attention. They stepped with more care. Weapons came up, the obvious ones plus the knife Reid had slipped up under the wristband of his thin jacket.

Tension spun around them. Reid could feel it with every intake of breath.

"You actually believe humans are the only human-like creatures walking the earth?" Parker snorted again. "Come on."

For once Reid welcomed this familiar nonsense conversation. "Do you ever listen to yourself when you slip into conspiracy mode?"

"I try not to."

"That's probably smart." Reid instinctively crouched as they started up the hill. No need to make himself a bigger target than he already was.

"I get it. You're a skeptic. It's naïve, but whatever," Parker said as his voice dropped to a whisper. "So, we're clearly not tracking Yetis or anything else that might prove interesting. Care to tell me what we are hunting?"

Despite the angle of the climb and the provisions, though limited, they carried in their packs, they moved up the slope without making a sound. "Humans."

Parker glanced over, but only for a second before his attention returned to the open space in front of them. "That answer should probably scare me more than it does."

"Which is why I brought you along instead of one of the others. You don't spook easily." Parker didn't shake. Reid liked that about him.

"You brought me because we live in apartments next to each other and you were afraid I'd just follow you when you left unannounced."

That part Reid didn't love. Parker skulked around. Could conduct surveillance and list every activity, down to the number of steps a target took to get to the bathroom, all without the target ever knowing he'd been watched. Reid knew because Parker had practiced more than once on him.

"You're a creepy little fucker sometimes." But effective. Reid had to admit that.

"Not the first time that's been said." Parker held up a fist. Whatever grabbed his attention had him spinning to the right and scanning the horizon. After a few

seconds of stillness, he nodded and they began moving again. "So, narrow it down for me. Which humans?"

As they got closer to the crest of the hill, they lowered their bodies even closer to the hard ground. When Reid dropped to his stomach, crawling along using his knees and elbows to move forward, Parker followed.

Reid's gaze whipped around behind him, seeing nothing but a grassy field with jagged rocks piled here and sticking up out of the ground there. "A science expedition."

Parker frowned but kept crawling. "Interesting, but I need more information."

Not that Reid wanted to dump a lot of intel right now. He didn't really have much to provide, since the expedition appeared to be on some sort of security lockdown. He only knew as much as he did because of some unauthorized data searches. The kind he knew he'd be called in to explain later.

But now he had a bigger problem. "It's gone missing."

"The expedition?"

"Yeah." But Reid only cared about her. He'd worry about the rest of Cara's team later, after he made sure she was safe.

"I thought we were supposed to be taking time off. Forced fun and happy times and all that." Parker shimmied to the top of the hill. He put his gun aside only long enough to reach for his binoculars.

"Such bureaucratic bullshit. As if losing one of our

own makes us want to take naps." The mix of fury and loss had the opposite effect on Reid. "I'd rather shoot things."

"And that's why I like you." Parker's head moved from side to side as he scanned the area. "Now, about these scientists."

The area in front of them remained dead quiet. Just more grass and rocks. Except for a flash of color off to the right side closest to the wall of trees, and a piece of something . . . material, maybe, blowing across the field every time the wind kicked up a bit.

"Stop." Reid grabbed the binoculars and took a long look at the area. Debris, and a lot of it. Some blended into with the deep colors of the land. Blue, but he also picked up on something orange and pointed it out to Parker. "What's that?"

"You mean what *was* it." Parker squinted. "No clue."

"Let's go in." Reid was already up in a squat and balancing his weight on the balls of his feet. "Keep your guard up until we know what we're dealing with."

"Roger."

Anxiety ratcheted up inside Reid but he fought it off and moved. His heartbeat pounded in his ears as he jogged down the hill to the small valley below. An impressive mountain, complete with jutting sharp rocks and an unwelcoming gray façade, loomed at the far end of the valley. Towering trees closed off the ready access to one side.

The place felt shut in. Deadly. Reid breathed in the stench of death, knowing it was his imagination but also knowing that something horrific happened right where they now stood.

The thought of Cara out here, alone or with a group. Subject to the whims of weather and whoever might hunt through here. For a second, blood-soaked visions bombarded his brain. He had to push it all away. Concentrate. She needed him now.

His jog broke into a run. Within minutes he shot down from the slope and raced to the spot where he'd seen the color. Depending on Parker to cover him, Reid stepped closer. So much damage. Notebook pages scattered over the grass. Down material shredded. The remnants of two tents, both ripped open and dragged out of shape with strips of tarp flapping in the slight wind.

Taking turns on watch, Parker studied one of the collapsed tents. Checked the poles and poked his gun at it as he lifted the remaining material and looked inside. "What the fuck happened here?"

"The tents." Reid spun in a circle, trying to take it all in. Looking for any signs of humans, and hoping like hell he didn't see any in pieces. "Clothes. Equipment."

"From the inside."

Reid froze. "What?"

"The tents look as if they're cut from the inside." Parker held the edges. Took photos.

Reid had no idea how Parker could make that assess-

ment so fast, but he didn't doubt it. Parker didn't guess or exaggerate when it came to judging real life danger. That was just not his style.

The reality of what that meant hit Reid hard enough to drive him to his knees. He put a hand out to stay steady. "None of this makes any sense. It feels like we've dropped into one of your conspiracy theories."

Reid kept talking, pushing out the words. The nonsense chatter kept his mind clear. Gave him room to think as he fought off the pooling dread that something awful had happened to Cara. That he'd gotten there too late.

"Not to make things worse, but some spooky shit has gone down in this area. Not right here, but same general area. A whole group of hikers in 1959—boom!—dead."

"You're an encyclopedia now?" Reid asked. For some reason, arguing with Parker eased some of the pressure building inside of him. This he could handle.

"The Dyatlov Pass incident." Parker dropped on his haunches, closer to the ground, and took more photos. This time of the food, some of which looked frozen. "It's famous."

Reid checked his watch, looking for the telltale red dot that should point out Cara's location. The malfunctioning blinking had stopped. Now he didn't get anything. Either something cut off the signal or . . . He shook away the rest of the thought. Once his mind

clicked off and the emotion turned on full force, he'd be useless to her.

"Maybe the Yetis did it." Right now he'd kill to see a Yeti just walking along with Cara.

"The hikers were found dead," Parker said. "Tents ripped from the inside." He stood up again. "Have you ever read a book?"

"This all happened more than fifty years ago. You don't have any conspiracy crap that's more recent than that? Something even a little relevant, maybe." Like who would want to harm a privately funded science expedition. That's what Reid didn't understand.

"There are rumors about labor camps hidden up here. Government experiments." When Reid started to interrupt, Parker talked over him. "Then there's the mountain folk. Lights in the sky. Sound vortexes that drive people insane. You name it and the Ural Mountains have a legend about it."

"Don't make me sorry I brought you." Reid walked around, mentally cataloging every stone and every leaf as Parker captured the scene in photographs.

"I can outshoot you but I do wish I could outrun you." Parker broke the usual protocol of securing the scene and glared at Reid. "Just spill it. Is this an actual assignment or not?"

"It's personal and . . ." His words trailed off as his eyes focused on the figure breaking through the mass of trees and heading right for them.

Parker must have picked up on the unexpected guest because he spun around and joined in the staring. They both watched as she got closer, stumbling and off balance, before stopping about ten feet away.

"One more step and I'll blow your balls off." Cara stood there, voice and hands shaking as the barrel of the gun bobbed around.

Relief smacked into Reid so hard that the breath whooshed out of him. He fought the urge to double over and rest his palms against his knees. He opted for putting his gun away instead, surprised when his hand trembled. "Thank God."

Parker scoffed. "That's your response to what she just said?"

"She's bleeding." The words kept repeating in Reid's head before he finally said them out loud. Then he really looked at her. Her dark hair hung half in and half out of a ponytail band. She wore hiking boots but her utility pants had a long gash down the thigh. Ripped clothes. A bloody shirt. No jacket. Shaking hard enough to make her body sway.

Parker took a step toward her then stopped when she aimed the gun directly at him. "She looks like shit."

Reid's gaze toured her body, looking for obvious injuries. A hefty case of shock seemed to be right on the verge of kicking her ass. Not good. He needed her calm. Had to get her warm.

With careful steps, slow and as nonthreatening as possible, he moved in closer. "Cara, it's me."

She nodded and kept nodding. "I know."

"Wait, you two are friends or something?" Parker asked.

"The threat still stands, Reid. I don't trust anyone, including you." She tightened her grip. "Do not move."

"I like her so far." Without any obvious footsteps, Parker had moved. Shifted his body until he drew almost even with her side. "Except for the part where she looks ready to pass out. Guns and fainting don't mix."

Reid agreed but didn't let his concern for her show. "She knows how to handle a weapon."

She glared at Parker. "And I've never fainted in my life."

Anger. Reid took that as a good sign.

"Do you have a mirror?" Parker asked, drawing her attention back to him. "You look like you've been ripped apart by mountain lions."

She frowned, as if sizing him up. "Weapons down and stop shuffling around."

"That is never going to happen, sunshine."

Her eyebrow lifted as her body seemed to steady. "Sunshine?"

Parker shrugged. "I thought I'd try flattery."

Just enough talk. Reid moved in. One lunge and he'd have her gun. He didn't want to rattle her or push her

any closer to the edge. Didn't want to get shot either. "Cara, look at me. I need you to lower that weapon."

"I can't." She shook her head as her words came out in a new wave of panic heavy breaths.

"We're here to help."

Her eyes turned a little glassy, as if she had trouble focusing. "Someone called in the Alliance?"

"She knows about the Alliance?" Parker asked, sounding stunned at the idea. "Clearly I'm the only one who doesn't know what's going on right now."

Reid ignored his friend. Blocked out the cool air and the danger involved in standing out there, exposed. Kept all of his attention on Cara.

"I came for you." And that was not a lie. He would cross oceans without blinking if it meant keeping her safe. Their rough past didn't change that.

She frowned. "How did you know where to find me . . . or to come now?"

"You're in danger." Reid thought the gnarled tent should make that obvious, but she clearly was not in a stable mental place to be able to reason things out for herself. "Cara, you have five seconds or . . ."

"Or what?"

"She asks a good question, man. What kind of threat do you intend to make next?" Parker whistled as he made one last move. He stood next to her with a hand close to her arm.

Reid waited for Parker's slight nod. When it came,

Reid knew they were ready. Both in position. They could disarm her without incident then get her help . . . and seek a few much-needed answers. But he needed to draw her attention first. "What the hell happened here?"

"They're dead." The desperate words sounded as if they'd been ripped out of her.

He forced his instincts back. Did not rush in or give in to the tension pumping through him. "Who, Cara?"

"My whole team."

That didn't really clear anything up for him or stop the tension shooting through him. "How did—"

"Reid." The hand with the gun dropped to her side and she rushed forward, closing the short distance between them. Her free hand came up and fingernails dug into the sleeve of his thin jacket as her gaze searched his. "We need to hide."

"I think she's tipped over." Parker slipped the gun out of her hand and checked it before tucking it away behind his back.

A wave of relief crashed over Reid, followed by an even bigger one of dread. "Let's calm down for a second."

She held on to him. Both hands now. Her fingers tightening around his biceps as her eyes and voice begged for help. "We have to go."

Reid agreed she needed to get out of there and relax. "Why?"

"They'll be back."

He glanced at Parker, who just shook his head and asked, "Who is 'they'?"

"They're coming—" Her words cut off as she dragged in deep breaths. "This time they'll kill me, too."

3

CARA COULDN'T catch her breath. Couldn't think. And there was no way she could deal with Reid. Not now. Maybe not ever, but certainly not while her head spun and the thoughts in her brain kept scrambling.

But there he stood, towering over her at six feet. His short hair straddling the edge between brown and blond. Muscles so defined she could almost see them through his thin jacket. Those protector instincts clicking into place as he morphed into this larger than life persona.

His edge remained. The wariness in those bright blue eyes. He held his body stiff, almost as if waiting for the next blow to come. None of that had changed in the months since she'd seen him. Little had. He looked even more fit, more toned, if that were even possible.

Just seeing him had her stupid heart flipping over. Through all the confusion and fear, his sturdy demeanor broke through and comforted her. Her insides

stopped jumping around and her whole body seemed to steady. Slowly, but she could feel the change.

Being with him had been a wild ride that left her reeling sixteen months ago. Standing in front of him now both knocked her off kilter and calmed her. It had always been that way with him. In every conceivable way he'd been wrong for her . . . and still so right.

She focused on his face and that intense stare that seemed to burn through her. Holding on to him, the world stopped its violent spinning. She inhaled, tried to settle what was left of her frayed nerves.

The last three days had been a nightmare. She'd been dragged and thrown around. Passed out. Even now she could only remember snippets. Fragments of the information she needed to piece together to find her team.

She forced her grip on Reid's arms to ease. A small shake continued to move through her. When she turned her palms over she noticed the blood.

Reid's gaze followed hers. "Let's get you washed up."

"You're not worried someone might attack us?" Time blurred on her but even now she looked around, unable to move and just waiting for the next attack.

"No."

Always so clear and sure of his capabilities. On another man the self-assurance would come off as cocky. On him—how he took every new problem in stride and handled it without any fanfare or need to shout about his abilities—the confidence worked. Made her feel

more at ease. "They came out of nowhere. I didn't see who or what."

"Understood." Reid nodded to the other man, apparently sending him some secret signal that had him taking off his pack before turning back to her. "We'll talk about all that later. Right now, we're going to make sure you're okay. And if anyone tries to strike while my back is turned, Parker will shoot 'em."

Parker nodded. "Damn straight."

She filed the name away and concentrated on the way Reid held her. Moving slowly and being more gentle than she remembered possible, he cradled her hands in his. The reassuring touch nearly broke her. Her mind shot back in time. The feel of those palms running over her skin. The hours she spent studying each scar and every callus.

She couldn't do this.

She stepped back and dropped her hands from his. "It's not mine. Cliff . . . he should be here."

Reid frowned at his friend then at her. "What?"

"The blood." The word stuck in her throat, but she punched it out.

The memories flipped around on her. The red, so much of it, pooling on the tent and running into the grass. The smears on the piece of tent she'd been wrapped up in when she woke up from the night of horror she couldn't quite remember.

Some parts floated back to her. She'd tried to rub

the blood off, in the grass and on her pants. The voice in her head that kept screaming to get it off. The haze, the stumbling and crawling. The useless search for her team. For any sign of life.

"It's not yours. I get it." Reid continued to study her. Those intelligent eyes roamed over her. Not in a sexual way. More of a I-need-to-knock-her-out-to-calm-her-down type of way.

Just the thought of that had her inhaling deeply as she struggled to bring her nerves and her brain and every other part of her back under control. "I'll be fine."

"Here you go." Parker handed her a towel.

"Thanks." She had no idea what pocket he pulled it out of. "You are? I caught the first name, but—"

"Parker Scott."

She nodded as she rubbed her hands. Raked the rough cloth over her skin again and again. Knotted it then unknotted it. "Part of the Alliance, I'm assuming."

"About that . . ." After a few seconds Parker grabbed onto the corner of the rag and pulled it out of her hands. "How do you know about the Alliance? We're not exactly in the phone book."

"No kidding." Not knowing what to do with her hands now and trying to ignore the burning sensation from rubbing them raw, she stuck them in her pants pockets.

Parker's eyebrow lifted. "So . . . ?"

She glanced at Reid, but he hadn't said a word. Just

stood there, watching and taking it all in. She might not remember what happened a few days ago right here at the campsite, but she did remember the way Reid stared. How he sized up every situation, work or personal. That last part had been an issue between them.

"I've seen you all in action." She waved her hand in Parker's general direction. "Well, not you, but the rest. Some of you."

Parker blinked at her a few times. "How exactly?"

That situation, being held hostage and the standoff, she didn't want to think about any of it. She could only handle one disaster at a time. At some point in the future she'd need to sit down and figure out how she kept walking straight into danger, but not today. Not while this one was still in motion.

After a few beats of silence, Reid jumped in. "She was involved in my first case with the team. You hadn't joined the Alliance yet."

"Wait a second." Parker held up a hand as he continued to stare at her. "This is the second time in like a year and a half that you've been in this kind of danger?"

Something about the stunned sound of his voice snapped her to attention. The rest of the haze clouding her brain cleared as anger settled in. "Are you trying to suggest that says something about me?"

Parker took a step back. "Nope."

"That's probably enough talk about the past for now." Reid picked up the other man's abandoned backpack

and handed it to him. "For the record, Parker tends to speak his mind, regardless of how scary or stupid his thoughts are."

Parker snorted. "Thanks, man."

"But you are part of the Alliance." For some reason she needed to be sure. One team member increased their safety. Two might make her nerves stop pinging and the constant need to double over and throw up subside.

"Yes," Parker said.

With that answered, her mind flipped to a new thought. She looked at Reid. "And I'm your assignment again?"

"Good question," Parker mumbled under his breath.

Reid took his time. Took off his pack and dug around inside. Handed her a jacket and glared at her until she took it from him and put it on.

Once she snuggled into the oversized sleeves and wrapped the extra material around her, she eyed him up. "Happy? If so, answer. I'm not going to forget what I asked."

Reid exhaled. "Your brother sent me."

She closed her eyes for just a second and let the news wash over her. "I should have figured."

It made so much sense. Of course, big brother Caleb. He had the resources. He could hack into any system and dig around for information without leaving a virtual footprint. She had no idea how and didn't want to

know the particulars, but none of this amounted to a surprise.

"Uh, who exactly is your brother?" Parker asked.

Reid talked right over him. "We don't have time for this now."

Parker cleared his throat. "We're going to make some time."

The back and forth made Cara's head spin again. She tried to focus on Reid as she pointed at Parker. "Which one of you is in charge?"

Reid nodded. "Me."

"Definitely me," Parker said at the same time.

Her hair picked that moment to lose the battle with the wind. She felt the last strands slip out of her ponytail holder and fall around her shoulders. She thought about running her fingers through it, trying to untangle the knots, and didn't even bother. Not when she had bigger issues plaguing her. "How did you know where to find me? No one is supposed to know our exact location."

Reid reached into his pack again. This time he brought out a satphone. "Not important."

But it was. Something about the way he ducked the question when he usually ran at them head on. He kept moving around, and not just conducting his normal surveillance. No, this was different. She likely wouldn't have noticed if they didn't have a history. But now, as the panic started to subside, she picked up on other things.

"I get that my brother tracked you down when our communications went down and I stopped checking in twice a day, but how did you—" Then it hit her. Anger stormed through her. Red hot fire burned from her feet to her head. "Reid Thomas Armstrong."

"Wow." Parker's eyes widened and he whistled. "That is a spectacular pissed-off female tone."

"The use of my full name is bad." Reid's voice dropped even lower. "Trust me. Even though it's not my real name, it's still bad."

She took a step forward until she stood right in front of him, just inches away. She poked a finger into that impressive chest. "You still track me?"

Parker's frown deepened. "Wait, what does that mean?"

"Okay, hold on a second." Reid's hands came up along with the soothing tone. "Calm down."

He had once admitted to her that it was a practiced law enforcement move. The lilt to his voice and comforting words. The whole thing where he settled down people who had lost the ability to function or think rationally. Brought them back from the edge. How he remained straightforward and logical, even repeated phrases and carefully picked his words.

Well, she wasn't in the mood to be soothed. Not about this. "Say that again and I will fire that gun right at your—"

"I don't always use the tracker," Reid said as his hands moved in front of him. "This was an emergency."

Parker looked from Reid to Cara and back again. "What tracker? What are we even talking about?"

"The one he implanted. In me." She jabbed Reid's chest one more time, half furious she hadn't removed the thing and half grateful for the failure.

Parker's mouth dropped open. "What the fuck?"

She was starting to like this Parker guy. "Yeah, that was my reaction when I found out."

"Let's go back for a second." Parker let out a sound halfway between an exhale and a harsh laugh. "How do you two know each other?"

"We used to date," she said. That didn't cover it, but she thought the explanation came close enough.

Reid glared at her. "We were engaged."

"Barely." And that was another subject she absolutely did not want to discuss. The quick proposal, the doubts, how it all fell apart. Memories of Reid had become a flashing warning sign in her brain. A testament to how not to get involved with a guy.

Forget that she'd loved him. That she still thought about him and fought off regrets. That doubts about leaving him pummeled her every hour at first, and still on a daily basis. The nagging sensation that she'd given up too soon and out of fear.

Yeah, forget all that.

"The length doesn't matter," he grumbled.

She almost laughed. "Typical guy response."

Parker nodded. "She's got you there."

"I figured out we made a mistake and left." Talk about a shortcut. She bypassed all the confusion and heartache and the very real sense that she'd waded into waters well over her head the second Reid jumped through that window and covered her body as the bullets flew all those months ago.

Reid's jaw clamped shut. "We've gotten off track."

Not as far as she was concerned, because the point was not about their relationship. It was about his controlling behavior . . . which kind of was about their relationship. "I broke up with him," she said to Parker, "but not before he implanted a tracker under the skin on my shoulder while I was out due to a knife wound."

Parker winced as he turned to Reid. "Do you do that with all the women you propose to?"

The thought of him . . . of being one in a line . . . She pushed the idea away and concentrated on the anger welling inside her. For the first time in days she felt like herself again. Not just like a zombie wandering around, waiting to drop from exhaustion or be carted away. "Good question."

"There was an ongoing kidnapping threat back then." Reid offered the comment as if it explained everything.

"How long ago?" Parker asked as he took the satphone from Reid.

"I dumped him sixteen months ago."

"Yeah, please keep saying it that way." Reid exhaled.

She shrugged. "It's true."

"Good thing I have a strong ego."

She didn't want to think about his ego or any other part of him. He possessed unbelievable skills with a gun, in the bedroom. Everywhere, really. He could even cook, when all she bothered to do was order takeout.

Focusing on her rage was the only way to get through this. "So, my brother told you he lost contact with me, and you turned on the tracker, or whatever you did to find me, and came out here."

Reid shrugged. "Sure."

No, that wasn't right. She sensed there was more to the story. Bad parts he wasn't telling. "You just happened to be in Russia?"

A huge grin spread across Parker's face. "Montana."

The answer didn't make any sense to her. "What?"

"We were supposed to ride to Montana. Luckily, we hadn't left DC yet."

She broke eye contact as she tried to process that bit of information. Papers blew around her feet. All harmless. The notebooks and laptops she'd collected contained the important information about the expedition. Unfortunately, most of the technology had been damaged and only the hidden notebooks survived *that* night.

"So, this isn't an Alliance assignment." Which meant they didn't have clearance. They didn't understand the import of what was happening out here or how a case

of missing scientists made more sense than they might think. She didn't wait for them to answer. "You have to leave. Now. Ten minutes ago, actually."

That didn't make sense, she knew, but there were protocols. In the event of an emergency, she needed to contact specific people, none of whom were Reid. But he could get the call out since she hadn't been able to raise anyone on either the satellite phone or radio back at the main camp. If he waited around until right before reinforcements came, she would not be upset about that.

Reid treated her to a second exhale. This one longer and more dramatic. "That's a ridiculous suggestion."

Parker made a face that suggested she wouldn't find a partner in him on this one. "It kind of is."

"You don't get it. This expedition is not . . ." Everything depended on her silence. Her team might need rescuing, but then again, silence might buy their freedom. She had no idea which choice to make.

She'd waited, in hiding, for the attackers to come back. For her to pick up some stray sentence that might explain what was going on and how much danger surrounded them. She'd tried to trek to their main installation that first day after waking up alone and terrified, but the buffeting winds and what she suspected was a head injury stopped her. This morning she'd made it there only to find the buildings cleared and abandoned . . . except for those hidden notebooks.

"Cara?" Reid skimmed his hand over her arm. "Finish the sentence."

"The expedition is not on the books. It is top secret and it's clearly gone sideways."

"Good thing we specialize in the not-supposed-to-be-happening type of situation." Parker walked a few steps away and started playing with the phone.

With Parker's attention drawn away from the silent surveillance he'd been conducting, Reid took over. He didn't say anything. Didn't even move. He just became more . . . aware. She couldn't explain it. But she sensed the exact moment when he flipped from intently listening to her to focusing on the area around them.

The strange covert tag team approach should have surprised her, but it didn't. From the second she saw them climb over the crest of the hill, she sensed they were in sync. Two men cut from the same mold. Parker, younger with darker hair and a bit less of a regimented feel to him. Reid, hot, lethal, and a constant diversion from everything she should be thinking and feeling.

Which brought her zapping back to reality. She wanted their expertise, but Reid could not do his usual rush-in-and-take-over job. "You can't be here. Hell, I'm not supposed to be here."

"And we're going to talk through all of that, but not right this second." Reid spun around and glanced at Parker. "Anything?"

Parker shook his head. "We seem to be in a dead zone, and I don't know why."

"I was having a problem with . . ." Reid glanced at her. ". . . other equipment earlier."

Parker kept fiddling with the phone. "That's not good news."

"Keep trying. We need to figure out if this is a normal technical blip or if something else is going on. Either way, we've got to get word to headquarters and arrange for an exfiltration for Cara and technical backup for us."

Ignoring the part where she was not leaving that way, with her research open to being stolen, Reid's orders qualified as the exact wrong way to handle this situation. The Alliance would swoop in and take over. Break her cover and possibly further endanger her missing team and the true reason for the expedition.

Maybe that was fine, and someone could tell her that, but until then she had to comply with the requirements given to her. But that didn't mean they couldn't help in another way. In a way that was much more important.

She took a step forward, putting her body between the men. "Instead of staying here or going to the main compound, you could investigate what happened to my team. That could be a violation of some oath I took, but at least you wouldn't be messing around with the research."

Being a good six inches taller, Reid looked right

over her head to Parker. "Good point. We'll need intel on the area and expedition parameters."

This side of Reid she remembered all too well. She grabbed his arm and yanked. Anything to get him to listen. "I'm standing right here, telling you there are limits on what you can see. Hunting for people, protecting them, is fine. I'm saying that has to be fine."

This time Reid spared her a quick glance. "You don't get to make assignments."

Air refused to fill her lungs. She tried to drag enough in, but her body wouldn't cooperate. Not when they stood this close. It had been that way from the start for her. "I'm not stupid. The idea of having a few guys with guns around here right now sounds pretty damn good."

A look of satisfaction crossed Reid's face. "Then we're agreed."

"Almost."

He eyed her up, ending the visual tour with a frown. "When you stumbled out here you were ten minutes away from going into shock."

"Not anymore." Determination and more than a touch of anger fueled her. The fuzziness that threw off her equilibrium slowly lifted.

But the details of that night refused to gel in her mind. She'd walked through every minute she could mentally grab and tried to connect it to anything. Remembered the wind and the tent. Cliff getting out his knife. Then the world went black and she awoke hours,

possibly a day, later. Somehow she'd survived the exposure to the cold. Animals. The attackers.

None of it made sense.

"She does look better," Parker said.

Reid shook his head. "I don't care."

That was it. The one commanding comment too far. "You are not in charge here, Reid."

"Oh, boy," Parker said as he mumbled something about her tone.

"And you are in charge?" Reid's voice had gone deadly soft while he looked at her. "Is that what you're trying to say? Because you look a mess, and last I checked this is not your area of expertise."

She had no idea what she was talking about, but she knew they needed to work all of this out before he called in the rest of his team with rocket launchers and missiles and whatever other weapons they had in their possession.

If she wasn't careful, something already awful could turn into an international nightmare. Escalate into an unsolvable political problem. "It's my expedition."

Reid opened his arms wide at his sides. "Then where is everyone? Why aren't the comms working? Why didn't you check in with Caleb?"

Smartass. "Those are points I need to figure out."

Parker held his thumb over a button on the phone. "You were attacked."

"Something like that." One of the many things she'd

lost during whatever happened was the expedition sat-phone. But she still knew how they worked, and she feared Parker was inching closer to making the call Reid wanted him to make.

Reid went back to studying her. Treating her like a target he needed to interrogate. "I don't understand that answer."

Parker nodded. "While you two work that out I'm going to keep trying to make that call to headquarters."

Each one was more stubborn than the other. She had no idea how to break through to them. "Listen to me. Seriously, we need to comply with my protocol on this."

Reid pulled her in closer. With his hands on her elbows and the heat of his body rolling into her, he stared down. "Say something that will explain why you're dancing around all of this, asking for help with some things but not others. Holding on to rules that don't matter right now."

He was right. There was no use playing games. She could put this in language he would understand. "The Russian government thinks this is a privately funded expedition. An investigation into the Dyatlov Pass incident for a documentary."

Reid groaned. "I had never heard about this so-called incident until a half hour ago, and now I've heard it twice."

"It's famous." At least she thought so.

"Told you." Parker dialed then tried again. "Like Yetis."

"Don't be ridiculous." She laughed, but when Parker didn't laugh with her, she sobered. "Wait . . . you know Yetis aren't real, right?"

"Parker believes in many things that will make your head implode," Reid said in a voice filled with amusement.

Parker scoffed. "Just because she's some fancy science type."

"You mean doctor." She put her hand in front of the phone and forced him to look up at her. She had full use of her mind and body now. She could probably kick if she had to. "A geologist."

"A doctor geologist." Parker nodded. "I guess I should have known."

These two had a habit of using a certain tone, sort of a know-it-all type thing. She knew she should chalk it up to their job choice and being at the center of all that danger, but it made her back teeth slam together.

That and he'd hit on a subject guaranteed to tick her off, depending on what he said next. "Meaning?"

Parker froze. "What did I do wrong?"

Reid actually smiled. "She's not a fan of the 'Asians are good at science and math' assumptions people make."

"I didn't know you were . . ." Parker's eyes opened wider.

And there it was. Her biggest pet peeve. Having a Chinese mom and a Caucasian dad sometimes left her in this nether world, one where neither side rushed to embrace her. Some of the older guys at work—the ones passed over for field assignments in favor of her—mumbled about her being a "token," and that was some of the nicer stuff she'd overheard.

"Don't I look it?" she asked, prepared for him to say the wrong thing.

Parker still hadn't moved. "I'm afraid to answer that."

She continued anyway. Might as well make all of this clear now. "No tiger mom. Neither parent is a scientist or math genius."

"I'm not sure what's going on." Looking hunted, Parker glanced over at Reid then back to her. "Look, I was saying I should have known you were a doctor because Reid said we were looking for a science expedition. Science, doctor . . . I made the leap of logic."

With that, her anger deflated. Ran right out of her. Sometimes her defenses rose before she could catch them. "That's fine, then."

"Now that we handled that." Reid nodded at the satphone. "Try explaining again. We need to get assigned to this case and move forward."

She inhaled nice and deep as she prepared to fight this verbal battle one more time without saying too much. "It's not that simple."

Reid held his gun as he looked around the valley. Then his gaze shot to the trees. "It never is."

She thought about what these men did for a living. How they traveled all over the world neutralizing threats and walking into danger when others ran out. "The expedition is here to investigate the unsolved incident."

The corner of Reid's mouth lifted. "But?"

"I'm investigating something else. Me and a few others on the team." She held up a hand. "And before you ask, I'm not going to spill every detail. But yes, why we're supposed to be here and why we actually are do not exactly match up."

Reid pointed at the ground and the broken flashlight by his foot. "You realize whatever you were really doing out here probably caused this."

"Smooth," Parker said over a fake cough.

"Yeah, Reid. I get that."

"And I get that you're trying to be professional and protect your work, but we're done. We're going to arrange for transport to get you debriefed and back to your brother." She tried to interrupt but Reid only talked louder. "Parker and I will secure this scene . . . stop shaking your head at me."

"I can't leave yet."

Reid stared at her but this time the harshness around his eyes softened a bit. "Your team. I get it. We'll find them."

"It's more than that." She couldn't even imagine where they were and what they were going through. If she let her mind go there, bile rushed up the back of her throat and her brain froze. "Yes, you need to find them and make sure they're safe, but there's also sensitive data I need to recover."

Reid frowned. "From?"

"Our facilities." Having a security crew get here probably violated some contract she'd signed before coming to Russia, but she never agreed to die for this job. She'd take the risk and apologize later.

Parker joined in the frowning. "What are you saying?"

"We have a site more than a mile from here. It's the main campground." She knew that was just the start. Once Reid started picking away at the details, she'd likely tell all. This undercover stuff clearly was not for her.

"Why are we just finding that out now?" Parker asked.

"We'll get to that later," Reid said. "Let's go." His jaw tightened and his voice dropped even deeper. "And do not fight me on this, Cara. This is what we do. We minimize damage, and we're going to try to do that here."

Right. They were experts and did this sort of thing as routinely as she collected soil and mineral samples. If there was ever a time to trust that expertise, it was

now. She couldn't win this battle anyway. He had the guns, the connections, and the muscle. And the idea of having a bodyguard sounded smart right now.

Before she could answer, Reid tried again. "I came to help, Cara."

"Which is why I'm letting you stay." How good he looked, how the steady thump of her heartbeat kicked up whenever he turned that intense gaze on her . . . those things made her think she should go. She'd never had much of a defense against him, and she needed to find one now. "Don't make me regret the decision."

"Trust me."

"You said that to me once before." And she'd paid a steep price for listening.

His gaze narrowed. "This time actually try doing it."

4

REID IGNORED the voice inside his head that said to rush her out of there, onto a plane and back to her brother. Anything to keep her safe and out of the middle of a mystery that could end with more missing bodies, or worse, a few dead ones.

First they had to retrieve whatever she found so damn important she was willing to risk being shot over it. He bit back a barking yell at her over but only because he understood the need to secure sensitive information at all costs. But that was his job, not hers. He didn't like the lines merging and blurring.

Since he'd never been great at outarguing her, he decided to focus on speed. With Parker's help they'd performed a quick search of the debris field, set a few triggers to tell if someone else came through after them, then took off. All that while trying to ignore the churning in his gut and the rolling tension that ran his blood cold at the thought of Cara being hurt or in danger again. He could tolerate a lot, but not that.

After the campsite was photographed from every angle and was as secure as they could make it in these conditions and with limited equipment, they headed off. Skimmed the line between the trees and the open land. The path left them less exposed as they stumbled over tree roots and rock piles.

Their boots crunched against the ground and fallen, scattered leaves. Now and then they'd see something from the campsite and Cara would bend down to grab it. He'd bundled her in his warmer jacket and now she filled the pockets with whatever she decided she had to keep.

Despite the sense that doom might come closing in, Reid tried to keep his walk at a steady pace. For him, it was almost like standing still, but he didn't want to shake Cara up any more than necessary by jogging the distance to the cabins, as she called them. She might have pulled back from the edge of shock, but he hadn't had time to check her for injuries, and wasn't fully convinced she'd escaped whatever happened with only bumps and bruises. One trip or overturned ankle could start her on a severe health decline.

Never mind that she'd regained her spunk, and sure had no trouble broadcasting all over the Russian countryside her decision to dump him. That fucker still stung. Yeah, the affair had been quick and his marriage proposal faster than what most might consider normal, but he asked because he'd meant it, and the fact that she never seemed to get it pissed him off.

She'd walked away, moved on and limited contact with him. Well, at first limited then cut it off completely. But here they were, back in the same cycle. Her work put her in danger, which put her under his protection.

He shouldn't give a shit about what she'd been doing or the lack of contact. He'd moved on. He'd had sex during the last sixteen months and learned a valuable lesson about proposing marriage. That particular act would never happen again. The whole commitment, love crap clearly wasn't his thing. The final text message from her on his phone telling him they should "take a break" served as a constant reminder of how much he sucked at it.

Parker pulled even with Reid, letting Cara venture out a few steps in front of them. Parker's constant surveillance of the area never ceased, even as he leaned over and dropped his voice lower than usual. "You're making growling noises."

That was nothing compared to the running commentary in his head. "Fuck off."

Parker laughed. "Yeah, clearly you're fine."

"Something is going on here and I don't know what it is. I hate not being in control of a situation." And not knowing what she was thinking didn't help.

She hadn't run rogue. For the most part, she listened to directions. She didn't strike him as the kind of person who sought out danger, but it sure did keep finding her, and he could not get a handle on why. She

was a geologist, not an undercover agent. He wondered if she truly understood that.

"Uh-huh. The 'situation' is the problem." Parker buried what he'd said under what sounded like a fake cough.

Reid knew ignoring his friend wouldn't help. Parker would just pick away, dropping comments until he started talking. Not that they could have a normal conversation right now anyway. Not with their attention on the area around them and the need to listen for any sounds, any movement.

"Just say whatever you've been holding in so we can get back to work before the FSB hunts us down." And there was no question the Russian security service would close in soon. The successor to the old KGB handled everything from border control to terrorism threats to general surveillance. Sneaking into the country put them firmly in all of the FSB's target areas.

Worse, the FSB had contacts everywhere. A missing expedition, legitimately investigating some old case or not, wouldn't go unnoticed. People talked. The Alliance not even knowing to look for them left them stranded and on their own. Reid could handle that but he didn't want Cara in the middle.

"Engaged?" Parker asked in a near whisper.

Loud or soft, the word scraped across Reid's already raw nerves. "Not anymore."

Seeing her again carved him inside out. The sight

of all that blood had hit him first. The torn clothes touched off a blinding fury at the thought of her being in trouble. Then instead of unraveling, which anyone else in her situation would have done, she grew stronger. She'd gained her equilibrium and started meeting his verbal shots with some of her own. That's when he'd really gone down for the count.

He'd tried several times over the slogging months since she left him to adjust the image he held of her in his mind. Chip away at his attraction to her. But no such luck. That round face and those intelligent eyes haunted him.

Seeing her again, he realized her self-confidence hadn't faltered. She wasn't one to back down from a verbal battle, and though he pretended that annoyed him, he actually loved that side of her. The energy. The way she threw herself into her work and enjoyed her off time with equal pleasure.

She fed on fresh air and craved the outdoors, just like he did. The bedroom, sweet damn the things she liked to do in there. The urge to strip her bare and throw her on the bed pounded on him the entire time they were together. There wasn't a moment when he hadn't wanted her. Fast up against the wall or slow and savoring every taste. Often he'd set the pace. Other times she'd seduce him merely by walking into the room and throwing him one of her sexy smiles.

The kissing. The touching. She could wear a body-

skimming dress that made his eyes cross one minute and dig in the dirt the next. And that tight body, toned from hiking . . . so fucking hot.

The good and bad memories collided in his head, knocking against his personal promise not to get lured in a second time. He fell for her once and that proved to be one time too many.

"I sense the breakup wasn't your choice at all." Parker lifted his hands in front of him, which just happened to be in the direction of Cara's ass. "I mean I get it. She's way hot."

Reid let his gaze bounce down, tour over her, for just a second. Then the frustration of her choices snapped his festering anger right back into place. "Find another topic."

"Yeah, I can see why you're getting all weird and stuff." Parker made a big show of exhaling and sighing. "At least this bit of history does explain your pathetic dating life for the last year."

That struck Reid as too much. Yeah, he didn't have a parade of women in and out of his door, but they didn't run screaming when they saw him either. "I do fine."

"Remember that I live next to you and see everything."

"Gentlemen." Cara stopped so fast they almost ran over her. She spun around and glared them both into silence before they could grumble about the interruption to their conversation. "I am not deaf."

"Okay." Parker made the word last for three syllables.

"Do you think you're talking in code? Because I can hear you." Her gaze switched from Parker to Reid but the severe frown never let up. "Every last stupid word."

Parker turned to Reid. "She rebounds from injury pretty well."

"Unfortunately, she's had some experience," Reid said, knowing better than to take his gaze off her when she hit this level of fire-spitting fury.

Parker frowned. "About the last time you needed the help of a super clandestine, no-one-knows-who-we-are organization usually reserved for hunting terrorists and madmen—care to fill me in?"

Slowly her shoulders fell. Some of the stiffness left her muscles as she turned around and fell into place between them as they started walking again. "A kidnapping. It was a wrong place, wrong time thing."

When Parker glanced down at her as if waiting for more, Reid jumped in. "You don't realize it, but you just described half of our assignments."

"Ah, I get that." Cara took a folding knife out of her pocket and passed it back and forth between her palms. "While on a government assignment in Egypt, a coworker saw something she wasn't supposed to."

Reid stared at Parker over the top of Cara's head. "The 'something' was an assassination attempt on the Egyptian defense minister while the guy was trying to

eat dinner in a dark, out-of-the-way restaurant with his mistress."

"Damn." Parker whistled, just as he usually did when faced with rough information. "That's some shitty timing on your friend's part."

"No kidding," Cara muttered under her breath. "Armed men followed her back to her temporary apartment, the one she happened to share with me at the time, and then windows exploded. Literally. Reid, here, flew through one."

"We'd picked up chatter about the plans for the attempted hit and were already on the ground. Bravo Team intervened but got pinned in the gunfire." Reid knew Parker didn't want the details, so he skipped those and went right to the heart of the mission. Bravo Team rushed in. Delta, Parker's team, provided backup. Parker could get all of that from the cryptic sentence. "The result was a three-day standoff until we fought our way out."

Cara opened her mouth, looked like she wanted to argue, but then snapped it shut again. "That's the highly abbreviated version that ignores the high body count, the unbelievable terror, and all the lies in the media about a neighborhood evacuation due to a gas leak or some stupid thing, but yes."

They walked in silence for a while after the intel drop. Parker continued his surveillance. Looked ready to accept all he heard and let the conversation go. But

no . . . "Did you propose between magazine reloads or wait until all the bad guys were dead?"

Reid had sensed the amusement and still couldn't avoid it. "Shut up."

"We got away," Cara said, "and he played bodyguard for a few more days until we received the signal it was safe to come out of hiding, that the people involved in the assassination were caught."

Now there was a pretty way of saying it. Reid remembered a lot of blood, too. "She means dead."

Parker nodded. "Got it."

"Right, that was the G-rated version. The one I can think about without wanting to hurl." She cleared her throat. "After that, he proposed."

"And you said yes. You seem to forget that part." She certainly backed away from the answer fast enough. Not that Reid remembered the details, except that he could recite every word of every conversation between the time she said yes and the time she walked out.

He'd assessed and reassessed everything he did and every sentence he'd uttered to figure out where they'd taken the left turn that ended it all. Sixteen months in and he still didn't have a damn clue where it all went wrong. He'd been spinning up, ready to tell the team and figure out the safety parameters they could put in place in light of her research, and needed time in the field. All while she was stamping her get-out-of-relationship-free card.

"We had a whirlwind few weeks then it fizzled," she said in a softer than usual voice.

That's not how he remembered it. He was about to launch into a lengthy explanation of how she pulled back and started with the "highly emotional situations never work for a romance" lectures when they rounded the bottom of a hill and were confronted with signs of life . . . sort of. "Buildings."

"What?" Her head snapped up and her gaze followed his.

"I think we're here." Parker pointed.

Since she looked ready to run toward the structures, Reid slipped his hand under her elbow. "Stay behind me."

"No arguments there." And for once she didn't. She slid back, using his shoulder as a shield, and slipped her finger through his belt loop. "You get to be in charge of this part."

"That's what I like to hear."

"Don't get used to it."

He nodded to Parker. "Swing out to the left. We'll follow along this side."

He reached back and touched her hand to let her know they were ready to move. They walked the length of a football field to get to the huddle of four small nondescript white buildings. All single story and boxy. The buildings sat in the middle of an open field with more mud patches than grass.

The two structures in the middle looked to be larger and connected, with limited windows. A small shed stood off to one side. The door to the structure, maybe twice the size of an outhouse, stood open. The wind lifted it and banged the handle against the wall every few seconds, with the broken lock hanging open.

Other than the steady knocking and the rustle of trees, Reid didn't hear any other sounds or see any signs of life. He couldn't even imagine why someone would put buildings out here, so far from anything and standing right in the shadow of the grim-looking mountain looming behind. There were hiking trails in and around parts of the Urals, but not here. Not on this side of the mountain, which consisted more of rocky outcroppings than anything else.

With slow steps, careful not to give away their location to anyone who might be lurking nearby, or to trample on something that could trip a wire, they made their way to the closest edge of one of the free-standing buildings. Reid pushed Cara back against a building and edged alongside of the window. Peeking in, he saw a similar scene to the one out in the campground. Papers everywhere. Smashed laptops. Add in clothing strewn across the floor and broken furniture, and they'd stumbled over something more than a burglary.

Reid could see from one side of the building to the other. No people inside. Whoever ripped the place apart had moved on, but that didn't mean they'd left.

He kept pressing forward, clearing every inch and stopping for a quick check of the other door near the middle of the building. Just a small bathroom. The one place that looked as if it survived a destroy-everything-in-sight search.

"This is the main building." Cara whispered the words directly into his ear in a voice so soft even he barely heard her. "The makeshift labs and collection areas. The communications center."

He nodded to let her know he understood. Then his gaze switched to the far end of the complex. Parker must have cleared the last building because he headed toward them just as Reid reached the set of double doors connected the two main units. He gestured for Cara to stop.

"Do not move." He wasn't sure if he said the words or just telegraphed them to her, but he could tell she understood. With wide eyes filled with fear, she inched back until she hovered in the doorway with her back tight against the doorjamb. Her hands tightened around the pocketknife until her knuckles turned white.

He winked at her, hoping she took that as a sign everything would be okay. And it would. There was no way in hell she was doing anything other than walking out of there. If it took his last breath, she'd leave Russia healthy and safe.

Parker went first then Reid slipped inside behind him. The open area was a replay of the other building.

A mess of broken equipment and shredded documents. Smashed rocks with piles of what looked like dirt on the floor.

He could make out muddy footprints. Boots, large, likely belonging to men with equally big guns. No spent cartridges or signs of shooting. Even more important, no blood. No sign that humans had been injured here.

After walking from one end to the other, opening the limited number of doors and searching under every desk and around every pile, Parker stood in the middle of what looked to be the main office area. "Clear."

"Clear." Reid didn't get what had happened or where her team had gone. Only the three of them stood in the building now. He motioned for Cara to come farther inside. "I think we can rule out that animals attacked you. This mess was done by men."

"Did you see any of them the other night by the tents?" Parker shot her an unblinking stare. "Any clue what we're looking for here?"

The devastation showed on her face. So pale and drawn. She bent down and picked up a stapler with shaking hands then set it on the edge of one of the desks. "I thought we were being hit by a freak storm. It was so loud and disconcerting and then . . ."

Reid ached for her, for what she'd been through. He knew if he'd lost his team without explanation it would hollow him out. The "no man left behind" motto meant something to him. "What is it?"

She winced. "I passed out. I remember the fear and bits and pieces, but mostly my memory picks up the next morning when I woke up wrapped in the tent with blood all over me and it."

Parker hissed through his teeth. "That's pretty fucked up."

Anxiety edged up on Reid. They'd been talking and walking and he'd missed a pretty big fucking step in the process. "I get the blood on your clothes isn't yours, but we need to know the rest. Were you injured?"

"My head was killing me during the storm, and for a day after." She touched her hair then dropped her hand again. "I was still hazy when you two arrived."

A huge grin lit Parker's face. "But seeing Reid made you snap out of it."

Reid thought this might be a good time to punch something. "Shutting up now would be good."

"Honestly? He's not entirely wrong." She went back to juggling the pocketknife in her palms. "From experience, I know I need to be awake and on my game to take you on."

"Thanks, I think." And that was enough of that talk. Reid nodded in the direction of the satphone sticking out of Parker's front pocket. "Anything?"

"Already tried and nope."

Not exactly the answer Reid wanted to hear. "The only possibilities for that other than malfunction—"

"The phone wouldn't dare fail on your watch." Cara

topped the comment off with an eye roll that suggested she didn't find either of the men in front of her all that bright.

"—are a signal jammer or weather." Reid stopped long enough to spare her a quick glance to let her know he'd heard her joke and was ignoring it. "I'm going with human interference."

Parker nodded. "Humans tend to mess up a lot of assignments for us."

"Someone is jamming the signal from a satellite?" she asked, as if mulling the words over, tasting each one, as she said them.

Reid once again fought back the urge to point out how much technology sucked and how often it failed. Refraining from stating the obvious made his head pound. "That's not quite how it works, but yes. They—whoever the hell 'they' are—can block us from using the satphone, but only within a limited range. We should be able to get far enough to break free of the interference."

"Unless this 'they' follows us." Parker emphasized each word.

Reid knew that was for his benefit. Sort of a this-is-your-fault thing. "Right. Then we can't get a message out."

"Which is a big fucking deal since we're supposed to be in Montana right now, so no one even knows to look for us here." Parker's mouth fell into a flat line

as he sat down on the edge of one of the two standing desks and glared at Reid. "This is the last time we vacation together."

"It's a shame no one implanted a tracker in you two." Cara went to work picking up laptops and checking them to see if they turned on.

Parker smiled at Reid.

Reid debated filling her in, but thought she might find some comfort in knowing where he'd learned the trick. "Actually . . ."

Her head popped up and she stared up at him with wide eyes. "Are you serious?"

He hated to squash her growing enthusiasm, but he was about to. "If we weren't supposed to be off the grid, with no one checking our trackers right now, that piece of technology and bit of required team protocol might actually be helpful."

She slowly stood up again. "When are you supposed to check in?"

Parker swore under his breath. "Not for another three weeks."

"Oh, good grief." She snorted. "Okay, so that's not going to do us any good. What do we do now?"

Reid's mind had already flipped into action mode. He looked at Parker and started barking orders. "You cover the outside while Cara gets whatever she needs in here. Then we're gone."

When he made a move toward the door to check to

make sure they were still alone, she caught his arm. He could have broken the hold with ease, walked away with little more than a flinch, but he knew where this was going and she deserved honest answers. "Yeah?"

"I know I talked about protocol, but the people are what matters to me. What about my team?"

"We'll be able to help them once you're somewhere safe and I have more feet on the ground and a communications system up and running." The plan made sense. Very logical. Except for the part where he had to come up with a way to actually reach the team first.

"You're calling in the Alliance." She didn't sound worried or upset at the idea.

Reid knew some people got twitchy about this sort of thing. Lethal guys moved in and some panicked. Not her. Not back then and not now. He couldn't think of anything more sexy. "You bet your sweet ass."

"Okay." Parker jumped off the desk. "This sounds personal, so I'll be outside."

"Stay close. She only has two minutes."

Parker nodded and left, closing the door behind him. The move left Reid alone with Cara. Alone for the first time in months and all he could do was watch her. Her movements remained jerky. Likely due to nerves and the fear of the unknown, but she kept it together. She walked around broken desk chairs and pushed a slab of some sort of rock around with the toe of her boot.

The silence fell and still she said nothing. Didn't

even give him eye contact. Didn't open any emotional door for him to walk through. If she hadn't been through a scare and still in the middle of who the hell knew what, he might have launched into a new round of verbal battle. Instead, he did what he'd been doing for over a year, tamped it all down, pushed it back and pretended he didn't give a shit. "We should try to figure out if we can recover anything because you're down to one minute."

She let out a long labored breath. "How charming."

"I've never been accused of that." By her or anyone.

"Reid—"

"Not now." He recognized the tone and held up a hand to shut it down. Fucking no way was he letting her set the agenda or say something lame about how leaving him was for the best. Any comment remotely like that would send his anger spiraling even more. "Not if it's about us or what happened or how you hate that I'm here. You can go back to hating me as soon as you're out of this open area and less of a target."

"That's the point." She bit her bottom lip.

He'd never seen her do that before. She didn't really do the whole fidget, nervous gesture thing. "What?"

She visibly swallowed. "I never hated you."

His heartbeat pounded in his ears. For a second he couldn't tell if he was furious or happy. His focus kept slipping. Something kept pulling his attention away from her. A noise or stray thought, he wasn't sure.

He guessed it was some sort of internal call for self-preservation and welcomed it.

He said the only coherent sentence he could form. "Could have fooled me."

"Reid—"

"Wait." There it was again. That "something" that sent his instincts ticking. He'd been so lost in looking at her, thinking about her, that he missed the quiet. The shadow. "Damn it. Get down."

The next second, what was left of the window exploded. The sound of crashing echoed around them. Shards of glass rained down. His only thought was to tackle her and roll.

Then the gunfire started.

5

FOR THE second time in days Cara curled into a ball. She wasn't the hide-and-weep type. She'd seen things, awful things, while out in the field. People fell off cliffs. Got bitten by snakes. She'd just missed being swallowed by an avalanche years ago, right at the beginning of her career. The kidnapping.

None of it compared to the sensation the last few days of being mentally tossed around and plowed under. The upheaval, the confusion—not knowing if her team members were alive or dead—the dragging sense that she got lucky and didn't deserve it. The emotions piled up, weighing her down, crushing her chest until she couldn't breathe.

Seeing Reid walk down that hill both terrified and excited her. She'd tried to move on, date a physicist here and that manic stock analyst there. But it was all noise, and none of it could drown out the doubts rolling through her head. But then she got swept up in a terrifying situation and common sense fled. The will to live, to connect, kicked in.

After a lifetime of doing the right thing even while her parents tried to pull her toward a life of art and music—two things she had zero aptitude for—she ignored every warning bell ringing in her head. Gave in to her attraction to Reid. Went on emotion and spun wild dreams. Forgot the comfort of facts and the reality that their lives were too different to make sense together.

Even though it shredded her, she had walked away. She refused to let the churning inside her draw her back in. She'd never been attracted to the bad boy, always-in-danger type, and refused to start as an adult. But no one had warned her how the pain would eat away at her. How she'd take increasingly riskier field assignments and shrug away any suggestion from her brother that the building need inside her came from Reid.

All of those past doubts mixed with the current fear as anxiety pounded through her. What could have been mixed with the reality of her life falling apart once again, until she could barely stay standing. She'd tried to force the emotions down and concentrate, go to a place in her head that felt safe, but the clanging rushed back on her.

When Reid slammed into her she lost her balance and they both went down. Her arms and legs tangled with his. She tried to reach out to slow their fall but his hand snagged hers. Her head would have bounced against the hard floor but he had them tucking and rolling in midair.

They landed with a crunch on his side. Her shoulder slammed into a chair as the rest of her weight fell against his stomach. His grunt vibrated against her back and echoed in her ears. One of his weapons jabbed into her side.

Then he was up. Boots smacked against the ground, right by her head. Bullets knocked into the walls and furniture stacked around her. Pieces of white brick kicked up around her.

She unwrapped her arms from around her head and peeked up. One man then another slipped through the broken window. Reid sprayed them with bullets, taking each man down with a sickening thud. Blood spilled across the floor. The all-black clothing the men wore, almost uniforms, crumpled around their still forms.

When she heard crashing behind her, Cara started crawling. On her elbows and knees, she scooted across the floor, aiming for the overturned desk. Some form of cover. Still, Reid didn't run or duck. He moved closer to the window, shooting into the open air. Slamming another attacker in the face when the man tried to grab his gun.

The whole scene took only seconds. Loud, draining seconds of pure terror. In her mind, every move passed in slow motion. The gunfire seemed to come from every direction. She heard yelling and grunts. Heard a crunching sound that seemed to start inside her. Felt panic freeze her muscles and shut down her brain.

She could not die like this. She could not let Reid sacrifice his life for hers.

She forced her mind to focus as footsteps thundered just outside. She had a knife. She had rocks. In this area, northwest of the city of Perm, the one thing they had plenty of was rocks. They'd collected all sorts of samples, including limestone and gypsum. Relatively harmless materials in their raw form. But she could throw them. Cause a diversion. Help Reid beat back the attack.

She slipped behind an overturned cabinet, ignoring the painful thump of her knees against the floor. She had just reached for a chunk of limestone when the front door blew open. The wood splintered and pieces flew through the air. Smoke poured into the confined space but the open window seemed to suck most of it out again.

She could smell fire and hear the crackling. She looked up, searching for Reid. The gray air blocked her view and made her eyes water. Her heart nosedived into her stomach when she spied the bottom of a pair of boots, legs flat on the floor where Reid stood just seconds before.

She blocked all of it. Refused to think about what that could mean.

Flames crawled up the cracked and broken door frame. She heard talking. Russian, she thought, but her mind started to blank on her. Just as she decided to curl

in, get as small as she could, a beefy hand grabbed her ankle. She slid across the floor. Stretching, she reached out to grab the biggest rock she could see, but it slipped out of her fingers.

With one final yank, her body flew toward the fire and the two men standing right there. With their faces and bodies covered, she could only see their eyes. No emotion showed there. Whatever they said to each other was muffled by the sound of the growing fire.

She kicked out, aiming to cause as much damage as possible. After two kicks to the shin of one man, her muscles barely seemed to work. One of them laughed as the other reached down for her. She shimmied and tried to crawl away, but he slammed her body against the floor by putting a foot in the middle of her back. Pain mixed with blinding panic, but she refused to give up.

Everything hurt. Every nerve and every cell. The smoke burned inside her throat and she started coughing. Even her hand hurt . . . her palm. The memories clicked together in her head. She uncurled her fingers and opened the pocketknife. A mental countdown started a second later.

When the attacker grabbed her arm and pulled, she spun around. Using all her strength, she swung the blade and dug it deep into his thigh. He yelled and kicked, nailing her in the cheek. Her head snapped back as she reached to grab the knife for a second stab, this time at the man swinging a gun toward her. Before

she could slash him, however, she heard the *whoosh*, the sliding sound of material, then a bang as the armed man fell to his knees.

A massive weight hit her just as the attacker dropped. The crash knocked her sideways. She tried to spin around, launch an offensive strike before her body fully landed. Whipping her head around she saw a blur, then watched Reid shift to his back and keep shooting. Both of her attackers slammed to the floor just inches from her and right where she'd just been.

One of the man's heavy arms fell across her ankle. Reid kicked it off.

"Are you okay?" His palm went to her cheek as his frantic gaze searched hers.

"I thought you were dead."

"You're not going to get rid of me that easily." He sounded out of breath. His chest rose and fell with rapid breathing.

When her eyes finally focused, she noticed the blood soaking his shoulder and the cuts all over him. She jumped to her knees. "You're hit."

"We need to get out of here."

The smell of burning wood hit her then. Flames licked up the walls and danced across the ceiling. The roar drowned out everything else. More men could be out there, ready to shoot, but they had to take the risk.

She struggled to her feet and nearly screamed when her knees buckled. But Reid was there, He caught her,

half carrying and half dragging her as they stumbled through the small opening in the fire and fell onto the dirt outside.

They rolled a few more feet, then Reid braced his body on his elbows above her and he scanned the area. Two more bodies littered the ground. She spied another set of unmoving legs in the distance. No car or truck. No obvious way in or out. No sign of more, but the attackers could just be waiting.

Her insides started to shake. Bile rushed up the back of her throat and she had to fight off the urge to throw up. A hacking sound filled the air, and it took her another few seconds to realize it came from her. Her lungs' way of choking out the deadly smoke.

Reid rested an arm across her back as she rose to her hands and knees and breathed in huge gulping breaths. "Cara, can anything in there explode?"

"Something blew up the door."

"That was a smoke grenade gone wrong." A coughing fit broke up his explanation. It took another few seconds for him to get his body back under control, and even then his voice stayed scratchy. "I don't think they meant to set the fire."

"There are explosive materials in there, but mostly just rocks that would need extreme heat to cause damage." Except for the popping of the fire, she noticed the quiet. Then she thought about all that shooting. "Parker?"

What little color remained in Reid's face leeched out. He pushed to his feet, wincing and holding his injured arm loose at his side. "Stay here."

He needed help and possibly stitches. No way was she letting him wander around on his own. "I'm not leaving your side," she said.

"I'll refrain from being an asshole and giving the obvious response to that." He reached a hand down and helped lift her to her feet.

Her boots had barely touched the ground when Reid shoved her behind him again. A second later his shoulders relaxed and he lowered his weapon.

Parker was aiming a hose, directing a flow of water at the fire. "There's a water tank in the back."

"That's our drinking water," she said, knowing that sounded ridiculous, but so was the sight of Parker dragging the threadbare hose, walking around and . . . Was he whistling?

"I don't think you'll need it." His gaze drifted over her and Reid. "You two look like shit."

Reid just shook his head. "You okay?"

Parker held up a hand and wiggled one finger. "I caught my thumb on that shitty gun you bought for me."

The laughter bubbled up out of nowhere. Cara almost doubled over from the force of it. Relief, hope . . . she wasn't sure what caused it, but the panic subsided and took what felt like most of her common sense with it.

Parker frowned at her. "She finally lose it?"

"Nerves." Reid stared into the dying fire. "I'm afraid whatever you wanted to collect is gone."

She didn't even try to hide her smile. "Wrong."

Instead of getting angry or issuing orders, Reid looked amused. "What am I missing?"

"The backup of all our findings so far is on a jump drive I hid in the bathroom of the one building not on fire or in danger of catching fire at the moment."

Parker nodded as he shut down the hose. "Impressive."

"There should also be supplies and some extra clothes in the cabin at that end." She pointed, hoping they were still there since the idea of walking around in bloodstained clothes made her physically ill. She knew she should have changed before, but her mind hadn't been working right. Now it was . . . so long as she blocked out the memory of stabbing a guy.

"Maybe I should put you in charge," Reid said.

"No doubt about it." She glanced to Parker, hoping to get an assist for what came next. "We need to check Reid here before he passes out."

Reid scoffed. "That will never happen."

And she had no doubt that he could make sure of that by using sheer will.

"We need to get moving," he said.

She was about to ask to where when Parker said, "They came off the mountain."

"Otorten." Just saying the name made her shiver.

Parker dropped the hose and stomped out the remaining flames, catching the few stray glowing embers. "Mountain of the Dead."

"Sort of." The folklore on that, as far as she could tell, was overblown. Probably dated back past the Dyatlov Pass incident and the propensity of people to want to make it into some sort of crazy alien conspiracy. "Technically, I think it actually means 'do not go there' in Mansi, the language of the indigenous people who live in this area."

"Oh, that's better." Reid's tone still contained a rasp but his eyes looked clearer now.

The last thing she needed was two people searching for whacky reasons to be afraid of an impersonal slab of earth. They had enough to worry about without taking on the mountain. "The point is, men—not the mountain—just attacked us."

Reid stood up a little straighter. "Speaking of which, that could have been the first wave."

"Of what, exactly?" She could not take on one more thing right now. Her body craved a shower and a bed. She needed a few minutes to clear her mind and come at the idea of finding her missing team from a different angle. Nothing she'd thought of so far had gotten her one step closer to an answer.

He didn't blink. "Attacks by the people who want you dead, or at the very least, with the rest of your team."

"Great." The word slipped out before she could stop it. A few more seconds and she might sit down on the ground and not get up again. She'd run out of energy and her emotional strength was all but drained.

Reid lifted the collar of his shirt to inspect his wound before glancing at Parker. "Any ID on these guys?"

"Of course not." Parker shrugged. "But at least we have more weapons now. Newer ones. These guys were trained and well-equipped."

"Probably military or at least former military." Reid grumbled something under his breath before talking in a regular voice again. "Take photos, just in case we can get something back to the Warehouse for face recognition."

She caught words here and there. None of them sounded too good to her. "Warehouse?"

"The official name of our headquarters," Reid explained.

She still didn't like the sound of it. "Seems ominous."

Parker slipped around her and headed for the still body closest to him. "Almost as ominous as being stuck in the mountains in the middle of nowhere with limited weapons."

She stared at him. "You're not really a people person, are you?"

Reid smiled. "Parker is better with Yetis."

Now wasn't the time to give the man a list of all

the reasons Yetis didn't exist. If these two insisted on watching over her and shooting men who wanted to grab her, she could put up with a little nonsense talk. "Even I would take a Yeti right now. So long as it was on our side."

"I knew you'd come around," Parker said as he started taking photos.

"I'm a scientist." For some reason she felt the need to point that out. It likely had to do with the fact nothing made sense or was within her control right now. Falling back on what she knew to be true gave her some comfort.

Parker frowned at her. "So?"

"Not a big believer in things that have no scientific basis." That summed up her life. Usually she was fine with that way of operating, but thanks to the blank stares she was getting, her confidence faltered.

"Like falling for some random guy and getting engaged in a few days?" Parker asked.

Reid groaned. "Parker, really. Shut the fuck up."

But the guy had a point. Of all the plans she'd made for her life, someone like Reid—lethal and strong and ready to die for a cause—hadn't fit in anywhere. She didn't generally get lured in by a fit body and gravelly voice. At least, not until Reid.

"I did, didn't I?" Those weeks still stunned her. Falling so fast and so hard had run counter to her practical nature. She'd backed out believing that sort of intense

relationship shouldn't morph into anything long-term. That it couldn't survive. And even if it could for her, there was no way it could happen like that for him. She just couldn't see it.

It all sounded smart in theory. In practice, leaving him left her in pieces. Fast or not, whatever she felt for him refused to go away quietly . . . or quickly.

"As you pointed out, whatever you felt didn't last for long. You wiggled out of it." Reid stared at her as if waiting for her to challenge him. When she stayed quiet, he pushed on. "We need a plan for this situation."

The man was six-feet-whatever of pure stubbornness. She walked over to him and peeled back his shirt. Both because he needed medical attention and because, in that moment, she needed to touch him. "Any ideas?"

She half expected him to shrug her off or insist he was fine. Instead, he stood there and let her fuss over him. Winced and glared but didn't push her away.

"Easy, I head out. Possibly draw out anyone who might be following, and go back to the last point where the communications system worked." When the shirt underneath his jacket stuck to the wound, he looked at her. "That doesn't feel great."

She assumed his calm comment meant that it really did hurt. She also knew they could be looking at much worse injuries if they went along with his dangerous plan. "So, your plan is to get shot. Take one for the team and all that."

He frowned. "Hopefully not."

"Hope? That's not good enough. Come up with something else. Preferably, a plan that keeps you alive." She tried to remember where they'd dropped their backpacks before storming the compound, then decided it would be easy to find supplies amidst the wreckage in the sleeping quarters. "And I need to sew that up, so don't think we're done with the medical part of this."

"It's a flesh wound. The bullet just grazed me." He lifted the shirt again and studied the area she just touched.

"Did you get a medical degree on one of your days off?" She knew he had limited training for just this sort of out-in-the-field issue, to get team members injured in action out. If possible. But that wasn't really the point.

"Did you?" he asked. But before she could volley a response at him, he changed the subject. "What if we made use of a labor camp? Off-the-books, Stalin era. Covert."

She glanced at Parker. When he didn't protest or say anything, she turned back to Reid. "That sounds awful."

"Russia insists it was something else. I don't really care, but from the aerial photos I studied on the way over, it shouldn't be too far." He started to shrug, then hissed in reaction to the movement before letting his wounded shoulder fall again. "More importantly, it's abandoned, or should be."

Parker made a humming sound. "That's a lot of 'shoulds' in that comment."

"Do we have another choice?" Reid asked.

"Huh." Parker shrugged. "Like I said, perfect."

He had to be kidding. They both did. She could barely control the fear rattling around inside her. "Do you know what that word means?"

"And that's why scientists aren't in charge of the Alliance." Reid squeezed her upper arm then let his hand drop again.

Not that she had any desire to be, but still . . . "Because we're practical?"

"You play it too safe. Sometimes you've got to take a risk to get the big reward."

The intensity of his stare almost knocked her over. "Are we still talking about this situation or something else?"

The corner of Reid's mouth kicked up in a smile. "I'll let you figure that out."

6

TASHA GREGORY stared out her glass-walled office and into the Warehouse situation room. High-end equipment hummed with life and covered table after table. Oversized monitors showing news from around the world and covert camera feeds from hotspot locations hung from the ceiling and lined the walls.

The space was modern and sleek. Very industrial. The career types who sat in the big building across the fenced-in grounds of Liberty Crossing, the home of the National Counterterrorism Center in Virginia, liked to testify in their secret congressional hearings about the Alliance being an example of true international cooperation between the U.S. and the UK. That was when they weren't too busy berating her in private for every little thing the Alliance did and every dime spent.

But the higher-ups liked a big public show, complete with lots of self-congratulations. They also felt qualified to make decisions without ever picking up a weapon or making a life-or-death spot decision in the field.

Both the Americans and their British counterparts micromanaged to an annoying degree. Tried to plan everything out, as if a national crisis came with the ability to call time-out to regroup. They spent a lot of time designing manuals and talking about protocol. Never mind that the setup of the Alliance outside of the CIA and MI6 meant the team was not hamstrung by the rules the intelligence agencies had to follow. And she would not have been able to convince her men to read operation manuals even if she ordered it, not that she ever would.

The Alliance could move from country to country with great freedom. She took the heat and played the game so her team could work with her as the only true oversight. Move in and out without being seen. Get the equipment they needed while standing in the middle of a firefight. Skate the very thin line between right and wrong as they assessed how to contain the damage. No one was better at any of that than her team.

To her, the fancy office space and Marine guards at the entrance gate amounted to pure window dressing. The real beating heart of the Alliance was the team members, and she trusted them to make the hard calls. She directed and ordered, but she listened and made adjustments. Right now most of them were out.

The place usually bustled with activity, but she'd sent the members of both Bravo and Delta out on mandatory leave. They'd lost one of their own and needed to

grieve, even though they fought the idea. Almost every one of them thought that heading straight out on a new assignment and concentrating on doing what they did best was the answer. Part of her agreed. But the higher-ups in the CIA and MI6, the intelligence agencies that trained most of the team members and sometimes supplied backup for missions, argued the point and she conceded.

There were fears about vigilante frustration and the potential for something catastrophic to happen. Having risen through the ranks of MI6 and set up the Alliance, Tasha had a high tolerance for handling catastrophe. Her team was no different.

She planned to call them all back in next week, reassemble and get back to work. It wasn't as if the gun runners and human traffickers and every other terrorist and piece of human garbage out there looking to cause trouble took the month off because Harlan Ross, lifetime British intelligence officer and Alliance administrator, sacrificed his life in exchange for saving a terminal of people at Paris's Charles de Gaulle Airport and the Alliance team members standing in the room with him. Including her.

No one outside the Alliance even knew about his sacrifice. And that was the part that ticked her off the most. All those years of service to the Crown, and he wouldn't receive even a star on a wall like the CIA did for their own. Harlan had been an MI6 officer before

joining the Alliance and there would be no public appreciation for him because he died after leaving MI6. That was a choice he'd made when he joined the Alliance.

Harlan wasn't the type to seek accolades and the job didn't allow for it, but the covert end for a hero still sucked. She wanted him to be recognized but knew it would never happen.

"Is it usually this quiet around here?" The deep male voice bounced around her office. Caleb Layne looked from one corner to the other, not trying to hide the fact that he was taking in the position of every paper clip and notebook.

"Actually, never." She gestured to the guard hovering in her doorway to leave. After a brief hesitation he did, closing the door behind him.

Once alone with her guest, she focused all her attention on him. That was no hardship. She might be engaged to an administrator in the Alliance but her eyesight worked just fine.

The phrase "tall, dark, and handsome" might have been invented to describe Caleb. He was a guy with a bit of a reputation. Outside of these walls, the public saw him as a technology genius who went from creating apps that made life easier, to building a gaming company that supplied the world with an endless stream of postapocalyptic role-playing activities.

Impressive but a bit ruthless, and inside these walls

a valuable asset. He excelled at creating what he called "pathways to further communication" but others would see as hacking or even potentially espionage. He could access systems that no one should be able to break. Closed systems. Top secret, lives-depend-on-no-one-knowing-this systems.

Which is why Tasha hired him to make sure the Alliance's system remained secure. The last time someone penetrated their internal communication it touched off a manhunt that led to many deaths, including Harlan's. That would not happen again. Not on her watch.

Caleb smiled as his gaze hesitated on the file open on her desk. "Is the world on fire and the rest of us don't know about it?"

Thirty, with coal black hair and something in his facial features that hinted at his Asian heritage. She couldn't quite nail that part down, but he did look just like his sister. Tasha just wished she could fully trust the man to tell her the truth rather than try to play her.

"Probably." She closed the unimportant file, letting him think he might have seen something when he hadn't. He was a man drawn to solving problems, so she liked to keep him motivated by giving him some. But she hadn't called this meeting. "I'm guessing that's not why you're here. You're not one to panic, and I sensed worry in your voice when you called."

His confident smile slipped a little but regained its full wattage before he leaned back in his chair. It

creaked under his trim runner's build. "Thanks for seeing me."

"You've done work for us. Tell me how we can repay the favor."

"This isn't just for me. It's for you, too."

That sounded bad. Like she'd missed something, and she did not miss things. "You've lost me."

"I can't reach Cara." Caleb stared down at his hands for a second before meeting Tasha's gaze again. "To be completely accurate, the science expedition she's on has gone dark."

His word choice didn't make much sense. It was a little too dramatic for Caleb's usual choices, so Tasha treaded carefully. "Where?"

"Ural Mountains."

She forced her body to remain still. At times the world felt as if it were on fire, with regional outbreaks of violence, and nations threatening other nations. For the first time in a long time, the Urals made the list of potential problem areas. Sixteen hundred miles stretching up to the Arctic, some of it home to small cities and towns. Much of it desolate and hard to investigate, and that didn't even take into account the difficulty in dealing with the country's leadership.

She leaned back, matching her relaxed position to Caleb's even though she knew they were both playing games here. "What kind of expedition is this?"

"The undercover type."

She mentally flipped through every briefing file and satellite photo from the last two weeks but could not place any mention of a field operation disguised as a science expedition. "And that's where I come in? You think this is something the Alliance either knows about or should?"

"Reid is there. I think he took Parker Scott with him."

Tasha could hear the air rattling around inside her chest. Feel the tension ratchet up as her body and brain prepared for battle. "Excuse me?"

Caleb blew out a long breath. "I lost contact with Cara and I went to Reid."

"You're telling me you lost two of my men." Two men she planned to strangle when she got her hands on them.

"I wouldn't say it that way, since you know how to use a gun, but yes."

Good thing she had plenty of fury to go around because right now it extended past the man in front of her to the two on the ground she trusted not to be so reckless. Apparently they were unclear on the concept of vacation. Since neither their real names nor any of their aliases tripped an alarm through passport or visa control, she had to assume they sneaked into Russia. Not exactly a country with the warmest regard for that sort of thing.

"Why?" And she didn't explain further. She knew Caleb knew what she was really asking.

"Cara has a tracker. I thought maybe Reid could find her faster than I could."

This conversation just got worse and worse. "You're saying Cara let him implant a device on her?"

Caleb winced. "'Let' is the wrong word."

"When Reid gets back and starts the mandatory refresher course on international travel restrictions I plan to make him take, I'll throw in one on consent as well." Reid's boundaries had never been great, but this . . . *damn it.*

"She's in Russia on a grant from the Bastion Foundation."

Tasha didn't even try to hide her frustration over that news. She grabbed onto the armrests and dug her fingernails in to keep from yelling. "Of course she is."

"What?" When Tasha gestured for Caleb to keep explaining, he did. "They are there under the guise of testing theories about some old hiking incident. One of those big unsolved conspiracies. But I did some digging—"

"I don't want to know how." Plausible deniability was a big concept in her dealings with Caleb.

"She's there for something else."

All the pieces fell together in Tasha's head. The CIA's insistence they had agents working to assess what could be a threat in the Urals, and the steadfast refusal to let her bring in the Alliance to help. Those idiots at Langley were using scientists, endangering people without sufficient training.

She exhaled. "Let me guess. You stumbled upon allegations that a faction within the Russian military—or worse, a private former military group—is using former Soviet era compounds throughout the Urals to do something weapons related, possibly nuclear but also could be chemical, it's not clear except that the complete takeover of the Ukraine seems to be the endgame."

Caleb's arm dropped and his hand smacked against the side of the chair. "I see you already got the memo."

"It's my job to know these things." And since she might need Caleb's backdoor assistance, she filled him in on the basics. "I'd been told there were assets in the region tracking truck movements and poking around to see if the Alliance should investigate. Then satellite access cut off. Signals are being jammed on the ground."

"Reid, Parker, and Cara are in the middle of all of that."

"I'm not happy about you using my men for your personal mission." Now there was an understatement. She'd firmly crossed over from frustrated to pissed, but with her people scattered, the Alliance being watched closer than usual after Harlan's murder, and the need to keep this off the intelligence community's radar for now, she needed Caleb.

"I didn't know about the alternative reason for the expedition until communication got cut off and I started investigating." He held up a hand in mock surrender. "I

really did ask Reid to go as a personal favor." Caleb shook his head. "He said something about having vacation time and motorcycles."

"The fact he still loves Cara probably weighed heavily in his decision to go." And that was the other unknown factor. Tasha had worked with her fiancé, Ward, in the field in the past and knew just how hard it was to keep the emotional separated from the mission in those circumstances.

"Reid insists that's over." Caleb shrugged. "That's what he *says,* anyway."

"Sure." Men really could be clueless. "I'm assuming you covered your digital tracks. The CIA isn't hunting you down right now, correct?"

Caleb snorted. "Give me some credit."

"Good, because we need to do an end run. Convincing the people I answer to that we should put a second team on the ground and risk pissing off Russia will take too long." Her bigger fear was in touching off an intelligence agency battle between the CIA and everyone else, where the CIA rushed to cover its ass and the science expedition became collateral damage. "You wouldn't believe the layers of bullshit involved in this sort of thing."

Caleb's gaze narrowed. "So, what do we do?"

"Go straight to Nikolay Murin." One of her least favorite people on the planet, and that was saying something.

"The head of the Bastion Foundation," Caleb said nice and slow, as if weighing each word as he said it.

"Niko and I have a bit of a history." She found her first smile since the conversation started.

"A good one?"

"I think so." She unlocked the safe behind her desk and threw a stack of files in it. Then she took out her gun. "I grabbed him and interrogated him about nine months ago. We made an agreement when he ended up accepting my blackmail terms. Things ended up fine."

"Does he see it that way?"

Tasha smiled for the first time since the conversation started. She stood up, ready to get this done. "Well, he's not in jail for fraud, and that's thanks to me. Me and his willingness to tell me everything I needed to know at the time."

Caleb shook his head. "I don't want to know about what."

"No, you don't."

"Maybe I should go in alone." Caleb said it more as a comment than a question.

"Even with your money and power, it's possible he'll never see you." The man was ridiculously paranoid about his protection. Refused public appearances and played the role of mysterious billionaire philanthropist very well. "But Niko will see me."

Caleb was slower to get up, but he finally did. "What makes you so sure?"

"He threatened to kill me." Niko had used harsher words than that, but Tasha was pretty sure she made her point, since Caleb looked like she'd hit him with a bat. "He will think he's finally getting his chance."

"Aren't you worried he'll actually try?"

She stifled an eye roll. "He's never been successful before. He won't be this time either."

7

WHEN CARA sighed at him for the fifth time, Reid knew he was in trouble. They'd told her the camp was "not far," and by that he meant five miles off any known path, including adding in extra time for doubling back and creating false trails just in case. In hindsight, he could have handled that information better.

After two hours of walking she tagged as vigorous and he viewed as unnecessarily slow, they came up to the back gate and fence surrounding the outside of what was once known as Norkosov, one of a series of possibly thousands of forced labor camps used mostly by the then Soviet Union up through the fifties. Some had been demolished. Others were turned into museums. This one, small by comparison, probably housed only a thousand or so men at a time, but that didn't make the horror of what happened here any less dramatic.

Guard towers still stood. So did the outside fence, a fact that started Reid's instincts ticking. Some of the buildings were little more than piles of rubble. Still, the

fence hadn't been torn apart, wasn't ripped in places. It and the lock holding the gate shut struck Reid as pristine. Not new and shiny, but not sixty years old and abandoned either.

"Just so you know." Cara glared at Reid out of the corner of her eye. "I hate you both. We walked around in circles forever."

Parker shrugged. "Not exactly a circle."

Not one to be overly cautious, Reid still understood there were times that called for the ability. He'd spent his younger years being passed from foster home to foster home. He learned how to maneuver, how to fight, and when to listen to the voice in his head as it warned about incoming danger.

He'd been on his own a long time, not depending on anyone or anything. He didn't collect people or things. But he did trust his team and his common sense, and nothing about what he saw in front of him looked right.

"We're not alone." In long strides, he walked along the fence line a few feet down for a better angle on the main building in the center of the complex, then returned.

Cara paled. "Meaning?"

"The fence. The truck." He noticed the front end of the older model vehicle sticking out from behind the edge of one of the buildings. Who knew what he'd see if he ventured farther. "The place is supposed to be rotted out and human-free."

"It could be kids hanging out where they absolutely shouldn't be, but I really don't see anyone." Cara peeked through the lines of barbed wire. "Nothing looks new or in working order."

Reid's gaze shot back to the long two-story structure running down the center of the camp. Faded spots of yellow dotted the white. Paint peeled from the outside walls. Pieces of concrete lay stacked in piles on the ground as if a section of the building had crumbled. But the windows, every single one of them, were intact.

"I don't like it." Reid watched Parker scan the area and focus on the ground and what looked like covered-over tire tracks.

Parker nodded. "Me either."

"Let's move." Reid didn't see cameras, but that didn't mean they weren't there. He grabbed Cara's arm, careful not to pull too hard, and marched them over to the small guard shack about fifty feet along the fence.

When they stopped, Cara sighed at them. Threw in an eye roll, too. "Is this a paranoia thing or do we really have a problem?"

"Fair question." Parker checked his gun then his extra ammo.

Looked like they were on the same page. The world worked better when that happened. Despite his fractured life before the Alliance, Reid was smart enough to know heading into danger alone sometimes just heightened it.

"We do a little surveillance." They might be there for her and to find her team, but if someone was starting up the gulag system again, Reid wanted to report back to Tasha. He really wanted to shut the shit down, but he had Cara to worry about. Speaking of her . . . "You're going to hide—"

She was already shaking her head. "No."

"Cara."

"I am not leaving your side." She gestured to indicate him. "If someone comes for me, they have to go through you. That's a plan that works for me."

"I think that's a compliment, but I'm not totally sure."

Her gaze traveled over Reid, as if assessing his strength and abilities just by looking at him. "I know for a fact those big shoulders are good for many things."

Parker nodded. "Very romantic."

"I'm practical."

As if Reid would let hers be the last word on the subject. "And untrained."

"Not to jump in the middle of a lovers' quarrel here . . ." Parker repocketed his backup ammunition. ". . . but if any of the scientists from her expedition are here, we won't be able to identify them. We actually need her help."

Logic. Just what Reid needed. "Shit."

"You picked her, man."

"And people think scientists suck at communication. Again, I would point out that you two need to work on

your people skills." She stood in front of both of them and held out her hand, palm up. "I'd rather keep you alive than charm you."

When she didn't drop her hand, Reid couldn't resist asking, "What are you doing?"

"I want a gun."

Parker snorted. Looked horrified by the suggestion. "Nope."

The idea of a novice with a gun made Reid twitchy, but Cara was no novice. "She can shoot."

Her eyes narrowed. "How do you know?"

Because he knew every damn thing about her. Caleb had filled him in on some of the details. Reid wasn't sure if that amounted to torture or matchmaking, but the truth was, he never lost touch with her. Not really. "You took lessons after we broke up."

"She dumped you," Parker said, sticking his head between them. "She's made that clear."

Cara pushed Parker back without looking at him and glared at Reid. "I'm going to ignore the fact that you know what I've been doing and how that means you've been stalking me, because in this case it helps me win the argument."

"Fine." And by that Reid meant the issue about stalking was closed.

She held up a finger in front of his face. "But we're going to talk about your knuckle-dragging behavior later."

Reid reached around, pulled out a second gun and handed it to her. "Once I save you."

She treated him to another eye roll. "Or vice versa."

Parker laughed. "I really like her."

Yeah, Reid was not getting into this argument now. He knew he sometimes missed the boundary lines others saw and easily navigated. Every now and then he went overboard. His protective instincts had been known to misfire.

He even understood that when it came to her, the desperation to keep her safe overwhelmed everything else. He'd tried to rein it in, and the first time he did she ran into trouble in the middle-of-fucking-nowhere Russia and he came running.

His need for her bordered on pathetic. He'd never been so attracted to a woman before. Never screwed up so much.

Time to get back to work. He nodded at the phone sticking out of Parker's pocket. "Check the comm."

"Already did and nothing."

"Damn it." That meant they had no choice about the closer investigation. Part of him wanted to bundle Cara away somewhere, but leaving her only opened the door to having someone sneak in and grab her. They had enough missing scientists at the moment. "Fine, you swing to the left. We'll take the right. This is intel gathering only."

"As opposed to what?" she asked.

Parker winked at her. “He doesn’t want me to shoot anyone.”

“Sounds like a good plan.” She checked her gun then moved her finger off the trigger. Refrained from sticking it in her pocket or something equally stupid.

Reid was impressed. Someone taught her well. “Not to me.”

With a nod, Parker took off. All those years of Army training paid off. He moved fast and low and without a sound. Combine that with his shooting ability and willingness to step in front of a bullet, if that’s what had to be done for the mission, and he was one of the most solid of the Alliance agents. Except for the whole conspiracy nut thing.

Reid dropped to his knees and reached into his pack to find a small leather pouch. He glanced over his shoulder at Cara as he went to work on the fence. “Be ready. I move, you move. No talking. Got it?”

Instead of stepping back, she closed in. Loomed over his back until her shins touched his ass. After a few seconds she shifted to stand by his side, bent over with her hands on her knees.

Her hair slipped off her shoulder and the ends blew around in the breeze. This close, stray strands skimmed across his cheek. He could feel the heat coming off her body and fought off a reaction in his.

“I’m going to assume you think you need to talk to me this way.” She whispered the words right into his

ear. "Even if so, you should stop doing it before I punch you."

The small puffs of air sent something raw and primal racing around inside him. He chalked the feeling up to the rush of the moment. Adrenaline pounded in his veins. The energy he needed to get them through the next few minutes built inside him. Grew stronger.

"Whatever you say." Opening the pouch, he took out the tool he needed and slipped on a thin pair of gloves. The kind that wouldn't interfere with his shot or limit his mobility.

The wire cutters sliced through what should have been old barbed wire only after he exerted some force. Instead of cracking into pieces, each strand broke with a clean snap. One more sign this compound was not as old and decrepit as someone wanted people to believe.

"Keep using that tone and you can count on it." She held out her hand and collected the cutter, putting it back in the small bag and then into his bigger pack. "The whole pissy alpha act turns me off."

"I thought women liked the hot and lethal thing," he said as he rolled back the sharp edges of the fencing, making an opening big enough for them to slide through without trouble.

"Stop talking."

It was good advice, so he followed it. Flattening the pack as much as possible, he set it on the ground, just outside of the fence. The extra weight could block his

shots and make it tougher for him to spin and shoot. He wasn't looking for more obstacles, so he abandoned this one for now.

Then he took off sprinting across the open space between the fence and the first building. He knew she followed right on his heels because he could hear the soft thump of her boots as they hit the ground. Keeping up wasn't a problem. The woman could run.

They landed at the side of the first building. With his back plastered against the wall, he motioned for her to join him and stay quiet. They slid along the length of building without any windows. When they got to the end, Reid checked the area around them then turned a corner, leading to a set of massive double doors. Heavy chains and two locks blocked their entrance. New locks.

Looked like his instincts hadn't failed him this time either. "So much for this place being abandoned."

Cara placed her palm against the door. "I hate to think of what happened in that building in the past."

Reid wanted to know what was happening in there now. Not hearing any noise and not having the time to get out the equipment he needed to pick the lock, he mentally added that to the list of things to check later and moved them on. "One down."

Low and fast they jogged to the nearest corner of the next building. The rumble of voices hit Reid first. Leaning toward the edge of the window, he saw a cube

positioned on the floor. It threw off just enough light to chase away the darkness but not enough to show through the windows or give him a good shot at what was happening inside. He needed a better angle.

He glanced back at Cara and felt her fingers tighten on the lump of his jacket she held in her fist. He tried to turn around but she held firm.

She put her mouth right against his ear. "Don't even think of leaving me out here alone."

The woman did pick the oddest times to pull him in close. At some point they'd need to work on her timing and the forty pounds of other baggage stacked between them. Unless she ran again, which he feared was inevitable.

He pointed at the window. "People."

"I know." She mouthed the words more than said them.

"I need one second. Promise not to go far." Now to make some identifications, or at least try to. He toyed with the best way to get her closer without endangering her more than he already was.

The body count came first. He'd expect guards. Hell, the place was set up with lookout towers and sight lines in every direction. When no guards appeared, he went with the possibility that whoever hung around inside expected to be alone up here. A logical assumption but a dumb one.

He held up his hand and gave her a thumbs-up when

she pressed her back tighter against the wall. After checking the ground for trip wires and the area around them for an unwanted company, Reid started to move. He headed for the door and stopped in front of it. Even debated taking the risk and opening it. Peek in, get a good look, and keep moving.

Too risky.

Another eight careful steps and he stood next to another window. This one provided a different angle, but the assessment wasn't good. One body on the floor, unmoving and with what looked like hair matted with blood. Four guards, all standing around fully armed and watching the action.

That guy was in trouble. Tied to a chair with his head hanging down. Reid put the man in his mid-fifties. Stripped down to his hiking boots and dark pants and in mid-interrogation.

Reid took it all in. Memorized every detail down to the silver watch on his left wrist and a wedding band. A black man, trim, with dark hair graying around the edges. Reid feared he'd just found one member of the missing expedition.

His gaze shifted to the man on the floor. All he could make out was blondish hair and a bright green shirt, probably a color he chose to stick out and be easily found. Now there was a fucking terrible calculation.

Backing up, keeping his gaze on the men inside who could move at any moment while watching his silent

steps, didn't faze him. He'd learned from the best at the Farm, the CIA training facility in Virginia, but that was only the start of his baptism into the covert world.

Explosives, hand-to-hand combat, apprehension avoidance—it all came naturally to him. His former career as a paramilitary operations officer for the Special Operations Group, a department of the special-ops division of the CIA, took him overseas to infiltrate terrorist cells and nationalist groups in Germany and elsewhere. He spoke four languages fluently and could hold his own in three others.

Danger didn't scare him. He thrived on it.

He reached the front of the truck he'd spied earlier and motioned for Cara to join him. She looked around, checked behind her—acted exactly how he'd teach her to act if he had the time.

Damn, everything about her impressed him.

Her boots crunched against the stones, but Reid doubted anyone inside could hear. As soon as she got close enough, he snagged her arm and brought her around to the back of the truck with him. Hunkered down and, balancing on the bumper, he described what he could of the men he'd seen.

"Are they dead?" Her voice shook as she asked the question.

Once they ventured down that road it would be hard for him to drag her focus back to the problem at hand. That wasn't a knock against her. It was human nature,

something else Reid had studied at length. "Tell me who you think they are."

She gulped in deep breaths. "Cliff."

"Which one? I need more information."

"In the chair. Clifford T. Jackson. Born and raised in the south. Fought for social justice his whole life. Put himself through college by day and arranged protests at night." She rubbed her hands together. "He's an icon in and out of environmental sciences. He's also the leader of the expedition. He's spent a lifetime in the field, first with the Forest Service then teaching at MIT."

"None of that is going to help him now."

"He's dead?"

"It looked like he was being questioned."

"So, not yet." She grabbed Reid's arm and held him in a tight grip. "Stop them. Go in shooting. Throw a bomb. Do whatever you have to do."

"Too many variables." He couldn't quite give her eye contact. The pleading in her voice already pulled at him. Looking at her would have him debating and taking risks. "The other man."

"Simon Dexter." She kept squeezing his arm. "There were four of us at the temporary camp."

"We have one missing. Describe him . . . or her."

"Glenn Cole. Really tall. Like, used-to-play-basketball tall."

"No one in there fits that description."

"You have to get Cliff." She was practically on Reid's

lap now. "He's a good person. He doesn't deserve whatever is happening in there."

Reid decided not to point out that this Simon guy didn't deserve to be facedown in a pool of blood either. "Once I get a look at the rest of the players."

She dropped her hands and backed away. Stood up, but kept her head ducked down. "We don't have time for this."

"I can do the math here, Cara. I could start shooting and have an entire army come up my ass." His explanation did nothing to ease the flat line of her mouth or the fury in her eyes. "This group isn't wearing the commando uniforms, but I see the same skills. Same weapons."

"Are they tougher than you?"

He decided to ignore the snap in her voice. "No fucking way."

Some of the tension left her shoulders. "Russian military?"

"Maybe."

"Do you know and aren't telling me because you're afraid I'll lose it?"

"I've never seen you lose it." Not in panic. Alone in bed with him, she'd let go. In public, when working or concentrating on a task she wanted to get done, she maintained a laserlike focus. "It's one of the many impressive things about you."

"I'm surprised you still find anything you like." She

tilted her head to the side and eyed him up, almost like a challenge.

No way was he taking that bait. "I'm not responding to that." He winced at the ripping sound of the Velcro as he undid the straps on his protective vest and handed it to her. "Here."

She stared at his hand but didn't make a move to take the vest. "What are doing?"

"You're wearing this." Before she could balk or list the top ten logical reasons why she didn't need the protection, he slipped it over her head and adjusted it on her shoulders.

She tugged at it, trying to lift it back off again. "You need the vest."

He rested his hands over hers. With one touch, she froze. Those dark eyes stared up at him and he had to shake his head, glance away. All those reminders about how she'd ripped him apart when she walked out disappeared from his brain. He tried to call them up—even one—and all he could think about was how good it felt to see her again. Be close to her again.

He'd clearly lost his fucking mind, which made no sense. Just like her focus never wavered, neither did his. He'd charged into battle more times than he cared to remember. Shot terrorists while they planted bombs. Retrieved kidnapped kids taken for ransom to fund more heinous acts. Stopped assassinations and threats that would have killed thousands.

Worse, he'd spent months undercover, sitting in a forest in Germany and watching weak men be indoctrinated into an ever-expanding hate group. Spending every minute fighting the urge to round up all the members and stick them in a hole somewhere. That mission had taken up the eighteen months prior to his joining the Alliance, and when it ended in a standoff and more deaths and arrests, he started doubting that he'd ever feel clean again.

He'd seen some awful shit. Starting with growing up in a series of homes, waiting for the next punch to come. Then he ran away to live in one dangerous hellhole after another. His career as a covert operative saved him but sent him on an equally problematic emotional path. Head down and eyes on the mission, he'd gone from day to day. No entanglements. Limited interaction with decent people.

Meeting Cara had made him rethink every promise he'd made to himself. Every vow about staying unattached and not dragging someone else into his life. With her, he wanted to try . . . and she'd walked away.

"No one is going to hit me." He said it and meant it. Believing someone could put him in the defense position seemed like a one-way ticket out to Reid.

"What with you being so small and all." She pulled the vest away from her chest. "You know you need this more than I do."

"I'm fine." Hell, he'd duct-tape the thing to her if

he had to. Just because she didn't want him in her life didn't stop him from wanting her safe.

She shot him a shaky smile. "Your confidence can't stop bullets."

That's not the lesson life had taught him. "We'll agree to disagree."

8

SHOTS RANG out before Cara had time to pull the vest tight around her. In the vast open space in front of her, she couldn't get a handle on the direction of the staccato sounds. She only saw a second of the stark landscape and the sky above before a hand touched the top of her head and pushed her to the ground.

Rounds of fire gave way to a constant volleying. Gravel crunched. Through it all she heard shouting and the thump of footsteps. Peeking up, she could see Reid's stiff shoulders as he shifted around the truck, taking turns shooting and ducking back. Every time he pressed against the bumper, he shot her a quick look as if to make sure she hadn't moved, then fired again.

The noises kept cycling: shots then the loud thud of what sounded like a body hitting the ground, then more shouting. She reached for her gun, thinking the least she could do was get off a few shots of her own. Parker could be anywhere and Reid would eventually run out

of bullets. She knew from experience it was all a numbers and timing game now.

Her hands shook as she slipped the gun out and held it. Firing meant moving into the open, and that idea made every inch of her rebel. The panic rose inside her, from the tremble in her muscles to the loud pounding of her heart. Tension ramped up as energy pumped in her veins.

Just as she started the mental countdown to suck it up and go, Reid reached over and grabbed her arm. With a fierce shake of his head he stopped her. Her adrenaline rush fizzled. Sitting there sounded good to her. Not safer. There was no safe in this situation.

"Fuck this." He mumbled the phrase as he dropped to his stomach. "Anyone comes near you who's not me or Parker, you shoot."

Before she could answer, he fired from his new vantage point under the car. Swearing and the sound of more falling followed right after.

Disable them. Smart. She debated waiting for a signal, a wave of men to storm in, but decided to join him on the ground instead. Just as she turned to lean down on her elbow, her head jerked back. A hand clenched her hair in a fist and pulled. Not subtle or a tug. No, this ripped out strands. She gasped as tears filled her eyes from the unexpected shock of pain.

Before she could punch or kick, an arm snaked around her neck and pulled her body back against a

hard chest. She could hear the man's heavy breathing. Smell the sweat on him.

"Stop." The command shouted past her ear in a thick accent.

Reid flipped around until he lay on his side with his gun pointed right at the person behind her. She grabbed at the arm choking her, pulling and digging her fingernails into his dark shirt. Nothing forced him to ease up on the hold. If anything, it tightened. Then came a rough shake that had her head spinning.

She tried to focus on Reid but his attention stayed on the face hovering over her shoulder. Fury radiated off him. Every inch of him promised pain. For some reason, his anger soothed the edges of her terror. She inhaled, trying to calm the bouncing in her stomach.

"Gun down or she dies," the attacker said in a thick accent.

There was no mistaking that threat. He practically spit it into her ear. One booming shot echoing from behind her. Next the footsteps would come . . . or they should have. She waited for the rest of the men to arrive, but no one else ran in. Just Reid and her and her attacker locked in showdown mode.

This amounted to a last-man-standing fight, one she doubted the man holding her had ever expected. Reid was not one to give up the high ground. He did not like to lose, and he'd told her more than once he never dropped his gun because that served as an invitation to die.

"Let her go." Reid shifted as he sat up. Every muscle tightened until he looked ready to snap.

The move put him eye level with her. She tried to plant her feet, get better traction against the rocks on the ground, but her boots just slid. Anxiety pumped through her. The gun she'd held lay by her thigh. Using it on the man holding her could mean accidentally shooting herself in the head.

She needed some sign from Reid about what to do. Anything.

Through it all, he kept his gaze on the other man. Stared him down. "You have five seconds to let her go."

The man barked out a harsh laugh. "Or?"

"You're fucking dead." Reid's voice morphed from vibrating with fury to flat. Firm but almost emotionless.

That was a bad sign. Reid getting quiet meant he hovered on the verge of blowing. They'd been together back then long enough for her to recognize that.

She tucked one hand between the attacker's arm and her throat, hoping to get a little breathing room. Preparing for whatever was to come. The man glared down at her just as a car roared to life in the distance. His grip eased. Not much, just a fraction.

Reid swooped in. One second she saw him sitting in front of her, almost bored, the next he was launching his body toward hers. She leaned to the side but the force of his impact drove her backward. Momentum sent them crashing into the mix of dirt and rocks.

Her shoulder took the brunt of the hit. The bounce shook her insides, but she didn't blink out. She didn't hesitate either. As soon as the attacker's arm fell away, she bolted. Rolled in the only direction she could, which wedged her half under the truck.

Feeling around and lifting her hips as high as possible underneath the vehicle, she found her missing weapon. Not that it helped all that much. Reid and the attacker were locked in battle. Punches thrown. Grunting as one blow after another landed.

She saw the flash of a gun then something that looked like a knife. After one harsh jab, Reid bent the man's arm back. She swore she heard bones crack. The man's yell filled the air but he did not stop fighting. He wrapped his legs around Reid's waist and tightened until Reid's back contorted at an odd angle and his breath wheezed out of him.

That fast, the advantage switched again. Reid threw his body to one side, taking the two of them away from her. When they stopped moving, she saw him straddling the other guy's chest. A gun wavered between them as they shoved and pushed. Reid yanked the other man's hand and something snapped. The man's arm fell useless to the side. Then Reid's two hands held on to the man's one and the barrel of the gun spun around.

Reid was going to kill him. Right there in the heat of the moment. Possibly before they could get answers. She had to stop him, or at least slow him down.

"Don't!" Her order floated into the air without either of the men seeming to notice.

Reid punched the other man in the jaw once, then a second time. The guy's head rocketed back but his hand stayed locked on the gun. Then Reid ripped the gun out of his fist as if the big blond bruiser weighed nothing.

Wriggling out from under the truck, she jumped to her feet and stomped her boot on the man's outstretched but wounded hand under the weight of her heel. His body jackknifed and his howl cut through her. She winced, trying to block the wailing sound from her head.

Parker slipped around the corner then, gun aimed at the man on the ground. "That was interesting."

Not the word she would use. "Are you kidding?"

Parker had the nerve to smile. "You were very impressive."

"Where the hell were you?" Reid wiped the blood from the corner of his mouth with the back of his hand as he shoved himself away from the downed attacker and stood up.

"Killing the guys you missed." Parker's smile faded a bit when he looked at her. "You okay?"

She nodded. Tried to answer, but the force of her breathing made forming sentences tough. A few more exhales and she got something half coherent out. "Did one of them get away?"

"A car took off from the other end of the complex. I couldn't see who was inside and didn't have my usual grenade launcher to stop them."

Reid aimed the gun at the attacker's gut. "Where are the scientists?"

The man stared up at him with eyes glazed. Instead of answering, he spit a wad of blood in Reid's direction, narrowly missing his boots.

Fear welled up in Cara. Every frame flashed through her mind, from the temporary campsite to now. Then her mind flipped back. "Cliff."

She started to move, thinking to run toward the building where he'd been held captive, but her gaze snagged on Reid's. He shook his head. "We all go. Together."

Yes, that made sense. Much smarter and safer, but the need to race burned inside her. It took all of her willpower not to shove him aside and run ahead herself. But after so much shooting, she knew there would be bodies, and possibly more fighting, so she forced her legs to stay still.

"I think Cara should stay behind," Parker said.

She recognized the tone. It might not be coming from Reid, but it had the same impact. The same goal: protecting her from something horrible. "What happened?"

He just shook his head.

"What is it?" Then the starkness in Parker's eyes hit

her. He might joke and talk about nonsense things, but that look spoke to a depth. To how often he saw death. "Oh, no."

Reid exhaled as he kicked some rocks with the toe of his boot. "Shit."

The hollowness of his tone confirmed her nightmare. "Not Cliff."

So much had happened. All that fear and uncertainty. Her body went limp. That fast, Reid was beside her, taking the gun out of her hand and wrapping an arm around her. She settled into his warmth, welcomed the touch, before glancing up at him. "I need to see him."

Reid hesitated for a second then nodded. He looked over at Parker then to the man curled into a ball on the ground and nursing his arm. "Bring him."

"Lucky me," Parker mumbled, agreeing, before grabbing the attacker under the arm and yanking his big form to his feet.

"If *I* do it, I might kill him," Reid said.

She barely heard the byplay. Walking to the building felt like stumbling through a battlefield. Bodies littered the ground. Sprawled on their stomachs, blood pooling into the stones. As they passed each man, Reid would kick his weapon just out of easy grabbing reach and check for a pulse. Each time he stood back up again his expression grew more grim.

Cara could hear Parker talking to the attacker behind

her. They argued back and forth, sometimes in English and sometimes in what she suspected was Russian. The man stumbled but Parker dragged him along.

When she got to the door to the building, she stopped. Everything inside her froze. She could have sworn she heard the air whistle out of her lungs. She opened her mouth to say something but couldn't get a syllable past her dry throat.

Reid's hand tightened around her shoulders. "I'm sorry."

But her mind couldn't process the scene. Cliff's perfect posture had abandoned him. He sat hunched over in the chair, leaning so far forward it looked like only the ropes binding him kept him from hitting the floor face first.

From her angle, his bowed head showed signs of bruising. Cuts with caked and fresh blood. She couldn't see much else, but recognized the lack of movement. No noise and dead stillness. No signs of life.

"Cliff." She wasn't even sure if she said his name out loud or if it played in her head.

She stepped into the open room. The smell of death hung in the air, new and old. The building almost groaned from the weight of its horrid history. Every scarred wall had deep holes, as if someone had tried to knock the place down but failed.

Ripped floorboards provided a peek at the dirt beneath. Other than a few chairs and a desk or two, there

was nothing in the building. A makeshift light the attackers had set up. Chipped and cracked columns holding up a crumbling roof. A few boarded-up windows and lights hanging from above, but dark and missing bulbs.

With slow steps, never leaving Reid's side, she drew closer to the man who had believed in her. A mentor who choose her for this assignment. Never played games. Having lived through so much discrimination, he'd aimed for an open workplace and didn't care if a member of his team was male or female. He'd given her a chance, and now this was his end. He deserved better. Much better.

As she watched, Reid cut the bindings holding Cliff upright. Lowered him, making sure to cradle his head as it touched the floor. His actions reflected the respect and reverence she'd seen from him before. Seen and loved.

But her fury festered. Breath hiccupped in her throat. She had to choke down the mix of anger and sadness balling in her chest. Up close, she could see the damage. One side of Cliff's face bore the evidence of a beating. The other showed the gunshot wound. The gaping hole.

Her balance wavered. She had to bite back the bile rising inside her. She heaved but refused to throw up. She would not let the attacker see her weak and vulnerable.

The pain fueled her. She spun around to face him. "You did this."

He didn't say anything as he continued to lean against the nearest column with Parker right at his side. Gun ready.

She closed in on the man. Watched him back up a step. Good, he should be afraid of her. She held her hand out to Reid. "Give me the gun."

Parker's eyebrow lifted but he didn't say anything.

Rather than hand it over, Reid stepped up beside her. "Where is the rest of her team?"

The man shook his head. Said something she couldn't understand.

"You already showed us that you speak English." Reid took a half step, putting his body just in front of hers. "Unfortunately for you, I know Russian. Talk."

The man jerked out of Parker's hold and lunged at her. Parker attempted to grab him but when the man got within a foot of Cara and the knife blade in his hand flashed, Reid fired. The shot filled the room as the big man's body dropped. No stumbling and no last words. He went down in a giant whoosh. Crumpled right in front of her.

The combination of death after death played in her head. Then the reality hit her. She grabbed Reid's arm. "What did you do? We needed him."

Reid didn't even spare her a glance as he dropped down to check to see if the man was still breathing and

then searched him. "He was going to stab you, and no one touches you."

"Then you aim for his leg. Right?" She'd seen the move on television shows a million times. Injure the guy and threaten him until he talked.

"That's a bad plan."

She heard Parker's voice and looked up to see him staring at her. "Why?"

"When a guy like that attacks, you aim to kill." Parker exhaled. "It's too dangerous to do it any other way. Too Hollywood."

That from the guy who believed in the unbelievable. "But . . . we have nothing. No information to go on now." She wiped a hand down her face. Tried to regain her composure. "I don't—"

"Where's the other one . . . this Simon guy?" Reid stood up, putting his body between hers and Parker's and pointing to an empty spot on the floor. "He was right here."

Her brain stuttered. She'd forgotten all about him. About the rest of the team. She hated that she could block the human toll from time to time. The thought that she'd become so detached made her feel sick all over again.

So much had happened in such a short time, she couldn't even catalog and assess it all. For the second time in her life chaos reigned. She'd grown up in a household where very little danger happened. Her par-

ents had scrambled for cash and chased their dreams. Her father would sing for money on the street.

They'd gifted her with a life full of music and art, and all she'd wanted was to break free of the uncertainty of limited paychecks and the aching of not belonging, or not being like everyone she lived with. Free-spirited parents who were disappointed that their daughter had chosen something as stereotypical as science. Who even now questioned her every choice and tried to sideline her career, until she'd had to build an emotional wall between them and her when it came to her professional life.

She'd spent so much of her life making excuses for them, silently resenting them . . . aching for her mom to be just a little bit like the stereotype people had about Asian mothers. Just once. Just for a little while.

But as she stood on the edge of death for the second time before reaching thirty, Cara missed them and who they were. Wondered if a simpler life would have taken her away from all of this. Wondered if maybe their mutual inability to understand each other had stolen something important from her.

For someone who craved the stability of a steady job—and she did—she kept landing in unstable situations. She wasn't an adrenaline junky or danger-seeker, but some part of her seemed to search out this life. No part of her feared Reid or questioned the life he led, even though being around him meant wallowing in danger. She didn't know what that said about her.

"I thought Simon was dead," she said, putting words to a thought her brain refused to accept.

Parker scoffed. "Apparently not."

"They're looking for something, Cara. They may be keeping Simon alive just long enough to get information." Reid's intense stare didn't ease. "Which means your time is up. As soon as we clean this place up, we need the whole story."

"Fine." She didn't see the need to disagree. They'd walked into a bloodbath. Right or wrong, the Alliance specialized in this sort of thing. She might not trust Reid with her heart, but she trusted him with her safety.

"The jammer is one building over." Parker reloaded his gun as he talked.

"Let's go." Reid didn't wait for his friend to finish.

With his hand on the small of Cara's back, they started moving. Careful steps took them out of the building and around the rest of the bodies. They reached the end of the main structure and glanced up at the black metal staircase that wound its way to the top floor.

"Already checked there," Parker said as he stepped up and took the lead.

They headed for the next building and didn't stop until they got to the far end. There, on the ground, sat a black box. Wires connected it to two antennas. Except for those, the whole thing looked small enough to carry around. There was even a cart resting nearby.

"It should be bigger." The idea made sense to Cara.

Something that messed up their cell phones and Reid's fancy tracking system and whatever else should at least take a truck to move.

"That's the kind of nightmare line a man never wants to hear from a woman." Parker dropped to one knee and opened the lid. There were switches and dials and he seemed to know what to touch.

Still, she didn't fully appreciate the joking. Not now. "People are dead."

"It's his warped way of dealing with the situation," Reid said.

The trucks, the men. All of the evidence stacked together in her head. She was a person who dealt in details and facts. Things she could test and analyze. The Alliance did the same, in a way. Which made her wonder how this happened. "Don't your people look for things like this? Movement where there shouldn't be movement?" She pointed at the antennas. "Those."

"Something this size would be hard to pick up via satellite image, and they—whoever they are—would have to be looking for trouble right here at the exact right time to discover the problem." When she started to argue, Reid nodded. "But you're not wrong. Having a communications blackout area should raise some flags."

Parker stood up and wiped his hands on the front of his pants. "Tasha could be trying to reach us right now."

"Which is why you're going to dismantle this thing."

Reid snapped into leader mode. Fatigue pulled around his mouth but he no longer spoke in clipped, angry sentences. "Then we need photographs of the dead and a safe place to put Cliff until our people can come and get him. I don't want anyone using his body as a political statement or as an excuse to start a war."

Parker's eyes narrowed. "Sounds like I got the shitty end of the to-do list again."

"We also need to collect the guns and ammo, so we're stocked." With that, Reid put the one he was holding in the holster by his side.

"And what are you going to be doing while I race around and play fetch and take photos?"

"Calling Tasha and getting an alternate place to hide out." Reid winced as he unzipped his thin jacket and peeled up the bottom of his shirt. "And letting Cara handle this."

Parker paled. "Oh, shit."

More blood. Red everywhere. Cara blinked, hoping the frightening image would disappear. But it didn't. Reid covered the wound with his hands, but the blood just seeped through his fingers.

"You were shot?" She knew it was a ridiculous question. She could see the evidence, not a direct hit to his stomach but a hole right off to the side.

"Again," Parker said. "I think this is the second time."

"On this mission." Reid shrugged. "I've had worse."

Parker moved closer to Reid. Took a packet out of the utility pocket of his pants and ripped it open. "No one tagged me. You losing your touch?"

Reid hissed when Parker touched the bandage to his open wound. "You're too busy playing it safe, hiding behind buildings and stuff."

Part of her understood Parker wanted to take Reid's mind off the pain. She got that. She just knew they needed to do some pretty serious first aid if they had any chance of getting Reid out of there on his own. She didn't have a medical degree but she knew enough. Knew he needed a doctor.

First she had to make sure he stayed stable. "Enough boy talk. You need to sit down and—"

"We're heading out." Reid held out a hand. Parker passed him a needle and Reid administered his own shot. "I want to be away from this area before I scramble a call to Tasha."

Before Cara could stop the back and forth, they were tending to the wound. Acting as if it was no big deal or like Reid was made of some sort of unbreakable metal. Not human. Immune to things like shock and death.

His nonchalance made her want to strangle him. "Have you lost your mind?"

Parker frowned. "Fair question, but we are trained for on-the-ground triage. Once you get the bullet out you can either sew him up or use some of the magic powder we bring along to seal wounds."

Reid pressed his hand against the edge of the bandage. “The person in charge of the men we ran into here could be watching. Certainly will come back.”

“Besides,” Parker put the pouch back in his pocket, “this will go faster if I don’t have to worry about Reid fainting.”

“Not happening.” Reid added a bit of name-calling before flipping back into leader mode. “I’ll get coordinates for a safe place then send them to Parker, who will be right behind us.”

She listened to the arguments and comments. Every one sounded so reasonable, as if they’d acted out this routine a million times. They had her thinking she’d blown his injuries out of proportion . . . until she remembered they were not normal. “This new safe house, or whatever it is, better be close because I can’t carry you.”

Reid shrugged and then winced. “I’m fine.”

“Yeah, you seem great.” *The idiot.*

“Not after Tasha gets done with you. ‘How did you get into Russia?’” Parker’s voice changed as he mimicked a higher tone. “I can almost hear her now.”

“I remember Tasha. Tough, in charge.” That gave Cara comfort. These two needed an ass-kicking. She was happy to start it, but she savored the idea of turning them over to Tasha for a second round.

“Remind you of anyone?” Parker asked.

Reid cleared his throat. “I’m still bleeding here.”

And limping, and walking half bent over. Cara saw it all now. Tried to ignore it and keep her voice steady. Letting him know how concerned she was about him wouldn't make the next few minutes run any smoother. "Just so long as it's not another labor camp."

"Knowing Tasha, it won't be anywhere near that nice." Reid wrapped an arm around his midsection. "Let's grab the bags and go. The time for finding temporary cover is running out."

9

TASHA SAT on one of the sleek gray modern couches strategically placed at odd angles in the middle of the Bastion Foundation's waiting room. At least that's what she thought it was. With its three-story soaring ceilings and spare monochrome décor inside, the scaling glass building shouted overpriced and trying-too-hard to her.

She sat on the second floor and squirreled away from the steady stream of visitors and deliveries coming through lobby doors downstairs. Out of the way and cold, like something a serial killer might find soothing.

When her cell beeped for a third time, she read the message and sent off a four-word response. The first emergency call provided the location she needed. The second requested supplies and backup. The third confirmed the coordinates she provided. Not bad for three minutes' worth of covert communication bounced back and forth through a series of proxy servers and pinged from one side of the world to the other.

Caleb glanced at her arm as she dropped it and pocketed the cell. "What was that?"

Tasha skipped right to the information she knew he wanted to know. "Your sister is fine."

That counted as an overstatement. Still, Tasha delivered the line with confidence, just as she'd been trained to do. Just as she'd done in numerous cases over the years. Reassure the loved ones so they stayed quiet and out of the way. Limited the potential liability.

"How do you know that?"

"A message from Reid." Telling Caleb his sister had gotten trapped in some sort of informal turf war—or worse—would not calm him down. He had the resources to get to Russia and get in Reid's way. Add in Caleb's hacking skills and whatever underground network fed him information and he could make himself a target without knowing it. Pulling out another Layne sibling was the last damn thing she needed.

"Ask him—"

"The message was coded and short, which means Reid is worried about communication right now." And that was already more information than she wanted to share. "To the extent your sister is in danger, he's protecting her."

Caleb left the seat across from her and started pacing. "You need to get her out."

"Reid will, as soon as he can." Tasha glanced around. There wasn't a single employee or security guard in

sight. That likely meant cameras and, knowing Niko, ultrasensitive listening devices and body scans.

"You trust your guy that much?"

An interesting question since Caleb was the one who contacted Reid and dragged him into this mess in the first place. Tasha decided not to dwell on that point right now and skipped to the truth. "With my life, with Ward's life. With the life of every member on my team. So, yes."

That part wasn't for show or a line in a training manual. Ward Bennett operated as her second in command in the Alliance, but he was so much more than that. He was her fiancé and the one person who could get her through even the worst day.

The rest of the team qualified as family. Better than blood relation in that she handpicked them and watched with awe every day as they amazed her with their strength and loyalty. Which was why they never left a team member behind and appreciated every sacrifice.

"If it's dangerous for her there, she should be on her way home. Let Reid stay behind and fix whatever is happening on his own." Caleb stopped behind the couch he'd abandoned and glared at her. "Hell, you can move your people in as her flight takes off, but I want her in the air and headed home."

All of that sounded good in practice. Tasha knew better.

She leaned back on the uncomfortable low-backed couch and pretended to brush some nonexistent lint off her knee-length black skirt. The one that hid the knife strapped to her thigh. "It's not as easy to get out of Russia undetected as you might think. Not when you're there on a supposed mission with people watching your movements."

"What kind of answer is that?"

"An honest one." She could almost see the wheels turning in his head. Unless she stopped him—and she absolutely would do that whatever way she had to—Caleb would do something reckless and launch the world into a new war. "You need to trust me. Your sister's life matters to me. I'm not writing her off as collateral damage."

Caleb exhaled, not bothering to hide his exasperation. "That's not very comforting."

Heavy footsteps stopped Tasha's response. A man appeared from the shiny marble hallway leading to the elevator bank. Tall and trim, objectively attractive but not too much, so he blended in. With the slight graying around his temples and conservative striped tie, he would have fit in at any business throughout the DC area. But he worked here, in the swanky offices on the edge of Georgetown, right next door to the high-powered sports management building.

"Mr. Murin will see you." The man delivered his message and started walking away, not waiting to see

if they followed. Barely giving her time to get off the couch.

But she'd played scenes like this before. The man was not just a man to her. She kept an eye on Niko and knew about those closest to him.

Michael Stoltz—Mickey to those who worked for him and had the displeasure of going against him—was the foundation's attack dog. He had some official title like Director of Security, but Tasha suspected his role was a bit less civilized. That would match his very hazy no-intel-to-be-found background.

Her heels clicked against the tiles as she walked past the first few elevators to the one at the end marked PRIVATE. The only one with a guard next to it. Looked like she'd finally found the one place the public riffraff could not visit.

They rode in silence to the penthouse floor. She'd yet to meet a big-name business mogul with an office on a lower floor. The elevator doors opened directly into the plush corner office. She and Caleb took a few steps into the room before Mickey held up a hand to stop them. The move put them a good twenty feet from him.

Gleaming hardwood floors partially covered with woven carpets that likely cost more than her car greeted them. But all she could see was the man standing at the opposite side of the room, staring out the floor-to-ceiling windows to the street. It was a dramatic entrance. Niko didn't even need to move to telegraph

his need to control the meeting. His I'm-in-charge vibe bounced around the room. Tasha was fine letting him live in that fantasy.

He slowly turned. The noted billionaire had just passed the threshold to forty. Never married and at the top of every "Most Eligible Bachelor" list out there. Tasha didn't see what everyone else saw. The temptation to roll her eyes nearly overwhelmed her every time she read his name in the paper or saw him on the news.

"I can't figure out if you're brave or stupid." He uncrossed his arms as he spoke.

She figured the goal was to show off his newly developed muscles. She half wondered how much he paid for those. "Probably a bit of both."

"I told you what would happen if I saw you again, yet you walk in here without a weapon."

That was adorable. It also meant all his fancy scanners could not penetrate the special sheath that held her knife. "What makes you think I'm not armed?"

Niko moved then. Took a few steps until he stood right behind his oversized black leather chair. "You're saying you beat my security measures to get into the building."

"I'm saying you shouldn't be so cocky." Much more of this and she might just shoot him to knock that smug look off his face.

But Mickey was already moving. He pushed away from the wall and stood right next to her. She almost

wished he'd try to touch her. Showing him that women could fight, too, would be a pleasure.

"It's fine." Niko waved his guy off then sat down in that big chair. Looked her and Caleb up and down. Didn't offer them a seat. "Tasha and I understand each other."

"Yes, we do." Instead of yelling across the stupidly big room, Tasha ignored the lack of an invitation and moved farther into the room. Got right up to the edge of the desk before she stopped and gestured to the man beside her. "This is Caleb Layne. You sent his sister on a death mission to Russia."

To his credit, Niko's eyes narrowed. "Excuse me?"

"We've known each other a long time, Niko."

"He's Mr. Murin to you," Mickey said from right behind her.

Niko smiled then launched into an introduction. "This is—"

"I don't care." She didn't spare Mickey a glace.

Niko leaned back in his chair. His gaze suggested he kept sizing her up. "That's a mistake because my head of security can be very protective."

As if that impressed her. "So, this is the guy you hired after I kidnapped you."

Niko sat up straight again. "What do you want, Tasha?"

"Answers."

"Go find them somewhere else."

She actually admired the response. Sounded like something she might say.

"My sister, Cara, is on your expedition to the Ural Mountains." Caleb's voice stayed even. Not exactly respectful, but not rude either. "The missing expedition."

The man had a flare for the dramatic. She admired that, too. "I told you that you'd want to see us," she said to Niko.

For a second, just a flash and then it was gone, Niko's self-assurance slipped. His forehead wrinkled and his look could only be described as confused. Then he returned to his usual I'm-better-than-you half smirk. "The expedition isn't missing."

Not a surprise he took this tack but still annoying. To keep from giving anything away, she kept her expression neutral and didn't fidget. Stood perfectly still. "Oh, really?"

"Everything is on track. She is working in the field and I'm sure once she gets back to the main station—"

"Two of my men are with her." She broke in because if she let this guy talk he might never stop.

"Isn't that interesting." Niko's tone suggested he found the new information anything but.

"I thought you would like that." She didn't. She planned to lecture them later, but Niko didn't need to know that. "Since you're not really funding some documentary about dead hikers from an incident years ago,

why don't you tell me what you're really looking for in the Urals."

"I do not have a hidden agenda."

She noticed he matched her neutral expression with one of his own. "Does that mean you no longer play with Chechen rebels?"

"That won't work." The faint stain rose from his throat and covered his neck then his cheeks. He looked wound up and ready to spring in that chair. "Because that never happened."

"You tried to overthrow the Russian government and help buy a new one." She told the story more for Caleb and Mickey's benefit than anything else. Well, that and to get Niko squirming. "Supplied weapons. Funneled money."

Mickey took another step. Stood right behind her, close enough for the front of his shoes to touch the back of hers. "You need to leave right—"

She talked right over him. "Problem was, you backed some pretty nasty people who decided they liked your money but not the strings you attached to it. They double-crossed you. Covered their Chechen ties until it was too late." She leaned in. "That's not exactly the group of bad guys you intended to support."

Niko's jaw tightened. "All of this is a fiction created by you for leverage. You lied then you tried to use me."

"I did use you." She smiled because she couldn't help it. "Let's be clear on that."

"No."

"You know you're not the only one with friends inside Russia, right?" she asked, ignoring the intimidation tactics. When her cell beeped she ignored that, too. This conversation was too important to push aside. Niko needed to know the power balance hadn't shifted in his favor. He might threaten but she was the one who would act.

He visibly regained his composure. Loosened his death grip on the armrests of his chair. "It is because of my family history that you can understand why I would fund an expedition to investigate a long-running question in Russia's history."

"Because a random relative of yours botched the initial investigation into the hiking incident all those years ago." Not that she cared. She didn't believe for one second this guy would spend that amount of money on something that didn't directly benefit his current bottom line. It's not as if this bit of family history was easy to uncover and trace back to him anyway. And, really, no one would care or blame him. He had enough things he'd done on his own that he should answer for first.

"You've done your homework," Niko said without even blinking.

Always. "I make it my business to know everything about you."

Caleb started to shift his weight around. He'd worked

for the Alliance on the side and off-the-books but never in the field. Being this close to the action seemed to rev up the tension and kill his patience. "None of this helps my sister."

"Working with Tasha is your mistake. One you will pay for," Niko said in a low, menacing tone.

"Then forget she's standing here and tell me what is happening with my sister's expedition."

"It's on track." With the rush of tension over, Niko's shoulders seemed to relax as he leaned back a bit in his chair. Then his attention switched back to her. "You need to remove your men from my expedition. Tell them to stand down."

Her smile only grew wider. "Not likely."

"There are factions within Russia who may be interested in knowing the Alliance is on the ground there." The amusement lingered right there on the edge of Niko's tone.

Tasha found the threat anything but funny. She'd bring the full weight of every agent and weapon at her disposal to stop him from harming one member of her team. "Are you telling me you plan to commit espionage and pass top secret information to Russian authorities?"

His smile faded. "I'm telling you that once again you're playing a dangerous game."

She could see the hatred in his eyes. He seethed with it. "I won last time."

"You won't this time."

She had what she needed. Now it was time to leave, so she gestured to Caleb to move. "We'll see."

"You did well in there," she said as soon as they were out of the building and on the street. Still under Niko's watchful eyes, thanks to his network of cameras, no doubt, but outside of listening range due to the audio jammer she'd disguised as a cell phone. She didn't know if Niko would try to hear their conversation but she wasn't risking it.

After a few minutes of walking, Caleb stopped with his back against the wall of the office building next door. "Other than planting the listening devices, what did we gain?"

That had been Caleb's job. She got Niko riled up and ticked off his watchdog while Caleb pressed tiny black dots smaller than the size of mints in strategic places, like just inside the door and under the lip of the desk. He'd eventually find them but she didn't need to ghost him forever, just for now.

"We know from Reid that the expedition is in trouble. Niko isn't going to share information, but he is going to act and it's going to be fast." He would hate that she knew anything about his business and try to close that loop.

Caleb leaned his head back against the wall. "You think the expedition is part of some renewed plan for regime change in Russia?"

She didn't know what was going on in Niko's messed-up brain, but she knew if he was involved with this, they were in trouble. "Possibly."

Caleb turned his head and looked straight at her. "So, now what?"

"I gave Reid the coordinates for a place to hide out. That will buy him some time while we work."

Commuters and tourists passed by on the sidewalk. A car horn honked as an especially loud car raced by. Caleb never looked up. He kept his gaze on her. "Doing what?"

With her team scrambled, and her needing to work under the radar until she figured out what was happening and who she could trust, she'd depend on Caleb and his special expertise. "It's time we put those hacker skills of yours to work."

"I'm not a fan of that term."

"Call it whatever you want, but your job is to help me piggyback whatever satellite, video feed, or intelligence—regardless of which country it comes from—we need to get me eyes on the ground." In the meantime she'd start working on their covert travel plans to Russia.

Caleb smiled. "You're not even giving me a challenge."

"Let's see if you think the job is so easy an hour from now."

10

THEY WALKED for about half a mile, skimming a line of trees and using boulders and whatever other natural barriers he could find to partially hide their presence. A straight path would have been faster, easier. This way qualified as smarter, but even Reid had to admit that he was ready to sit down.

The way his shirt stuck to the skin around the open wound, pulling and tugging, almost guaranteed a fresh surge of blood when he tried to rip the material off. Just what he needed. Getting shot twice in one day didn't even qualify as a record for him, but then this wasn't supposed to be a dangerous mission.

"We need to stop." Cara did it right after she said it. Stood out there in the open as if it didn't matter who stumbled by.

So much for subterfuge and trying to keep the tactical advantage. He was about to point out their lack of both when her eyes narrowed. Her hand went to her throat as a sudden wariness washed over her.

His instincts flipped to high alert. "Are you okay?"

She rolled her eyes, a feat she was annoyingly good at. "You, not me."

"Do I look like I'm having a hard time walking?" The idea of showing any weakness ticked him off. His side was killing him and his shoulder ached, but he thought he was doing a pretty good job of covering those issues. Wasn't dragging behind. Didn't press his hand against his side, though that would have stemmed some of the thumping there.

Clearly Cara just didn't appreciate the male ego and feeble attempts to preserve it.

"You've been shot twice," she said, as if he didn't know that.

He waited for her to continue, but she stopped and resumed staring. "Typical day at the office for me."

"Don't go all super alpha moron on me." She pointed to a pile of three rocks and then headed over to the area before he could argue. "Come with me."

No question her initial confusion had passed. The haze cleared. Hell, she'd even gotten over what he originally suspected was a concussion and flipped right to the bossiness ordering-him-around part of the program. The hot part.

Some men might be intimidated by strong women. He was not one of them. He loved that she didn't take his shit. He just wished she'd wait until they got to their intended destination before unleashing her stubbornness.

"We need to keep moving." He reached out to catch her arm. The move pulled along his side and had him wincing. The only good thing is that she was too busy rummaging through her backpack to see it, so he fell back on reason. "The coordinates Tasha gave me will put us at a cabin. We can regroup from there."

Cara's head shot up as the paper from the bandage wrapper crinkled in her hand. "How exactly does Tasha know about some obscure cabin in the middle of the Ural Mountains?"

"It's her job to know." Cara just stood there, but Reid didn't have any other intel to add. "That's really my answer."

"It's not a helpful one."

He leaned back against the rock. An edge jutted into the middle of his back but the warmth of the stone eased some of the tightness in his tense muscles. "She has contacts everywhere. Even now she's arranging for a supply and weapons drop. Talking to her people, who talk to other people, who arrange to get us things."

"Like an army of guys so we can fan out and find the rest of my team?" Cara tugged on the bottom of his shirt as she peeked up at him.

Reid bit back a hiss of pain as his material stuck to the skin around his wound. The ripping sensation vibrated through him but he fought to keep his voice steady. "You're saying I'm not enough?"

Her hands froze in midair. "I don't want anyone else to die."

That sobered him. He dealt in death and blood every day. Hell, he practiced how to escape from being tied up and submerged underwater. How to bury a body on the run. He chose this sick life. For some reason, it kept finding her.

He took her cold hand and rubbed it between both of his. "I'm sorry about Cliff."

"This job . . ." She blew out a long breath but didn't continue.

Reid lowered his head, trying to get her to meet his gaze. "What?"

"Office politics are not my thing." She slipped her fingers through his.

He didn't understand where she was going with this, but he went along. "I bet."

"There's a presumption that I don't have to work hard. Like, that I was born with math and science knowledge. As if it's part of my genetic makeup or something stupid like that." She treated him to a sad smile. "Then there are the whispers about how I'm sent out on fieldwork because the team needs a token woman."

The one thing working for Tasha drove home for him was that women could kick ass. He might be stronger but she could outthink and outplan him, and that was saying something. "Geologists aren't very evolved, are they?"

"It's not a geology thing. It's more of a group dynamic where the people in charge have old ideas."

Reid read between the lines. "But not Cliff."

She let go of his hand. "No, he got it."

The pull away. Not this time. He reached for her again. "Come here."

He wrapped his arms around her. Lifting the injured one sent pain surging through his side, but when she rested her head against his chest, he didn't care if his muscles went numb.

For a few seconds the only thing that mattered was the weight of her body. The way she sank into him. Her hair had the hadn't-been-combed-in-weeks thing going on. She still wore the ripped pants, even though she'd grabbed a fresh Henley back at the compound and threw that on.

She'd never looked better. She'd probably smelled better, but that kind of crap didn't matter much to him. Not as long as she was alive. Now he had to keep her that way.

Just as his mouth went to her cheek, she pulled back. Put a few feet of distance between them. Cleared her throat. Basically threw up every emotional wall between them. In a flash she morphed from soft and open to all business.

"Let me check your injuries." She lifted his shirt again. Acted as if the tear along his side was the most interesting thing in the world.

The moment came and went, leaving him with a familiar kicking in his gut. She shut down, pushed him

out. The cycle of hot to cool left him reeling. But this wasn't the time to argue it out or debate her communication skills. He needed to be on top of his game and get her out of the danger zone before they could dissect every moment of their fucked-up relationship.

Until then, if she wanted to stay serious and on task, he'd give her that. "You have two minutes."

"Fine." With minimal supplies, she cleaned the wound. Patted and disinfected. Poked until he suspected the jabbing went beyond actual medical assistance.

He refused to squirm. Concentrated on keeping watch instead. "If you insist on doing this—"

"I do."

"Then I'm going to use the downtime to ask you a few questions."

"Of course you are."

He could hear the smile in her voice but didn't let it sidetrack him. "Tell me about this expedition."

She peeked up at him for a second before returning to whatever she was doing that seemed to cause more bleeding than it stopped. "The cover is the documentary."

"On that old hiking incident." He now had heard more about this dead hiking group than about her real reason for being here. That wasn't annoying or anything.

"Right." She stepped back and frowned at his side. "The bullet went through but you need stitches."

"No time." He gestured at her backpack and was surprised when she handed it to him. Before she could change her mind, he pulled out the packet of sealing powder. "Use this."

She stared at the envelope but didn't take it. "Do you want to die?"

"Not especially."

"Then stop fighting me."

"You've been in the field for your work. I'm sure the medical person who comes along has some version of this." He turned her hand palm up and put the sealant package there. "It will form a scab until we can get somewhere safe and take a closer look."

"No one shoots anyone while I'm in the field."

He decided not to remind her about the last two days. "Just do it." He met her glare with one of his own. "And keep talking about the real reason you're here."

After some head shaking and general mumbling, she applied the powder to his skin. It immediately mixed with the blood to close the wound. But she kept dabbing. "We were conducting other experiments while we're here. They—"

"Who is 'they' in this context?" he asked, because that struck him as a pretty integral piece of information.

She shrugged. "Someone like you. Covert types."

That really didn't help him at all, but he wanted her to give him whatever intel she had, so he stopped after one question. "Ah, I see. Go on."

"There was a lot of activity at an old work camp way up north in the Urals. The place is icy and desolate. It's one of those camps that's not supposed to exist and certainly isn't supposed to be active now, but there was a lot of in and out. Trucks and personnel."

With the adrenaline rush gone and the tension ratcheted down to nonlethal levels, his muscles started to burn. He leaned hard against the rocks behind him in an effort to conserve energy. "Military."

Her eyebrow lifted. "Armed men protecting scientists."

Not the answer he expected. And he hated that. "What?"

"The camp-that-wasn't-supposed-to-exist appeared to be a place to conduct experiments. Then it blew up. A month later word leaked that an entire village of Nenets died."

He knew a little about the region. Enough to get by when an assignment called for him to travel to Russia, but that word didn't jar his memory. "I don't understand."

"An ethnic group indigenous to the northern Urals, near the Arctic area of Russia. Mass deaths without explanation. Russian authorities blamed it on some sort of delayed reaction to a meteor strike from 2013."

He remembered something about the meteor strike and all the destruction. He'd been undercover in Germany at the time, but that sort of news played everywhere. Splashed on the front page of every newspaper.

Still, the explanation raised lots of red flags. "That sort of delay doesn't sound even a little believable."

She pocketed the empty packet. "I still need to sew this up."

He twisted a little to get a better look but stopped when he felt his skin tug and pull. "It's fine."

"I'm the one with the doctorate, so I decide."

Talk about convenient. "Your degree isn't in medicine."

"As between the two of us, who gets to be called doctor?"

"That's a terrible argument."

She shot him a triumphant smile. "It's also a winning one."

"Once the powder seals there is a whole process before you can stitch me up. You can't just grab a needle and start ripping into my skin." That was sort of true, so he went with it. "Keep talking about the expedition."

"They—and by 'they' I'm still referring to some sort of intelligence type like you—worried Russia was developing a new weapon." She pocketed the rest of the medical supplies and zipped up her backpack. "Something that has a lot of people who do what you do for a living very scared, which was why I agreed to take the position and come up here and run some tests."

Tasha hadn't briefed the team on any of it. One more reason mandatory time off sucked. Now they'd have to double-time it to get caught up and set the network in

place to investigate all of these allegations. He hated being out of the loop and one step behind.

Then there was the issue about the source of the intel. Someone hired this team. The "they" Cara kept referring to. Likely some idiot at the CIA who thought endangering untrained scientists was a good way to get the needed intel.

He'd yell about that later. Right now he had to pull the rest out of her. With her practical nature and adherence to rules, she didn't exactly volunteer information. "Go on."

"Specifically, I'm here to check for radioactive materials, any indications of chemical weapons." She wrinkled up her nose. "The usual."

"Shit." That was some rough stuff. Just hearing about the possibility sent a new flash of energy pumping through him. No time to recuperate and analyze. They needed to move . . . and that meant keeping her on the ground with him until he could get the needed new samples. Bringing another geologist in from the U.S. didn't make much sense when they had one standing with them on Russian soil. But that didn't mean he liked the idea. "Why did you have to be chosen for this task?"

"I'm going to ignore the part where that sounds a little insulting."

He hadn't even realized he'd said the words out loud. "I didn't mean you weren't qualified."

"This area, all of the Urals, is sort of a geologist's playground. It's rich in coal and minerals. Gold, precious metals, oil. You name it." She crossed her arms in front of her. "I've been here several times. Spent a lot of time in and around Perm, a city to the south. That experience got me on the team."

Reid had been scanning the area during their entire talk. He took a second and looked over the top of the rock pile. A new attack could come from any direction. But the firmness of her tone brought his attention zipping right back to her. "You don't need to read your résumé to me."

"Kind of feels like it."

There was no way to win that battle, so he didn't even try. "Did you find any evidence of weapons?"

The answer to that question would determine how much risk he took with her safety. His inclination was to keep that probability as close to zero as possible, which meant limited field time and not one second spent alone.

"It's not that easy." She held up a hand as she bit her bottom lip. "Okay . . . I'm not sure how much you know about this."

He felt a lecture coming on. In this case that might not be a bad thing, since he knew almost nothing about geology. "Talk to me like you're explaining the science to a kid for the first time."

"Radiation is all around us. Some of it occurs natu-

rally. Some is man-made. Then we have the problem that plutonium plants in this area used to dump radioactive waste into the surrounding rivers."

"That sounds bad." But not even a little surprising. Governments thrived on secrecy. The former Soviet Union, with this vast swath of unchartered land along the Urals and through Siberia, had a geographical advantage in the secrecy game.

"Like, three-legged cows bad." She slipped the pack over her shoulders as her gaze wandered over the open land. "On top of that there were a series of explosions which further polluted the entire region. That was back in the forties and fifties, and the testing still puts the exposure above normal limits on certain areas."

He was starting to wonder why anyone came to this part of the world. "Don't drink the water. Got it."

"My point is that field testing equipment doesn't always give the whole picture. The plan was to gather samples from a wide area and then test them at the makeshift lab in our compound."

He searched his memory. Ran through the mental layout of the compound. "I didn't see a lab."

"We can add that to our list of problems, because there was one and now it's gone."

"Great, now we have more things to find." The fact that the Alliance wasn't already on the ground and moving on this problem had his temper ticking up. "So, to sum up in nonscience language, you had only started

your work when the attack—or whatever—happened out here. Now your team, equipment, and samples are missing."

"That's pretty much it." She nodded. "Yes."

"Which suggests someone doesn't want you and your team investigating." There was no other conclusion to draw. She was too smart not to get that, and he wasn't in the mood to make up less end-of-the-world-sounding scenarios to explain the reality away.

"That's how I see it."

"Who hired you?" That was the key. The one piece he needed to know and get back to Tasha so she could start banging heads together.

"Cliff."

This was the wrong time for practiced ignorance. "You know what I'm asking, Cara."

"The assignment came through the U.S. Geological Survey. A government job." She wrapped her fingers around the strap to her backpack. "I didn't find out the real job until I had been interviewed, vetted, and was on the plane."

Not the way the Alliance did business. Not the way anyone should, but he needed to take the assignment-handling up with Tasha or the CIA regional director. Someone who wasn't Cara.

He searched his mind for the right words to ask the next question but nothing came to him. In the end he went with straightforward and clear. He didn't have

the energy or time to do much else. "Do you remember any other details about the night of the attack?"

Her grip on the material in her palm tightened. "It's a blur. Pieces come back, like I have this vision of Cliff shredding the inside of our tent with a knife."

For some reason that information shot through Reid. Pierced something deep and hollow inside him. "You shared with him."

She tilted her head a bit. "Do you have a question you want to ask?"

That was a dare and he didn't take it. "Nope."

"It was work only."

Relief whooshed through him. He pretended it had more to do with them evading capture than anything she'd said. "Right."

"But I can date whomever I want."

The words sliced into him. "We're not going to argue about that now."

"As if you haven't dated anyone since we broke up. Parker already said otherwise." She shifted to stand next to him. Leaned against the rocks and looked out over the landscape. Didn't give him eye contact.

"You left me." She'd already driven that point home and now had him saying it. Wasn't that fucking great?

She turned to face him. "Reid."

It was not the time or the place for this. They needed to move. Focus on the job. Get her to safety then double back for her team. Still . . . all good in theory. In prac-

tice, he wanted to be clear that she ripped them apart. Her, not him.

"We were engaged and you got up one day, packed everything and took off." Visions of half-open drawers and stray socks littering the floor filled his head.

He could call up a memory and see the position of every stick of furniture and every item she'd taken with her. Not much. Neither one of them collected things. He could fit most of his life into two oversized duffel bags. That probably said a lot about him. So did the fact she never unpacked the boxes of books she brought with her when she moved into his place before she took off again.

"You know the reality of what happened."

Women always said things like that. Expected him to pick up cues and understand arguments that made absolutely no sense to him. This time he wanted the long version of his sins. "Explain it to me."

"I tried to talk to you back then. I wanted us to pull back, stay engaged while we did the sort of dating normal couples do." She lifted her hand as if she wanted to touch him, but then let it fall again. "Make sure we were compatible. Admittedly, that would have been hard with your schedule but I wanted to try."

He remembered every argument she made. Each one boiled down to the same thing: *I want out*. "No, you *wanted* to put off the wedding."

"I was asking for the time for us to get to know each other."

Excuses, nothing more. "You suggested we live apart."

"Are you not hearing me?" Her voice rose, getting louder with each word. "God, Reid. What I felt for you . . ." Her voice faltered and she stopped.

"What?" He didn't want to care about the rest, but he did.

"It was so big. So overwhelming." She shook her head. "I fell so hard, so fast."

She could not sell that. Not to him. "That's not true."

"There I was, going under, and I didn't even know if you really loved me."

"How can you say that?" He was not shouldering the blame for that. He'd told her he did. Repeatedly.

She'd said she loved him. Cried about how she worried they'd rushed into the engagement and made a mistake. Asked him all those questions that didn't really matter for their future. He'd tried to reassure her, but she still left.

Later, when he turned over every sentence, every minute, while sitting in the shadows looking at a sneaker she left behind, he decided she'd never felt anything for him but sexual attraction. Even that had been fleeting. Because she hadn't just walked away. She cut off all contact.

But now, looking at her, seeing the pleading in her eyes and stark pain written on her face . . . "What are you not saying?"

"It—us—took over everything. Every part of my life." She gulped in a huge intake of air. "When it came

down to talking things through, actually communicating and fitting our lives together, we couldn't."

"Did we really try?" Sure, he hadn't seen the need to discuss every little thing about his past. Still didn't get why she couldn't accept the man in front of her and leave it at that.

"Maybe not enough." She shook her head. "I should have stayed and fought, but I really thought I was the only one fighting."

"I don't understand how you can say that." But he could tell from the hurt in her voice that she did.

"You refused to see that anything was even wrong." Her voice returned to a safer whisper. "This crazy high-adrenaline situation happened. We got whipped up and excited. I kept thinking we jumped in too quick, made a rash decision."

"And you still see our relationship that way." He didn't have to ask because he knew the answer.

"I don't know what to think." She glanced away, talked into the wind. "But I didn't go in looking for a way out. The doubts and worries that we made a bad decision came and I couldn't shake them off."

Every word cut and shredded him. "You."

She looked back at him and frowned. "What?"

"You mean *you* made a bad decision." He stood up straight, putting full weight on his fatigued muscles and clamping down on a groan that rattled up his throat.

"Us."

"I didn't ask you to marry me as part of some sort of adrenaline afterburn." The idea sounded ridiculous to him. He dealt in danger and death every day and had proposed exactly one time in his entire life.

Right when he would have walked around the rocks and restarted their journey, she put a hand on his arm. That's all it took to stop him. All it took to thaw the deep freeze that had settled inside him when she left.

"You act like I didn't feel anything for you."

The lukewarm statement made his head pound. He had to force his body to go numb, to not feel anything. "You did? Lucky me."

"You have to agree the situation back then was intense and unreal."

The words clicked inside him. Threw a switch that he could not turn off again. "You were the one woman I ever proposed to. So that we're clear, it was pretty fucking real to me."

And that was all he wanted to say on the subject. He told her he loved her, she said it back and then a few weeks later ended it. Gave him this speech about how they didn't want the same things and how the danger colored everything.

She'd moved on. Fine, she could keep on walking . . . just as soon as he got her back home.

"Reid, I need you to know—"

"No." He moved away from her when she went to touch him.

Actually, he had one more thing. It crept up on him

and demanded he say it out loud. "For the record, I have dated since you. Parker didn't make that up."

"I didn't think he did."

"I've had sex once. Exactly one time. That's it." And it sucked. Nine months after she left, he'd gone into a bar in France, just after an Alliance assignment ended. Drank too much and went looking for a one-night stand. The woman was nice, attractive . . . and he felt nothing except guilt. As if he were cheating on Cara. That's how wrapped around and fucked up she had him.

Her eyes widened. "In sixteen months?"

The number shocked him, too. He'd toyed with a screw-her-out-of-his-system plan. The idea of entering into a series of no-strings one-night stands, running through woman after woman, sounded shitty to him. Like a nightmare for any woman unlucky enough to find him attractive during that time.

"Yeah, so next time you're tempted to give me a lecture on not being serious about you or my feelings, save it." Because loving her had shut him down. Even now the idea of being with anyone else left him feeling numb.

Now he really was done with this topic. The argument recharged him. Got the blood and anger flowing. He was pretty sure he could take on an army with one hand and no weapon if he had to.

"Reid . . ."

Problem was, he still didn't know if he could handle being this close to her. He started walking. "Let's go."

11

THEY WALKED in silence as hours ticked by . . . or so it seemed. Cara guessed no more than fifteen minutes had passed, but spending even one minute with a pissed off man while he tromped across the field, shaking his head every two steps, made the seconds pass like an eternity.

His long legs gobbled up the distance. She had to speed up to nearly a jog to keep up. She understood the need to keep moving but was pretty sure he'd ramped up the pace for other reasons. Maybe he thought she'd be winded and unable to talk. Nice try, but no.

After what he'd said—about not dating anyone else—she should be out of breath. Right now she was stuck on confused as hell. Back then she'd looked at him—who he was and how shut off from anything and anyone but her and his team—and tried to get him to talk. When he acted as if everything was fine, always fine, and he pushed her concerns away, she pictured a long, lonely life of waiting at home while he ventured off to save person after person.

She knew he'd never share much, because he never did. The only hint about his past came from an offhand comment about growing up in the foster system. No clue as to what happened or the life experiences that brought him to the Alliance. Hell, she didn't even know his real name. It was as if he marked time from the point at which he joined the team and expected her to do the same, ignoring the rest. Ignoring every hard question and all of her doubts.

She got it. She understood how the work he did shaped the man he was. Part of her also knew that a certain type—in command, protector, loner—went into that line of work. But she needed more, then and now. Relationships weren't her thing. Opening up and loving someone made her feel raw and vulnerable. She'd tried with him, but when he met her every moment of doubt with a cursory "It's fine," she gave up. She had to own that. She'd been the one to walk away, but she'd always felt as if he'd pushed her.

Having been smothered growing up, her parents insisting that only artistic pursuits mattered and she needed to enjoy and *feel* each minute, Reid was a refreshing change. They were both driven and practical. With him, she didn't hear constant reminders about how she'd almost died as a kid and needed to "respect the second chance life had given her." She could almost hear her mother say those words.

Reid had admitted from the start that he didn't know

anything about science, but he made it clear he thought it was sexy that she did. For the first time, acceptance for who she really was rather than the sick kid who once beat cancer defined her.

But the practical side of her had balked. Doubt sparked. She'd wanted to accomplish so much more. The idea of being his sidekick, the woman he wandered home to now and then but never really confided in, made her stomach roil.

She walked away right then, because waiting even one more day would have made leaving him impossible. She'd already started justifying in her mind the idea of giving up her dreams and what she needed from him, and that change to her personality had scared her into moving out.

Seeing him now brought all those feelings of loss and longing she kept buried rushing up. She'd talked about how what they had couldn't be more than adrenaline-fueled attraction because to say more would be to admit how hard she'd fallen in such a short time. How much she loved him. Loved him with every part of her. Not something her rational brain could accept. But she loved to look at him, touch him. His loyalty and decency in the face of astounding evil appealed to her on a very fundamental level.

Staying away from him for all those months had been the hardest thing she'd ever done. She'd thrown herself into work. Took one field assignment after an-

other, each one more dangerous than the one before. She knew the choices amounted to running from her feelings and the gnawing sense of loss that consumed her. Knew it and ignored it. Pushed down all her churning confusion over him and tried to pretend it didn't exist.

And now he was back . . . and she still loved him.

Nothing about him spoke to a need for revenge, even though he had every right to be angry with her. She hadn't exactly left the relationship in the best way. It worked for her, but it must have bruised his ego. That hadn't been the plan. She left for survival, before she got in too deep. Before wanting him became more important than the plans she had for herself and her life. Still, he'd ended up as collateral damage, and while she knew he'd gotten over it, that didn't mean she didn't owe him more.

Since he'd stepped back into her life just hours ago, she'd already seen him prickly and vibrating with fury. Wallowing in sarcasm and emotionally crouched down, ready to leap into a new round of verbal battle if she said the wrong thing. Now he whistled. For some reason that nonchalance irritated her more than the rest.

She was about to comment on his new talent when he stopped. He held up a fist, and she assumed that meant she should match her steps to his and halt. Not that she intended to go out exploring anyway. Despite their his-

tory and the ton of baggage piled between them, she wasn't stupid. In a situation like this you stayed close to the guy with the gun and the training.

When nothing happened except more staring from Reid, she leaned in close to his ear and whispered, "What is it?"

"The rumbling."

She had no idea what that meant. The only sounds she heard came from the swish of the branches in the wind and the pounding of her heartbeat in her ears. He was the cause of the latter. "Could you be more specific?"

"This way." Before she could answer, he had her hand and pulled her with him. They veered off to the left and kept going toward a steep slope. The same one he'd warned her about a few minutes ago. "You still run every day?"

She was almost afraid to answer that. "Maybe."

"Good." He tightened her backpack straps then nodded. "Get ready."

"For?" Instead of answering her, he broke into a jog, pulling her along with him. She tried to stop and skid, but his grip didn't ease.

Her foot slid as he dragged her over the crest of the hill. The landscape in front of her dropped away and the view morphed into nothing but gray sky. No horizon. Just a forty-five degree drop to a rocky gravel bed and a snaking stream carved through the bottom of the valley.

Her knees buckled as she fought to get her footing. A stumble would hurt and gravity would drag her the whole way down. The thick soles of her boots grabbed onto chunks of hill then gave way. She fell hard on her hip but her body kept going.

Reid wrapped his arms around her, stopping the painful slide. His weight anchored them there, a quarter of the way down. Hanging from the hillside.

After some tugging, her bag slipped off her shoulders and he tore it off and shoved it farther down the hill. If not for the way he draped his legs over her, she would have slid along with her things. She looked up to say something but he was already moving. He flattened her on her back. A second later he moved over her, not bothering to give her any space or ease up on the pressure.

Their bodies met from chests to thighs. Heavy breathing wound around her. Not his, hers. He remained still, covering every inch of her like a human shield.

Her chest ached and a new round of banging started in her head. She put her hands on his chest to push him up a bit and catch her breath. Then she felt it. The stiffness of his body. How alert and primed for action he was. He held a gun and another lay in the grass by her shoulder.

They had company. She didn't need a signal or an explanation. Understood his body language.

She strained, keeping still as she tried to pick up

whatever stray sound had tipped him off. The creak came first. Then the sound of tires bouncing against rocks and uneven ground. An engine growled as a car or truck or whatever it was pulled closer.

Reid wrapped an arm around her head and tucked her even tighter beneath him. With his face this close, she could see every whisker where the scruff around his chin had started to fill in. Heat rolled off his body, and with his head ducked low their cheeks almost met.

The brakes squeaked as the vehicle chugged to a stop. Voices floated above them. She looked up, seeing only a patch of sky peeking out around Reid's shoulders. He still covered her but she sensed he was ready to pounce if men spilled over the top of the hill and headed toward them.

She waited for the footsteps. Tried to pick up some of the conversation from the little Russian she knew but the words raced by so fast she couldn't understand much. She immediately regretted not taking some sort of speed language course before heading out here.

Male laughter rose into the air. The guttural sound sent a pained tremble racing through her. Panic blocked her throat. She tried to swallow the lump back but couldn't.

A car door banged. Then another.

Reid leaned up on his elbow and aimed. Tension pounded off of him. She thought she could feel his heartbeat hammer against her.

She didn't know the plan but the end result would be the same—more death.

More talking. Right above them now. Near the top of the hill. If the men stepped to the edge and looked down they would see Reid's body. Maybe not hers, but Reid's would be enough to cause the world to break into chaos once again.

She thought she heard the word for body but wasn't sure. She'd stopped breathing, or tried to. She dug her fingers into Reid's side. He didn't even flinch.

A few more seconds passed and the world began to spin on her. The dizziness hit her out of nowhere. So did the need to roll to her stomach and throw up. The tension tightened until the air choked off inside her. She wanted to scream but the words stayed locked in her head.

She closed her eyes and counted to ten. Tried to inhale without making a sound. When she got to eight, another door slammed. This time a string of angry words came fast and furious. Yelling, shouting orders maybe. Footsteps thundered against the ground. They'd been spotted. That had to be the explanation. She had no idea how fast Reid could shoot or how many he could hit, but she hoped his training proved half as good as she always dreamed it had been.

Forcing her hands to unclench, she felt around on the ground beside her for the extra gun. Her fingertips touched the metal as the vehicle sputtered to life again.

The vehicle idled . . . right? She concentrated, sure she heard the unmistakable sound of an engine. The voices faded and tires crunched.

Reid exhaled as he raised himself. He held up a finger, which she assumed meant to stay quiet. As if she needed that warning. Then he crawled, not making a sound. Somehow, he moved his impressive body around, all that muscle, as if he weighed nothing.

He got to the top of the hill and looked around before he slid down toward her again. Instead of sitting next to her, however, he climbed on top of her, balancing most of his upper body weight on his elbows.

"They're gone." His whisper barely registered over the sound of the soft breeze.

She'd picked up that much. It was the rest of his actions that had her wriggling underneath him. "Then what are you doing?"

"Making sure there isn't a second truck or group following behind on foot."

That stopped her movements as well as the relief flowing through her. "I was hoping you wouldn't say something like that."

His fingers brushed through her hair. "It should be fine but we'll wait for a few minutes to make sure."

She couldn't break contact with the gun sitting right next to her. Her fingers rested against the barrel. She thought about grabbing it just in case. "Are you sure they left?"

He eyed the extra gun then nodded. "You did great."

"Since my job was to lay here and not cause trouble, yeah." She tried to smile but couldn't manage it. Probably had something to do with the way her teeth were chattering. The aftermath burn was going to kill her one of these times.

"It's easy to panic in that type of situation. Most would." His voice sounded so reassuring. Smooth and deep and so sexy. "But not you."

Yeah, nice try. "It's cute that you think I didn't."

Some of the tension left his face. "A smart person knows when to worry, and you're pretty damn smart."

The conversation headed to a strange place. Since they kept getting thrown into the middle of shoot-outs and lethal scouting parties, this level of strangeness shouldn't have been a surprise. Still, they needed to work together, and that meant clearing the air. Or at least trying to unmuddy it a little. "I think we should talk about this."

He frowned. "The truck?"

"This." She waved a hand in the small space between them. "Us."

He shot her a you've-lost-your-mind look. He actually excelled at that expression. "Now?"

"You said we shouldn't move."

He straightened up high enough to glance around then ducked his head again. "Or talk. Did I not mention that part?"

"We both know you threw that in as an afterthought just now to shut me down." He had to know from experience that she took his directions pretty seriously at times like this. She didn't doubt he'd use that prior knowledge to his advantage if he didn't want a challenge from her.

His face went blank. "After sixteen months, now you're all chatty?"

She couldn't read him, but the word "chatty" made her back teeth grind together. "We talked back then."

"No, you talked." Anger vibrated in his whisper. "You decided we should have been a short fling. Sex, fun, adrenaline. Done."

His voice had turned singsongy. She guessed he was trying to mimic her, and she fought the urge to punch him in the shoulder. Not that she could get off a good shot from this position anyway. "That is not true. I tried . . . Forget it. We are not plowing over that same ground again."

"Fine." His voice suggested her explanation was anything but.

"The point is, we knew each other for about a week before you proposed."

He frowned at her. "So?"

That would be a sufficient explanation for most people. "What kind of answer is that?"

"Apparently not a scientific one."

He was in fine sarcastic form today. She would have

complained, but something about battling with him brought her body kicking back to life. The aches faded and the fear eased. But the frustration? Yeah, that hit her full force.

"You wouldn't entertain the idea of dating, but you're saying you intended to go through with it." She didn't ask it as a question because the suggestion was ridiculous. Not after the way he'd brushed off her questions and concerns.

A guy like him did not meet a woman, fall for her in a few days, and change his whole life. That was like a plot from a bad Hollywood rom-com. Real people didn't act like that. They were rational and used common sense. Tempered their attraction with a heavy dose of reality.

His body relaxed into hers. "Through with 'it'?"

She ignored how good he felt and concentrated on the question. There was no way he didn't understand her point. "The marriage, you dumbass."

"How could I not want to, what with you being so charming and all."

Their voices had grown louder and she struggled to return to a whisper. "We had great sex."

For her it was so much more than that, but the comment seemed strangely safe. Their attraction sparked and consumed. They may have sucked at talking, and she needed work on how to get through to a stubborn male before giving up, but she could not deny the power of his kiss. Of all of him.

"Finally, we agree on something." He lowered his hands until they lay on the ground on either side of her head.

One shift and he'd be touching her. Like so many times before, he could frame her head in his hands. Lean in. That would all be bad. Very bad. But the memories lingered and she could not blink the visions away.

"The attraction between us was . . ." Her mind blanked on an appropriate word. They all sounded too big in her head, and since she was trying to calm things down, *big* might not be the right answer here. "Strong."

"Could you find a more lame word?"

She'd actually tried and failed, so no. "You describe it."

"On fire."

Heat sparked in his eyes. She suddenly became very aware that he had her pinned to the ground with his body over hers. He no longer crushed her in an attempt to play the role of human shield, but his weight did rest against her. She could feel him. All of him. Every muscle and one very obvious bulge that wasn't there a few seconds ago.

She cleared her throat as she tried to think of a dignified way of squirming out from under him. Not that she was afraid or didn't want to touch him. She needed out because she *did* want to touch him. All over.

The need snuck up on her. Kicked to life and wouldn't fade.

A memory punched through the Reid Keep Out

shield she kept firmly in place in her mind at all times. His stomach. Rippled and lean. It was a work of art, and she'd spent a lot of time running her fingers and tongue over it.

Stupid adrenaline.

She tried to swallow but apparently had forgotten how. "Okay, yes. That's a fair way of putting it."

"It fucking raged between us."

Those shoulders. That tight ass. She'd almost instituted a no-clothing rule when they were together because of the way he looked. Not pretty. Strong and lethal. His body bore the scars of his work. Something about all those marks reminded her of a warrior.

Primal feelings bubbled to the surface. She blamed adrenaline for that, too. "I'm not disagreeing with you. The attraction ran both ways."

The corner of his mouth kicked up. "Still does."

Much more of this and that bulge would become a huge distraction. "Because we're back in a high tension situation. See? You're proving my point."

He exhaled as he dropped his head. His hair ticked against her nose. She wanted to push it away from his forehead but didn't dare. There was enough touching going on without either of them using their hands.

"You know what I did on my last job before taking this supposed vacation?" He lifted his head again and pierced her with an intense stare. "Performed a quick in and out. Extracted a diplomat being held in Yemen.

The region became unstable and he was in the exact wrong place at the exact wrong time and got caught. Some rebels wanted to use him to extort cash before killing him."

She had no idea what that had to do with anything, but since the turn in the conversation might get them out of here without ripping each other's clothes off, she grabbed onto it. "And?"

"I didn't have sex with him." A stark silence followed his words. "That's your theory, right? The adrenaline pumps through me on a job and I release it by having sex. Then I propose to the person standing closest to me. In this case, that person would have been this guy. A thirty-year-old nerd who was so scared he wet himself. That guy."

"You're being a jerk." He also had a point, but she refused to admit that out loud.

"I was summing up your argument." He sent her a level stare. "I can't control myself when the postrescue fever has me in its grip."

"Be honest. How many other times have you had a 'thing' with someone you rescued?" She almost winced as she asked. The answer might kill her, but maybe it would finally drive home what her brain kept telling her—they were not meant to be.

"Never."

That . . . Yeah, her stupid all-knowing brain had no response to that. "Oh."

"Kind of kills your hypothesis, doesn't it?"

Blew it into a billion pieces. She had no idea how to process that. "Are you using what you think are science terms as a way of winning the argument?"

"Am I winning?"

The back and forth. The burst of energy that sparked when they sparred like this. She experienced it all with him. Never with anyone else. She'd dated before him, had good sex, enjoyed dates. But this, the pulsing as if the air came alive when he walked into a room, she'd never had that before or since.

Laughter raced up inside of her. She let it out, let it wash away the tension that had been ratcheting up and spinning around between them. "You haven't changed at all."

"Neither has how much I want you, even though you did dump me." He pushed up. Lifted his body a little more. Just enough to look down at her. "Guess that shows what a dumbass I am."

This was the wrong time and sent all the wrong signals, but she couldn't help it. In that moment, the idea of him getting up shredded her. She wrapped her arms around his waist and brought his body back against hers. "Stop talking."

He didn't pull away or continue arguing her to death. He leaned down, all muscle and mouth, and kissed her. Not sweet and not testing. He really kissed her. Lips crossing over hers again and again, with the kiss deep-

ening with each pass. His tongue licked against hers and a sigh raced up her throat.

His fingers slipped into her hair as he held her still for more. He kissed her until a familiar hunger burned through her and her fingernails dug into his back. Energy whipped around her. She'd been sucked in and now she didn't want out.

As if he heard her thoughts, he broke the kiss. Lifted his head and stared down at her. All emotion gone from his face. "We need to get to the cabin."

The words hit her with an icy splash. Her body dropped back against the ground and her hands slid off his warm body. "That's your response to the kiss?"

He winked. "Did you think I'd propose again?"

Something about the combination of his amused expression and his questioning voice made her want to smile. She bit it back. Wouldn't give him the satisfaction of knowing he won that round. "I should punch you for that."

"You absolutely should." This time he pushed all the way up. Leaping to his feet in one swift move and taking her with him. Once her feet hit the ground, his hands dropped from her sides. "And if you didn't need me right now, you probably would."

"Let's go," she said, repeating his earlier words back to him before she said or did something she'd regret.

"Fine with me." He reached down to grab their bags.

"And keep your lips to yourself." Sure, she'd started

it, but—damn—the man could kiss. He threw his whole body into it. Concentrated and emotionally overpowered her until her breath hiccupped in her lungs. It was almost unfair how good he was at it.

"Agreed." He held her backpack out to her. Wore a far too knowing grin. "For now."

12

NIKO MURIN did not get to his position in life by playing scared. He certainly didn't earn it by letting women like Tasha best him.

Descended from a long line of men who stood up to threats, he felt the weight of responsibility to carry that torch. He'd built his pharmaceutical company and sold it for billions before all the public whining about drug prices could lower his bottom line. Now he spent his days running the charitable foundation and continued to collect the tens of millions owed to him each year from the new business owners under a contract that guaranteed him more money than most countries would ever raise.

The charity funded a wealth of worthy causes, but privately he focused on one goal—to drive the current leadership out of Russia and replace it with men with vision. Men who understood being an international threat only worked if a man wasn't also an international joke. Niko had spent millions under the table while maintaining an outwardly supportive role.

Tasha once threatened to expose him, but she'd been neutralized when he gave her the intel she needed on another matter. At some point, though, he would need to remove her completely from the picture, but not yet.

His choices and reputation, not to mention his money, allowed him to move freely in and out of Russia as he built his network to further his cause. Getting a documentary crew into the Urals proved easy enough. The plan had been simple. He would ride in and explain a years-old mystery. Be the hero. Get press attention while he undermined the government's stability behind the scenes.

That would be his legacy. Rebuilding a strong Russia, economically sound and militarily unbeatable. Restoring its stature in the world. Ridding the leadership of the incompetency and corruption that allowed other countries to gain power over it. His ancestors deserved nothing less.

No one questioned his motives there. No one dared.

Then Tasha walked into his office. Her words breezed past annoyance. She raised issues, talked about things she shouldn't know. He'd sent his people into the Urals. They had the training for the documentary, yes, but some of them had other work to complete. And he'd lost contact. The fact that Tasha knew suggested she had people on his team. She admitted as much. That, he could not tolerate.

After a knock, Mickey Stoltz walked into Niko's

private office. Being the foundation's head of security afforded him certain rights others did not have. Chief among those being the kind of direct access Niko didn't grant to many people.

Mickey also possessed special skills Niko appreciated. Having been a young officer in the Stasi—the East German secret police—when the Berlin Wall fell, Mickey excelled at information gathering and infiltration. In his twenties he had proven to be a dangerous and determined man. Now, in his fifties, still in good shape with all his old contacts in place, he led a life that put him in a business suit and behind a desk most days. Niko had reformed him into a useful member of the team.

But Mickey had failed in the Urals. Very unusual for him. His job was to track the people on the ground and analyze their findings. That was difficult to do if he couldn't find them.

"Your plane is ready." Mickey stood at the door, as he always did. He didn't sit or try any of the food or liquor sitting on Niko's desk, just as a man who understood his place should do.

"I want to reexamine the file on every member of the team." Niko paged through the report in front of him. It was a detailed account of how and why Mickey had lost contact with the team. The conclusion seemed to be an unexplained communications failure, which Niko viewed as an unacceptable answer. "Provide me

with each member's exact location at the time of our last communication with them. I'll see what I can piece together."

Mickey continued to stand at attention with his hands folded together in front of him. "Yes, sir."

"Restore satellite communication now." Niko glared at his security officer over the top of the paperwork. "Do not tell me it's down or give me any excuses. Do your job or I will find someone who can."

Mickey nodded. "Of course."

"And then I want a specific plan on how you intend to deal with Tasha."

The security chief's perfect posture faltered for a second. "Excuse me?"

"She will be on the ground as soon as we are. She is not one to let others step in. While this is usually an annoyance, you should be able to use it to your advantage." Niko closed the report and threw it on the desk in front of him. "She is not to get in the way of you resetting this team and getting them back to work."

"Russia is going to let her in without question?"

"Either that or she will sneak in. That's what she does." Because she was a resourceful bitch. It was the one thing he admired about her. "I get invited through the front door. She sneaks in the back. Stop her."

Mickey visibly swallowed. "Right."

"However you need to do it, get it done." Niko didn't say anything more. He didn't have to. His job was to

demand results. How his staff decided to interpret his orders was not his business. He maintained deniability by carefully documenting each move in the way guaranteed to relieve him of liability. His cousin, the foundation's lawyer, oversaw that part of the operation. "I must say I like the idea of her doing something that would land her in Black Dolphin Prison among the terrorists and serial killers Russia houses there."

Mickey didn't even blink. He'd been trained to harass and entrap citizens. Force them to turn on one another. Whatever conscience he once possessed, if any, had abandoned him long ago. Niko depended on that.

"Where will you be?" Mickey asked.

"In Moscow. I have some government business." A discussion about FDA requirements that would include members of the U.S. State Department and be played in the media as a goodwill trip. "I expect a report within five hours after you arrive at your destination."

"I'll get communications back up and running."

Niko didn't want details. "You better have good news." He spared Mickey one last glance. "You're dismissed."

As they got closer to the cabin, Reid noticed how the tall grass was flattened in places. The trail wasn't exactly hard to decipher. He pointed at one of the more obvious signs of treads. "Tracks."

Cara glanced up at him. "That is the first word you've said in an hour."

"We haven't been walking an hour." He could recount every minute. Between the fuming woman beside him and the sizable nick in his side that sent a new gush of blood soaking into his shirt with each step, he hadn't exactly enjoyed the journey.

The careful surveillance and walking under constant threat of being seen stole most of his remaining energy. He had stamina and a stubborn streak, but the second gunshot wound of the day took something out of him. He'd lost a lot of blood and a good deal of his strength. Nothing a good twenty minute power rest wouldn't fix. He just needed to restore his strength, and that meant he had to stop walking and being on edge, waiting for the next attack to come.

She sighed at him. "Do you need to argue with everything I say?"

She almost made it too easy. "No."

"Reid, look at me." She stopped and forced him to join her.

"What?" he asked, letting her hear his exasperation in that one syllable.

"Use your words."

That wasn't insulting or anything. Never mind that he just assumed she would have figured it out by now.

He pointed to the ground. "Tire tracks."

Her snarky grin faded. "From Tasha's people?"

"I doubt they'd be this sloppy." He knew they wouldn't. She dealt with agents on the ground. Con-

tacts who knew how to get her the equipment and manpower she needed. Tasha didn't pay for amateurs.

"Maybe the guys we avoided on the hill?"

"Possibly." Reid swore under his breath, frustrated he hadn't gotten a good look at that group. He just couldn't risk popping up at the wrong time and getting shot in the head. He had enough to deal with right now, like the red blotches and drops stuck to the grass. "Blood."

The color left her face. Drained right out of her. Her body even swayed a little. "No."

He glanced up at the cabin sitting about forty feet away. A log structure with a sturdy looking door and no windows that he could see from this side angle. Trees lined the back, providing cover for anyone who might be hiding there.

He waited for any sign of movement. Walked them close enough that someone should start firing, but no sound came. The blood trail thickened from stray drips and a broken line to wide swaths of red. If he had to guess he'd say a body—or more—was dragged along the clearing toward the cabin.

That was a bad fucking sign.

He reached for her hand and pulled her behind him. The move left her back unprotected but there was only so much of him left to cover a 360 degree view. "You stay right there. Got it?"

Her hands tightened in his jacket. She tugged on the

material until it stretched against his chest. "I'm not leaving you."

"Good plan." He could feel her trembling but didn't comment. He needed her to believe they were going to get through this just fine.

When they reached the small outlined area outside the cabin's front door, which operated as some sort of makeshift patio, she made a strangled noise. Kind of like a gagging sound. "The smell."

The scent hit him hard. It was one you didn't forget. Decomposing flesh. A sick, rancid smell that stuck to everything.

He lifted the bottom of his jacket and tried to press it against his nose, but it didn't reach and the wound limited his flexibility. He had to power through or risk a rush of bile traveling up his throat.

"Put your back to the wall and yell if you see anyone coming." He tried to talk without breathing. Inhaling only made things worse.

Her hand covered her mouth and nose but she nodded.

He reached into his pack and took out an extra T-shirt. "Take this." He held it up to her face. "Breathe through your mouth, not your nose."

Her eyes watered. "I know that smell."

"So do I."

He didn't stall another minute. After a brief internal countdown, he pushed the door open. A new wave

of stale, rotting air washed over him. Putting the back of his hand over his mouth didn't help. Nothing would block the stench.

Even while coughing he fought to keep his focus. It took a second for his eyes to adjust to the relative darkness inside the cabin. A heavy curtain covered the one window. He could make out a cot and a small kitchen area at the far end.

None of that mattered once his gaze fell on the bodies. Dumped side by side. Lined up in a row, two with eyes still open in shock. Ripped clothing. Blood matted in their hair. Four men and no movement. What looked like stab wounds. One had a gunshot blast to the head that tore away half his face.

Red smeared across the floor. Rough old blankets thrown over them, but Reid could see enough. Brutalized bodies. Cuts and bruises. Total destruction.

He looked for a second longer then stumbled back into the door, slamming it shut and trapping him inside with all that death. His hand slipped on the handle as he tried to get a grip and rip it open. His muscles refused to work. No matter how hard he tried, he couldn't look away from the gruesome scene in front of him. If these were some of the scientists—and he guessed they had to be—they'd paid a heavy price for their interest in a trip to study a decades-old mystery in the middle of nowhere.

He finally got the door open and rushed outside.

Kept going until he stood several feet away from the house. Stood there and gasped in big gulps of air. Tried to purge the memory of that scent from his brain.

He could hear something and knew he needed to open his eyes. Then it hit him. Cara's voice.

She hovered next to him with an arm draped across his waist. "Reid, what's in there?"

"Give me a second." He blew out a long labored breath. Looking at her made saying the words harder, but he had to get them out. "We have bodies."

Her hand flew to her mouth. The tears spilled over her eyelids. "Oh my God."

"Four men." He tried to keep it clear and concise, as if he were giving a report instead of telling the awful truth about the end of people she likely knew.

She shook her head. "My team?"

Her voice sounded so distant, so lost. He tried to comfort her but the words wouldn't come. "I don't know that yet. I'll take photos and run facial recognition."

"It's so bad in there that you don't think I can identify them?"

The thought of having her march in there and witness that scene firsthand tore at him. "I don't want you to have to look."

He picked up on the footsteps and heard a faint whistle. She spun around, aiming her gun at the corner of the cabin with a shaking hand.

"Whoa." He reached around and lowered her arm. "This one's with us."

Parker stepped around the side of the cabin. He carried two bags and didn't look even a little winded, though he had to be double-timing it to make it to the cabin this fast.

"How did you know?" she asked as she peeked over her shoulder at Reid.

"He was making a lot of noise." Just as he'd been trained to do. Sent the code through their communications system on their watches then announced his arrival with the whistling. Made no attempt to cover his tracks or the noise he made on approach.

"On purpose." Parker's gaze switched from Cara to Reid. "What's wrong?"

"We weren't the first ones to find this cabin." Reid waited for Parker to pick up the hint.

When he didn't say anything, Cara spoke up. "Bodies."

Parker took a step toward the cabin but stopped when no one joined him. "Have you ID'd them yet?"

"Cara isn't going to look." She wasn't going anywhere near the place, if Reid had his way.

Parker frowned. "But we need—"

"Hey, Parker." Reid didn't try to hide the frustration in his voice. "No."

"It's okay." She shook her head and seemed to snap out of the stupor she was in. "I can do it."

"No." Reid vowed not to back down. There were some things a person couldn't unsee. He'd seen some awful shit on this job, but that didn't mean Cara had to see humans treated like discarded pieces of garbage.

"The sooner we get confirmation, the sooner we know what we're looking for here." Parker said the words nice and slow, as if explaining new information.

Reid understood how recon worked. The timing made sense. Everything Parker wanted to do followed protocol. But sometimes the playbook on these things missed the human toll.

"We need to get her out of here." Reid emphasized each word in a not-so-subtle message to his friend and team partner.

"You know that can't happen right now. We've got bodies stacking up and—" Parker's voice cut off as he winced. It was as if he'd only just noticed how pale and close to the edge Cara looked. "Sorry."

Finally. Ignoring Parker, Reid turned to Cara. He rubbed his hands up and down her arms. The stillness and the chill coming off her muscles worried him. "Your job is the same. Stand here. You're our first warning."

Tension pulled around the corners of her mouth. Stark pain showed in every line of her body and in those dark eyes. "What are you going to be doing?"

"Talking with Parker." Possibly killing him for being so damn clueless.

"I have a feeling that's a nice way of saying what you'll really be doing," Parker mumbled under his breath.

Damn straight. But Reid didn't want to startle her. Today had been a nonstop roller coaster of pain for her. He didn't want to add to it.

He kissed her on the forehead. "Stay here."

She nodded. "Don't be long."

"I'm not leaving you." He meant right then, but he worried that he really was talking about forever.

"Okay."

He gave her hand one last squeeze then forced his fingers to let go.

13

REID FOLLOWED Parker back inside the house of death. He didn't welcome the second trip, but this couldn't be avoided. As much as he hated the idea of forcing Cara to look at photos, Parker was right. They already had so many unknown variables. If they could understand how many people they needed to find, that would at least give them an idea of how to use their limited resources.

"Fuck me." Parker looked around as he wiped a hand through his hair. "This is some pretty horrible shit."

Not the worst they'd seen. Not by far, which is the part that really sucked. Reid had lived most of his adult life being other people. He'd been undercover in CIA special ops. Pretended to be everything from a terrorist to a white pride nationalist. Literally watched a man get ripped apart while tied to two truck bumpers. Saw another get buried alive.

That didn't even touch the endless parade of dead bodies, some of them at his hands. So many visions

haunted him, and he didn't want that for Cara. "Now you know why I want her out of here."

Standing there with his hands on his hips, Parker glanced over at him. "You sure that's why?"

"Don't be a dick." They had bodies to handle and a mission where he still didn't understand the end goal. The last thing he had time for was a game of verbal gymnastics about Cara.

"I'm just saying you two got back to kissing really fast." Parker's voice lowered as he took a step closer to Reid. "Be careful there, man."

"You think she's the killer?"

Parker shook his head. "You know that's not what I'm saying."

"Okay."

"I think she will fucking flatten you if you don't watch your back."

"She weighs half of what I do." Reid knew that's not where his friend was going, but this was not the time for a discussion about his love life. There was never a good time for that.

"Emotionally, you idiot."

The comment hit a little too close. When she'd walked out, he shut down that side of his life. Made a vow to keep things with women light. Make sure they knew the score up front and not get involved. Work was his priority. Staying in peak condition. Covering his team. Analyzing data.

It all sounded good until he'd gotten that call from Caleb. One suggestion that Cara might have walked into danger—again—and Reid blew every promise he'd ever made himself. He turned his life upside down and brought Parker along for the ride.

So much for swearing off women. For swearing off *this* woman.

"Does she look like she's capable of doing anything right now but throwing up?" The look on her face, the vulnerability, ate at him.

"So, you're going to swoop in, be all caring and shit, and then what?" When Reid started to respond, Parker talked right over him. "I'll tell you. Boom! You're knocked on your ass a second time."

"I'm concentrating on the job." Not that he even knew what that was. They'd come to Russia expecting one thing and walked into something very different.

"We don't actually have an official mission." Parker slipped his gun into the holster on his thigh and reached for the phone in his back pocket.

Reid couldn't argue with that, so he went another way. "Do you want to go home?"

"Nah, that bullshit is not going to fly." Parker crouched down and started taking photos of the dead. "You want me to get pissed off so we can trade verbal jabs and you can maybe throw a punch or burn off whatever is riding around inside of you."

Parker might say odd shit but he was not dumb. Reid

had recognized that from the beginning. The guy had street smarts, and for being on the socially awkward side, could read people faster than most. "Do you know how many metaphors you just mashed together?"

Parker shuffled around the floor as he got each shot. "I barely know what a metaphor is."

"You can't sell the dumb hick thing to me." Reid didn't buy it at all. "Yetis, snowmen . . . I know you believe in some weird stuff, but you're rock solid."

Parker glanced up. "Do you know why I believe?"

"No clue."

"Because when you see shit like this you should believe anything is possible." Parker stood up. "If humans can do this to other humans? Hell, I'll take my chances with Yetis."

For the first time, Parker's obsession with conspiracies made some sense to Reid. "Fair enough."

"Now about Cara . . ."

"I'm not going to fall for her again." Reid thought saying the words might make him believe them. Something about repetition making it so.

Parker smiled. "Too late. Actually, it's probably more accurate to ask when you un-fell for her."

"It's been one day." Had he really only been next to her again for a few hours? That didn't seem possible. Within seconds they'd fallen into a rhythm. They argued and debated, but he enjoyed the challenge. Man, she messed with his mind. "A really long day, but still."

"You never fell out of love with her."

He had to be. He could not be so pathetic as to hang on after she left him and never looked back. "What do you know about it?"

"I know when a guy is about to do something stupid when I see it." Parker flashed the phone's screen. "Hell, you were already thinking about wasting valuable time by not having the one person who could make these IDs actually do it."

"I wanted to spare her this." Reid took one last look at the motionless bodies. "I mean, Jesus."

"We've seen worse."

And that was a fucking shame. "Which says a lot about us."

"I need to know your head is on the mission. I count on that." Parker thumped his fist against Reid's chest. "Count on you."

That trust went both ways. Reid depended on Parker to have his back. That's why he needed Parker to understand about Cara. "It is, but we can make this work without exposing her to more danger."

"We'll see."

Three sharp knocks sounded at the door. "Gentlemen, once again you forget I can hear you."

Reid almost groaned. Her muffled voice from the other side of the closed door served as a stark reminder of how on top of each other they were. "Shit."

"She's got voodoo hearing." Parker sounded impressed by that fact.

"No, just the normal kind," she said.

Parker laughed. "I'll grab the rest of the photos, what little forensics I can. You go handle her."

Reid opened the door and almost slammed into her. She stood right there, frowning.

"You were listening in," he said, stating the obvious.

"Actually, I tried to hear all of it but you guys kept whispering." She rolled her eyes. "What? As if you wouldn't have done the same thing."

The door opened again and Parker slipped outside to join them. "She has a point."

"I could only pick up a few words, but I get that you're ticked off." She looked at Parker. "Why?"

"I'm supposed to be in Montana right now."

She nodded. "Makes sense."

Reid watched their back and forth. The practical science type and the conspiracy nut with a near perfect shot. They shouldn't have gotten along but they seemed to understand each other. Reid had no idea what to think about that.

He switched topics, trying to pull them all back to the problem they needed to handle first. They could deal with all the other problems later. "We need a new safe house."

"I can take care of that," she said.

Reid ignored the idea of dragging her any deeper into this than she already was as he made a mental list of all they needed to accomplish and started assigning tasks. He looked at Parker. "You need to handle these bodies."

Cara exhaled as she moved a few steps away from the front of the cabin. "That sounds awful."

"We don't want them sitting out here," Parker explained.

She winced. "Them?"

"How many were on your expedition?" Reid asked, needing to clarify the number of bodies they needed to track down.

"Eight, including me. Only four of us were at the temporary site when whatever happened there happened."

Parker glanced at Reid. "Eliminate Cara and Cliff and that Simon guy, and we're still missing one."

Her mouth dropped open. "What?"

Parker joined her. "Here."

Standing next to her, he flipped through the photos on his phone. Head shots only, but still gruesome. The looks on their faces, the blood. With each flick of Parker's finger, Reid could see the color drain from her face.

When her balance faltered, Reid took a step in her direction. "Cara?"

"They are on my team . . . were." She looked up at him. Her dark eyes were filled with sadness. Strain pulled at her mouth. She swallowed twice before listing the names of the dead men.

From experience, Reid knew the best way through this was to stick to the facts. He hoped she'd appreciate that idea. "That leaves two unaccounted for. Simon and—"

She filled in the blank. "Brad Byron."

"At least we've seen Simon." Reid turned that information over in his head, trying to figure out what that meant.

Simon wasn't moving when they spotted him. Dragging around a dead body didn't make sense. The attackers wouldn't do that unless they needed him for something. That pointed to him being alive. But there were still so many unanswered questions.

Reid tried to mentally chart out the locations they'd been to. He thought they formed a triangle. If there was a bull's-eye area for whatever was happening, they might be standing in the middle of it. Then there was Cara's intel about the rumors of scientists being moved around out here with military escorts.

"Five dead and we don't know exactly why." He didn't mean to say the comment out loud, but it wasn't exactly a secret.

Parker nodded toward the cabin. "I'll handle this."

"What does that mean?" Cara asked.

"Tasha arranged for one of her contacts to meet me and take Cliff's body. We'll do that here, too." Parker made the comment as if it answered everything.

From the way Cara's mouth dropped into a thin line, Reid guessed it didn't and rushed to explain. "We need to get them out of here. Home where they can be autopsied and then returned to their families."

"That's the worst sentence ever." She shook her head

and walked even farther away from the cabin. Still close and likely not away from the smell that soaked through the walls, but as if she needed some mental distance from all the death.

Parker watched her for a few seconds before saying anything. "I'll get in touch with Tasha, take care of this and get to the drop site."

"What will we be doing?" Cara asked.

"It sounds like I do all the work, right?" Parker winked at her. "Because that's true."

Reid skipped over that and answered her question. "Finding a place for us to meet up and figure out where we go from here. Trace the steps, look at maps. It's a lot of overview work."

"You could listen to me." Some of the color flooded back into her cheeks. "I told you I have a place."

"In Russia." He didn't even fight to keep the sarcasm out of his voice.

"I'm a geologist. I know the area."

Interesting that she waited until now to make that announcement. "We aren't going to hide in a cave."

"That wouldn't be so bad." Parker shrugged. "We've slept in places that make a cave look like a fancy hotel."

She looked back and forth between the men. "Like what?"

Reid worried Parker might actually describe the scenes for her. "Not now."

"Fine, then how about an abandoned mine?" From

her voice it was clear Cara thought she'd won this round.

And she had. Reid remembered something about mines, but she would get them there faster. That meant less time out in the open. He only hoped the attackers—whoever they were—hadn't gotten there first.

Parker whistled. Looked even more impressed with her. "Even better."

"You need to start trusting me." She glared at Reid as she talked.

She might have good ideas, but they had a past. He wasn't quite ready to forgive and forget. He didn't move on as fast as she did. "Easier said than done."

She stared at him for a second without saying anything. Eyed him up as if she were assessing his mood. "Then I guess I'll have to earn it."

One of Parker's eyebrows lifted. "Are we still talking about finding a safe house?"

"Yes," Reid said, because that had to be the case.

This time she shrugged. "Good question."

14

CARA TRIED to calm down. Her heartbeat kept jumping around and a headache pounded in her temples. Every time she closed her eyes she saw Cliff's lifeless form. Now visions of the other men on her team played in her head.

The blood. The obvious beatings. She couldn't even describe what Ken's face looked like. As if the bone had disintegrated. Eyes open. Other eyes closed. The evidence of the horror was right there. A piece of it would stay with her forever.

She leaned against the tunnel wall within the abandoned mine and inhaled the stale air. Almost choked on the hint of mold she drew in with each breath. Her muscles shook, making the gun hanging loose in her fingers tap against her side. She could barely hold on to the thing and her hand refused to tighten around it no matter how many times her brain screamed for it to do so.

Reid had said to stay here while he ventured deeper

into the shaft. If that meant avoiding whatever new terror lurked around the next corner, she would listen. Never one to blindly obey, this time she was fine with it.

She looked up, following the line of the arching ceiling soaring above her head. The stone walls had been painted white in places. The color peeled away, revealing patches of gray. No matter the color, the walls trapped in the cold temperatures. A chill filled the air.

The glow sticks Reid dropped onto the dirt floor gave the place an eerie glow but let her see her surroundings. Wires ran the length of the wall and connected to lights above her head. The box attached to the wall across from her was rusted and the door hung half off its hinges. Streaks of orange stained the space around it.

She guessed water had touched and possibly shorted out the electrical panel at one point. A very bad thing, but there was one bright spot. No bodies. No sign of blood.

She wanted to call out for Reid but didn't. Anyone else could hear and she didn't want to invite company. Not without Reid standing right next to her, ready to shoot. He'd had to snap the old lock holding the main double doors to the mine so they could get in, but that didn't mean they were alone in here. She didn't trust any obvious sign anymore.

Instead of fidgeting or exploring, she waited in the main section of the mine. Just around a slight bend, so

the front doors were no longer visible and right before two tunnel openings into what she thought of as rooms. Within one of these, she could see a huge pool of water blocking further passage. An old mining cart stood in the entry of the other tunnel opening, which Reid had slipped past before disappearing into the darkness to hunt for potential attackers.

"Please don't find any," she whispered to herself as she pushed off from the wall. Nervous energy had her needing to move. She had to burn off some of this adrenaline before her mind started spinning and her imagination ran wild.

She picked up one of the glow sticks and walked toward the standing water. Something drew her to that spot. Maybe the creepy atmosphere or questions about the unknown. Sometimes she couldn't turn off the scientist brain, the need to know and explore. To venture outside of her boundaries and test.

Her footsteps echoed through the damp space as she walked to the edge of the pool. The darkness hid most of the secrets of this tunnel. She held up the glow stick and looked across the dark water. The stillness haunted her. No ripples. No movement.

The pool was not the result of a leak. It was a huge hole, one intentionally carved into the ground, which likely filled with water from underneath. It stretched a good thirty feet along the sides and was cut into a perfect rectangle.

"Hey." Reid whispered the greeting as his hand slipped under her elbow.

The whole scene should have had her jumping out of her skin and headfirst into the dark pool. But she'd heard him coming. She was beginning to pick out the difference between his quiet don't-want-to-be-heard walk and the noisy-for-him version that tipped her off to his entry.

He wasn't the type to intentionally scare her. He didn't get off on seeing women cower in fear. She'd dated an asshole like that once. As if he needed to prove his manhood by showing he was so much tougher than she was. Not Reid. He didn't play those games. Didn't overwhelm her with his strength. He could probably pick her up with one hand and throw her over his shoulder, but he respected boundaries so long as he didn't think her safety was at issue.

He seemed to prefer ordering her around. For some reason that made her smile.

It was Reid's turn to hold up the light and study the tight quarters. He frowned as he did. "What am I looking at?"

"They flooded this shaft." Not an unusual practice. It tended to dissuade trespassers and kids seeking excitement from plunging in. "They filled the space with water so no one goes down there looking for gold, or whatever they were fishing out of this mine before closing it down."

The water could also signal a radiation issue. The Geiger counter in her bag wasn't ticking. She'd turned it on to get a reading on the confined space and so far they were fine. But that didn't mean she wanted to enjoy a long swim.

"Do you know what they were digging for here?"

"Could be anything." She guessed coal, but gold and precious gems were just as likely. The mineral rich area provided what seemed like an endless supply. Once one mine dried up, they moved a mile or so to one side and started again.

"Let's see what's under there." Reid threw one of the sticks into the water.

It floated on the surface, casting the pool in a green glow. The water was clear, deep. From one tiny light she could see a good distance down. The sides were carved into the stone and evened out. Stacks of what looked like wood and ladders sat in a junk pile just under the surface. Steps led down beneath the debris, with lights hooked to the wall to illuminate the way.

She pointed at the steps. "That must have been a way up and down, to go deeper into the mine."

"I don't see tracks for the carts."

"The prisoners likely had to climb in and out." She felt Reid staring at her and explained. "Most of these mines were built by the men trapped in the gulag system. The prison work camps."

Reid nodded. "An endless supply of free labor."

"Exactly. If a man fell to his death—and that happened all the time, I'm sure—the guards would grab another one and send him down in the deceased man's place." No one bothered to measure the human toll because they didn't care.

"While the world ignored it."

The comment sounded dramatic but actually wasn't. The history books referenced the hard life of political prisoners and anyone unlucky enough to land on the wrong side of those in power but couldn't really describe the horror. Records were falsified and information buried. "That's why we have people like you now."

He frowned. "Meaning?"

"I'm thinking if Russia started up a modern-day labor camp and used prisoners to mine or as subjects in weapons' experiments, you guys would know." For some reason, she slept better thinking that. Knowing he and his team were out there made her feel safer. Twitchy and more than a little concerned about his safety, though Reid was the most competent man she knew.

An expert with weapons. Smart in planning. Not one to rattle. While the bossy thing worked on her nerves, there was something very sexy about how in control he stayed under pressure.

"Which makes me wonder why the government sent scientists in to handle this rather than us in the first place." He shook his head as he stepped back from the

edge. "We should have had dependable recon on this and set up protection before you and your team ever hit the ground."

"There might not be anything to find." Despite all the death and danger, she needed to conduct her experiments. She couldn't imagine getting back to work, but she also refused to let her friends' deaths be in vain.

He scoffed. "The dead bodies suggest otherwise."

The reminder zipped to her stomach like a shot. "Right."

He did a double take. In one step he stood back at her side. "Shit, sorry. Let's go back out into the main area. At some point you need to eat something."

At the thought of eating, she almost choked up the protein bar she'd forced down for breakfast. "That is not going to happen."

"Cara . . ."

"I'll eat when you agree to sit down and let me examine you, stitch you up, and give you pain pills." She stared at him, challenging him. Waiting for him to blink.

"So, the timing is wrong for food." He nodded. "I get that."

She ducked her head and smiled as they walked out of the damp room and into the drier main entrance tunnel. "Did you see anything down the other opening?"

As he walked, rock-filled mounds of dirt and shards of wood cracked under his steps. "No."

"Would you tell me if you did?" She stopped and

spun around until her back hit the cool, white-painted wall.

He balanced a palm against the wall right next to her shoulder. "We're safe here. At least for now."

"So, it's okay for me to fall apart." She almost hoped he'd give her permission.

"Do you need to?"

"Sort of." She prided herself on holding it together, but she'd been down this road before and knew her mind could only handle so much strain. The kidnapping left her afraid to fall asleep for months. Back then Reid left the condo and she waited on the couch for his return.

She hid it all, of course. Pretended she bounced back without trouble. But even now, more than a year later, a stray sound could send her flying into the corner, holding her gun for protection. She'd taken lessons and practiced at the range.

For most of her life the only thing that helped to ease the tightening inside her, the churning panic that started in her stomach and could turn her entire body into a shaking mess, was to bury her mind in work. Run off the spiraling tension or hunkering down to review research. Fill her head with anything else.

Then she met Reid. With him she found the one thing that mattered as much as her work. The one person who could sweep her up and away. And that had scared her. Looking back now, she wondered if that's

why she ran when Reid wouldn't talk. Took the first opportunity to flee and dredged up every excuse to justify her choices.

The weight of all she needed to apologize for and explain nearly suffocated her. She was right to be frustrated with him. Thinking her love for him would just disappear had been the huge mistake.

"Cara?" His voice sounded so soft. So soothing.

It mesmerized her. Almost had her swaying. "Huh?"

"Fall, if you need to." He leaned in and cradled her cheek in his palm. "I'll be right here."

"I thought men hated to see women cry." Not that she planned to, but she probably could if she eased up on her self-control the tiniest bit.

"Some men are losers."

She dragged her hand down the front of his jacket. Let her fingers linger over the zipper. "Not you."

"I wish that were true."

She felt the pang through every part of her. An odd sensation that made her desperate to comfort him.

"I didn't leave because you were a loser." And that was the truth. He had faults. They both did. But he was a good man. Better than he knew or would admit. With her single-minded focus, maybe better than she deserved. "You absolutely are not a loser."

"You clearly left because I was such good husband material." He pushed away from the wall, put a few feet between them.

She hated that. Grabbed a fistful of his jacket and drew him close again. "You really didn't have any doubts about us? After the way we started out, hiding for days, all intense and dependent only on each other?"

"No."

"We skipped over dating and went right to sex and then the engagement."

His eyebrow lifted. "The one you never told your family about."

She heard the thread of anger in his voice. A bit of disappointment seemed to linger there, too. "How did you figure that out?"

That hadn't been an oversight but it wasn't really on purpose either. She'd kept waiting to tell the big engagement news, thinking she'd get some sort of sign or her mind would just somehow *know* that he was the one. She felt it in her heart, in the way her breath sputtered every time she saw him, but she'd never been the type to believe in curl-your-toes love. When it happened to her, she discounted it.

Looking at him now, she wondered why she hadn't fought harder for answers. That doubt never entered her mind before. Even though leaving him hurt—ripped her in two and had her fighting for air—she'd always needed to believe she made the right choice for *them.* Not just for her.

But now questions swirled. She wanted to blame the situation and the adrenaline, but the way her heart

flipped over from just seeing him told her those feelings she'd convinced herself were so shallow really weren't.

"Caleb asked why I left you." Reid's expression stayed blank. Unreadable. "I didn't bother correcting him or defending my choices."

"He thinks we were dating and it didn't work out." Because that's what she told her brother and her parents. Rather than bring home the lethal undercover operative no one expected, she kept him away and silently insisted she'd saved him from family drama.

All of those choices that seemed so right at one time now jumbled in her head. She spent most of her workdays analyzing data and coming to reasoned conclusions. She'd applied that same logic to her relationship with Reid. Now she wondered if he defied explanation. If he was the one variable she could not account for.

"I'm guessing you used my controlling behavior as the reason we broke up." He didn't sound judgmental as his hand brushed up and down her arm.

Cara pulled back. Almost slammed her head against the wall by accident. "Did Caleb say that?"

"He knew about the tracker."

She refused to apologize for tattling about that. "You have to agree it was over the top."

"I did it because you were still under a kidnap threat." Reid's fingers slipped along her chin. "Until all the men involved were caught, I needed to know where you were."

The gentle touches had her aching for more. "That all sounds logical."

"See?"

She ignored how breathy her voice sounded as she took his hand in hers. Didn't push him away, but held on. "Except for the part where you forgot to tell me first."

"Admittedly that wasn't a great move on my part." He lifted their joint hands and kissed the back of hers.

With a wink, he broke contact and walked over to his bags. He cradled his injured side as he bent down and grabbed a few things out of them.

The way he held his side made her want to kick her own butt. She was about to order him to stand up so she could check the wound when he dropped a coat on the ground. Then a blanket. Next he slipped an extra sweater out of the bag and set that down on the pile he made.

"What are you doing?" she asked.

"Making a place for us to rest for a few minutes." He used the toe of his boot to move the pile around. Kept doing it until he seemed satisfied.

"Is that smart?" He might think she was talking about safety, but no. She meant because the gathered material on the ground looked big enough for one, which meant she would be sitting on his lap. Which meant facing a new round of temptation she wasn't convinced she could handle.

His head shot up and he pinned her with a sly grin. "Are you afraid I'm going to propose again?"

She tried to stand still and not shift her weight around. "That joke still isn't funny."

He slid to the floor. Winced then covered it up with a fake smile. "I have to laugh about what happened back then or . . ."

Anxiety welled inside her. "What?"

"Never mind." He patted his lap. "Come here."

This idea had trouble written all over it. "There's that adrenaline issue again."

"Do I look on edge to you?"

So smooth. He handled this like he did everything else—without flinching. "No, but you're a bit of a freak."

He frowned. "Thank you?"

But she sank down. Somehow her knees bent and her body dropped. She blamed a momentary loss of common sense. There was no other explanation for why she ran right into the same situation that broke her heart before.

Trying to be smart and failing miserably, she sat up straight. Didn't touch him or lean back.

He was having none of it.

A screeching echoed through the space as he opened the Velcro straps at her sides, then slipped her protective vest off. With his hands on her biceps, he pulled her back and settled her against him. "Just relax."

"Easy for you to say."

He laughed and the sound vibrated in his broad chest beneath her. "In this position? Not really."

He wrapped his arms around her, letting one rest on her upper thigh and the other fall on her stomach. He didn't make another move. Didn't try to kiss her or take them another step.

"This does feel good." She brushed her fingers over his as she debated her choices and tried to turn off her mind.

Something about him reeled her in. The warmth of his body, the husky coaxing tone of his voice. A churning started inside her, low in her stomach. A need that kicked into gear whenever he touched her or looked at her. In their months apart she could call it up just by thinking about him. It made her forget the pain of losing him.

His fingers rubbed over her stomach in small circles. The touch burned through her layers of clothes to her bare skin. Her nerve endings tingled to life. The memories of what he could do with his mouth and his fingers bombarded her. Need whipped up inside her and she didn't want to beat it back.

Couldn't. Not this time.

The words she wanted to say but shouldn't stuck in her throat. She debated saying them anyway. Opening her mouth now could change everything, and she knew that . . . and didn't care.

"You could help me feel even better." She whispered the words as her palm traveled up his arm.

His hand froze over her stomach. "Is this the aftermath talking?"

He deserved the truth, so she gave it to him. "Maybe, I don't know."

"You've regretted what we've done during these times in the past." His lips touched her hair. His mouth wandered down the side of her head to her ear.

She shivered when a warm breath blew across her skin. "Never."

"Cara, I was there." His voice rumbled against that sensitive area near the bottom of her ear.

She hated to break contact, but for what she meant to tell him, she needed to see his eyes. Slow and calm so she didn't spook him or make him think she was running away, she turned around and faced him. "I never regretted our time together. It scared the hell out of me. My feelings for you . . ."

"Yes?" His intense stare didn't ease up.

"I need you to touch me." She took his hand in hers and held it against her chest, just below the base of her neck. "I mean really touch me."

For a second he didn't say anything. His gaze toured her face then down her neck. When it bounced back up to her face again, heat flared behind his eyes. "Lean back."

His hands slipped up and down her sides as she turned with her back to him. When his palms reached her breasts, he stopped to cup them. Rubbed his thumbs over her hard nipples through her clothes.

Her head fell back against his shoulder as he lowered her jacket zipper. And those fingers kept traveling. Over her stomach to the fly of her pants. Instead of plunging inside, he rubbed his hand over her from on top of her pants. Round and round, the heel of his hand passed over her. Pressing and grinding.

Without any thought from her brain her hips moved. Up and down to the beat of his hand. Every time he eased up on the pressure, she lifted up seeking more. She grabbed onto his forearm and tried to drag his hand even lower. Put his fingers where she needed them to be. But he didn't move faster. He kept his steady rhythm. Circled over her most sensitive place until the air hiccupped out of her lungs.

Needing more, she opened her thighs. Brought her knees up and rested the bottom of her boots flat against the floor. Every movement was an invitation, a silent request that he do more. Her body was primed and her control hovered right on the edge. It wouldn't take much to throw her over, and he had the skills. Boy, did he have skills.

His mouth lingered over her neck. His tongue licked and his teeth nibbled on her skin. The combination had her hips bucking even more.

Just when she thought she'd have to scream and beg, he opened the button of her pants. The zipper ticked down and his hand slipped inside. Over her stomach and then under the band of her sensible cotton under-

wear. Lower and lower and until his middle finger slid over her. Then he slid it out again. Not just a little either. He brought his hand to his mouth and plunged his finger deep inside, wetting it.

The move, so sexy, had her squirming, and when he slipped his hand down the length of her again she gasped with relief. That long finger pressed inside her. Pushed in and out, over and over. She met each thrust. Grabbed his hand through the outside of her jeans and held him deep inside her.

His thumb slipped over her, teasing her as his other finger worked. Within seconds her deep breathing turned to excited pants. She squeezed her thighs together, trapping his fingers inside her. Clenched her internal muscles and willed her body to let go.

Still, Reid plunged his finger inside her. He rotated between pushing and rubbing. Pleasure kicked up inside her. The crushing need wound tight. Every muscle in her body begged for mercy as she hung on to the edge of coming.

When he slid a second finger inside her, she lost it. Her body moved and her fingers tightened on his arm. The orgasm slammed into her, stealing her breath. Her head fell forward as he held her. She could hear him whispering something to her. Soft words that merged into a hum, a sound that made it even easier for her to relinquish control.

Her body pulsed and her skin caught fire. Every

inch of her came alive, and when it was over, she fell back against him again. Through it all he never stopped touching her. His hands traveled over her and his fingers inside her. His mouth caressed her and his words encouraged.

With him she was beautiful and powerful. Not broken or someone who needed coddling or to be sheltered. He treated her as a woman and celebrated when she enjoyed his touch.

She had no idea how she was going to leave him again . . . or why she ever thought it was such a good idea to do it in the first place.

Rather than run through all the reasons to be careful, she cocooned her body in his warmth. Put her hands over his arms where they wrapped around her and snuggled in closer.

The loving hold relaxed her. Every muscle loosened and her eyes eased closed. "I can barely move."

He kissed her temple. "That was sort of the goal."

"What about you?" She knew she should get up and let him have a turn. She had to wake up first.

He laughed and the rich sound washed through the room. "I'm fine."

"I can feel you." His erection pressed into her. Then she thought about all that moving around and her screaming. "And I haven't forgotten about your injuries."

"The bleeding stopped. We're good for now."

"We shouldn't risk it." She looked around for her pack and shifted so she could grab it.

He held her still. "Close your eyes for a few minutes. Parker will be here soon enough. You should catch some sleep while you can."

She'd been running on fumes for days, afraid to sleep. All the fear and exhaustion caught up with her. She fit her head into the crook of his neck and closed her eyes.

"I'm sorry." It took all of her strength to move her jaw and get the words out.

He skimmed his lips over her hair. "For what?"

"Not ending it better. I truly thought I was doing what was best for both of us. Not just me. You, too."

The words sat there as silence fell. She thought he might answer, and when he didn't she let her body drift off. She'd almost fallen asleep when she heard his whisper.

"I wish you were sorry for ending it at all."

15

TASHA CIRCLED around the parked truck and stepped right in front of Mickey. He'd been back inside the private home in the small city at the base of the Urals for about thirty minutes. She already had her people back in Virginia checking out the address and names of the people inside.

She waited until he was almost on top of her to speak up. "Interesting to find you here."

His head snapped up and his frown deepened. "I was thinking the same thing about you."

If he'd discovered the listening devices she'd planted in Niko's office, this visit would have been expected. She knew about this trip, Niko's plans and his stupid idea of setting her up for an international prison sentence. It had been so easy that she'd made contingencies in case he identified the device and was setting her up. Looked like that was an undue worry.

There was nothing worse than a man who thought he held all the power.

Mickey pocketed his keys and the piece of paper in his hand. She didn't have enough time to read the handwriting. The urge to wrestle him to the ground for it did hit her, but she refrained from launching an attack.

Well, not a physical one. "A German accent on a man working for an American who has an unhealthy obsession with Russia." She looked him up and down and made sure to show him an expression that telegraphed she didn't like what she saw. "It's like a bad logic puzzle."

There was nothing wrong with him, in general. The whole blond-haired blue-eyed thing didn't do much for her. Her fiancé and fellow team member Ward was the tall, dark, and dangerous type. He wasn't a former Stasi errand boy like Mickey either. Mickey had a dicey past with some questionable activities in it. It shouldn't surprise her that Niko tracked him down and hired him. Nothing should surprise her anymore.

"My boss is an—"

"Egotistical asshole." That was the easiest fill-in-the-blank she'd ever done.

Mickey folded his arms in front of him. "Why are you here?"

A fair question. She'd been following Niko. When he walked into a private meeting at this house and Mickey veered off, she decided to follow the more interesting of the pair. The guy most likely to actually get his hands dirty.

A wild car ride and an hour later, she'd followed him to a nondescript building that claimed to house a trucking business and back to the private home again. She assumed Niko was still inside as she and Mickey stood on the street outside. Interesting Mickey would find his way around the area and back to his boss again without any trouble.

"I'm looking for my men and your boss's science expedition." She also wanted answers, but she'd get those with or without his help.

The CIA briefing she demanded on the way to Russia had filled in some mission intel holes. As expected, they'd gotten wind of a potential weapons production and planted assets on Niko's documentary team. Whether Niko knew or not didn't matter to her. *She* hadn't known. Never mind that she was in charge of the best undercover, off-the-books team either the CIA or MI6 had right now.

The whole thing reminded her that intelligence agencies in the U.S. didn't like to share information or risk losing credit. She'd come to the Alliance, created it, after her time in MI6, British Intelligence. Having to dig around for intel on this problem in the Urals that should have been discussed with her before a plan was ever put in place ticked her off.

One of these days the suits in the CIA would learn to play nice with others. She just hoped they didn't get any more scientists killed in the meantime.

"Stay away from Niko's people," Mickey said with more than a little menace in his voice.

That order almost guaranteed she wouldn't.

She leaned against his car. Lifted her heel and made sure to scrape it along the paint. "Or what?"

"Some men are intimidated by women who act tough, who pretend they are as strong as men." He looked her up and down, almost as if he welcomed a fight. Wanted one.

No thanks. This guy spent a little too much time in communist lockdown in his younger years. He'd forgotten to move forward like the rest of the world had. "This is a fascinating story."

"I am not one of those men."

She wasn't impressed with whatever he was and whatever he intended to get out of this men-are-better bullshit conversation. "Are you intimidated by women who are tough and don't have to pretend to be like men because they like being women? I fit into that category. The can-kick-your-ass category."

He leaned in, baiting her. "Try it."

That was so tempting. "You're a bit too eager."

"You should leave the country while you still can."

"Or?" She watched Parker walk up the sidewalk behind Mickey. For a guy who had been trained, Mickey didn't seem to notice he was being stalked.

"I dunno, Tasha. That sounded like a threat." Parker clapped Mickey on the back as he walked by him and came to a halt next to Tasha.

Mickey's eyes narrowed as his attention switched to Parker. "Who the hell are you?"

Tasha talked right over him. "Please continue. I should leave or . . . what will you do?"

"Imagine what certain government officials would do if they found you hiding in the Urals."

There it was. Niko's big play. Pin her down here somehow then call in his bigwig friends. As if he was the only one with friends in this country. "For the record, I never hide."

"Then I hope you know how to run."

Before she could say anything, Mickey took off. He ignored the car and stalked his way to the end of the block. Turned the corner and disappeared from view.

They didn't run after him or panic. Didn't have to since Parker had pressed a tracker on Mickey's suit jacket when he said hello . . . or whatever that was.

Parker stared into the empty air where Mickey just stood. "He seemed nice."

"Niko's lapdog." Tasha looked at the GPS on her watch and followed the green dot as it moved along the street grid on her map.

"He was trying to get you to go after him."

"Obvious, right?" Tasha didn't like that part. Niko wanted a bold move to discredit her. She understood that but coming to the Urals right after they talked about it seemed ballsy even for Niko. "Niko is determined to leave my body in Russia. That much is clear."

"Are we worried about that?"

"No." Even if she were, she would never show that in front of her men. That was Admin 101 stuff. "Did you enjoy the ride?"

"I was really enjoying the snowmobile. The helicopter wasn't as much fun."

She'd needed him to get to her fast and be able to head right back out to Reid. That meant emergency transportation. "Be happy I didn't make you walk."

"Blame Reid. He's the one who dragged me here." Parker glanced around. "Where's Caleb?"

"Holed up in a hotel room running illegal computer programs."

Parker nodded. "Hacking."

"Apparently that word offends him." Tasha hadn't signed up to deal with the Layne siblings, but they kept making her life difficult. "How are Reid and Cara doing?"

Parker smiled. "He's injured and she's driving him crazy."

"How crazy?"

"I like how you skipped over the injured part."

"I assume if you were worried about that he would be with you." A big assumption since Parker seemed to think the entire team was invincible. But getting shot and bleeding out might be an easier road for Reid than dealing with his feelings for Cara. "I'm more concerned with the part where he's still in love with her."

"You figured that out, huh?"

"It seems that only Cara doesn't get it." Tasha knew that wasn't fair. The Alliance men were not easy. Still, her instincts screamed to protect Reid. To protect all of them. Keep them happy and doing their best work.

Not that she could speak to what went on behind closed doors. The one thing she had learned on this job was that people were not always what they pretended to be. But she refused to believe Reid fell into that category.

"You're not a fan of hers," Parker said.

"I actually am. She's tough and smart. She doesn't balk about the realities of Reid's job. She's had some crap thrown at her and never backed down." In other words, perfect for Reid. He needed a woman who would challenge him. Cara could be that.

"But?" The amusement was right there in Parker's voice.

"I need him to concentrate on this mission." Having a team member put more emphasis on handling relationship squabbles than following mission directives was her administrative nightmare.

"What is the mission exactly?" Parker studied the dot moving on his watch.

"To find out what the Russians—government sanctioned or not—are hiding in the Urals that's worth killing people over." Then get rid of it. The CIA likely had a different strategy, but that was hers.

Parker lifted his head and took a few steps to get out

of the way of a crowd of schoolboys approaching on the sidewalk. "Where does Niko fit in?"

If anyone else had sent the documentary crew to Russia, Tasha would have found it innocent. But with Niko, a man driven by self-centered motivation, the answer blurred. He had an ulterior motive. And unless the people at the CIA briefing her were lying, and doing it well for a change, no one there knew Niko's team had anything other than a documentary in mind.

It looked as if both the CIA and Niko were using the scientific expedition for different reasons. That left it to her and the Alliance to get those scientists out alive. "I'm going to spend the next few days figuring out everyone's end goal."

"What will I be doing?"

"Helping Reid track down the missing scientists and figuring out who's holding them. Once we know that, I'll call in other team members." They'd already been briefed. When she knew more, so would they.

Parker shrugged. "There aren't that many left to find."

And Tasha didn't ignore the human toll. Someone would need to answer for getting so many smart, decent, well-meaning folks killed, and she would make sure that happened. "That's part of the reason I have Delta team on standby in Germany."

"You could bring them in now."

"Too many agents on the ground and the CIA will

crawl up my ass for messing up their fake scientist scheme." The last thing she needed was a red tape nightmare.

The Alliance didn't have the same restrictions as the CIA or MI6. Her team worked undercover and off the books. Only a few even knew of the team's existence, but those at the very top of the CIA did, and that made for some awkward in-fighting.

She didn't have time for that nonsense. Not when lives were at stake. She'd apologize for stepping on toes and bruising egos after everyone was home safe.

Parker joined her in leaning against Mickey's car. "I'm guessing Cara is a CIA plant on the documentary expedition."

"I would only know the answer to that if I looked at confidential files I shouldn't have seen." The same ones that included mental health and physical evaluations of Cara, as well as a host of security clearance information.

"So, yes?"

She liked Parker's refusal to guess at an answer. "Yes. I hate when we're out here fighting for information from the same people who are supposed to be on our side."

Parker nodded. "Amen to that."

"So, let's clean up the CIA's mess, neutralize whatever bullshit Niko has planned, and get Cara and whoever is left of her expedition back home again." Being

successful in all of that would result in all sorts of paperwork and meetings and internal investigations, but Tasha didn't really care. She had a job to do and she would do it.

"Then Reid can figure out what he's going to do about her." Parker shook his head. "He's not exactly thinking straight right now."

Cara had rattled the usually solid agent once before. Had him tied in knots months ago and making uncharacteristic mistakes until a few of his team members took him out on a weekend mountain retreat. Tasha didn't know what they did back then to straighten him out but she didn't want a replay of the after breakup mess either. "Any possibility he's over her?"

Parker made a face. "Not a chance."

"I was afraid you were going to say that."

"Yeah, well." He shrugged. "Love sucks, or so I've been told."

She smiled. Couldn't help it since she had a fiancé back at the office in Virginia, barking orders and insisting she travel with backup. "It doesn't have to."

Parker threw up his hands in mock surrender. "Tell Cara and Reid that."

"Let's hope I don't have to."

16

THE TENT flapped in the strong wind. Cold whipped up around her. She heard a scratching sound. A rip. A tear. She tried to focus. To lift up and stick her head out of the safety of the sleeping bag. She'd bundled in so tight that she could barely breathe.

The tugging by her feet didn't stop. She felt a pull then a rough yank. A scream raced up her throat right before pain shot through her head and the world went dark. Time passed, she didn't know how much, but her body bounced against the ground. The dark night flashed by her.

Dragged. The thought formed in her head and she struggled to free her arms from the bag. The zipper smacked against her cheek as she struggled to push a hand out.

"You need to hide." The harsh whisper echoed around her.

She opened her eyes to see Cliff hovering over her. Ripped clothes and blood dripping down his arms. Fear mirrored in his eyes.

She squirmed and flipped around, trying to see the rest of the camp. She heard yelling in the distance and thought she saw a light. The tents looked so far away. Then the dizziness overwhelmed her. Sucked her down . . . and the darkness swallowed her again.

Reid relaxed back on the tunnel wall, enjoying the feel of her curled up in his arms. Her head rested against his shoulder and her hair fell across his chest.

The high-pitched scream made him jackknife, almost throwing her off him. The anguished cry stabbed right through him. He moved and felt the tear along his side. Not that he cared.

"Cara?" He shook her. "Honey, wake up."

She sat straight up with eyes clouded with fear. She spun around. Her gaze bounced around the area and finally fell on him. The harsh rise and fall of her chest slowed as some of the strain drained from her face.

"Are you okay?" He knew she wasn't. The confusion showed in her face and jerky movements.

She turned around and faced him. "Cliff."

The fact that she said the wrong name sent a spike of panic through him. He wasn't one to worry or invited trouble, but there was no way she confused him with Cliff.

"What?" He kept his voice soft because he didn't want to scare her. The fine tremor running through her suggested she was only barely holding it together.

"I remembered being dragged out of the tent. I was in my sleeping bag and kicking." Her voice sped up as she talked until the words tumbled over each other

He rubbed a hand up and down her arm. "Okay, maybe we should—"

"You don't understand." She grabbed his hand and squeezed. "It was Cliff."

"He tried to hurt you?" Reid already regretted making sure they'd retrieved the body and arranged to have it sent back home.

"He was trying to *save* me."

Nothing she said made sense. She'd blocked most of what happened that night or had been unconscious. The facts weren't clear. But now she talked as if she knew. Reid couldn't help but wonder if she was merging a dream and reality.

But he wanted the details. "I don't understand."

"I thought attackers were all around us, but it wasn't that." She pressed his hand to her chest and kept talking at maximum speed. "The strange panic and the pain. The sweating and the increase in blood pressure. It all makes sense."

Maybe his wounds were worse than he thought. Either that or she wasn't saying everything she was thinking. "It does?"

"Infrasound."

He blew out a long breath and reached for the patience that sometimes failed him. "Remember when it

comes to science I need you to talk to me like I'm five. Baby-step me through your logic."

"It's low frequency sound. It can happen naturally, like with an earthquake. Some animals use it to communicate." Her words slowed down, became easier to understand. Even her breathing leveled out. "These are sound waves below the range of a human's natural hearing."

He almost hated to ask the question, but . . . "What does any of that have to do with you being covered in blood and the ripped tents?"

"There are frequencies that actually interfere with human emotion."

Now she sounded like the in-control scientist she was. The stark panic had left her eyes. Except for the wild hair, which she kept touching and combing through with her fingers, she settled in as if giving a lecture.

Not that he fully understood what she was talking about. "I have to admit that has a science fiction ring to it."

"It's real. Governments have tested sound waves for years, sometimes with permission and sometimes on prisoners." She released his hand and started gesturing with hers as she talked. "These sound waves induce panic. A sort of fight-or-flight mentality."

That sounded familiar. "I've heard of experiments in terms of weapons, but—"

"That's one use. Some people think that ghost sight-

ings in houses are caused by infrasound." She draped her legs over his thigh. "The dose I got was far worse. My mind had me thinking we were under attack and being dragged around."

"Damn." About her sitting position. About the information. Two different needs walloped his brain. He had to separate out one from the other.

"If I'm right we might be able to prove it. NASA has a site in Virginia that measures infrasound."

He knew about the weapons part and the NASA Langley facility. Didn't know everything what went on there, but it sounded as if the facility had some impressive toys. "The whole way from there?"

"It detected and recorded the sound of a meteor strike in Russia a few years ago."

Damn. And this time it was about the power of science. "You sold me on the theory. But the Cliff piece?"

"My guess is he wasn't as far gone as I was. He dragged me away from the tent." She toyed with the zipper on her jacket then slipped her hand over his thigh. "Don't you see? He saved me from being caught."

Reid put his hand over hers to keep those fingers from wandering any higher into the danger zone. A man could only take so much temptation, and even now, after everything, she was his ultimate weakness.

"The attackers didn't actually attack the camp. They used the infrasound then rounded you all up," he said, restating the theory, making his brain work.

"I got lucky." She jumped to her feet. "And now I think I'm going to be sick."

He called up his energy reservoir and followed her. "Whoa."

"I need fresh air." She paced around in circles.

He caught her and lowered his head until he got eye contact. "This is not a good idea."

Armed men roamed the countryside. They had more weapons and vehicles. An entire battalion could descend on them before he could hide them away. It was too dangerous and not necessary.

She held on to his thin jacket with both of her fists. "Please."

The pleading. She never begged for anything except for a few amazing times in the bedroom. The self-reliance he found so attractive was about to kick him in the ass because knowing she needed him crushed his common sense.

"Do you still have your gun?" he asked, and immediately regretted it.

She scrambled away from him to her bag and pulled it out. Handled it like a pro. "Yes."

This was a stupid fucking idea. They were safe, or close to it. Where they stood now allowed for only one logical way in and out. That shifted the advantage to his side if attackers showed up. Out in the open they were targets.

He was about to change his mind and call this off

when she reached the entrance doors to the mine and pushed against one. He stalked over and pulled it shut before she could slip out.

She glared at him over his shoulder. "What?"

Nothing in that expression suggested weakness. She didn't look sick or emotionally beat up now. She had the stiff stance of a warrior.

Looked like he'd been played. That should have ticked him off but it didn't. He loved her spunk. But he refused to see her hurt.

He held a finger up in front of her face. Knew she hated that, but at least he had her full attention. "I go first. You do not move until I give you the signal."

"Which is?"

"I'll stand in front of you and tell you it's safe to come outside." And if he saw one blade of grass out of place that would not happen.

She rolled her eyes. "Subtle."

It had been a while since she treated him to the dramatic gesture. He actually missed it, which proved he'd lost his damn mind. "That's the deal."

"Go!"

The cool fresh air smacked into his face as he stepped outside. They'd made it through the night. The morning sky was painted in bright blue and orange hues. The early light peeked through the dark clouds in places, but he could smell rain. Overcast skies signaled an overcast day. The weather might limit the number of

attackers outside, but moving around in a Urals storm could be tough, injured or not.

Maybe it did make sense for her to come out now. Catch a few minutes of the day before the downpour came. But he had to make sure it was safe for her to venture out.

Gun in hand, he followed the line of the mountain. The mine doors were tucked into the side, but the scaling rock walls continued in a steep slope high above them. He doubted anyone would take the risk and launch an attack from up there. The sharp edges and lack of obvious hiding places made it a bad tactical choice. That still left a significant amount of land to cover.

He continued along the flat part of the valley, scanning the area around him. Trees grew in bunches off to one side. The open land stretching out in front of him made an attack from that angle possible but also stupid. It was hard to hide face-to-face.

That left the right side and the dip down the hill to the stream below. An easy place to hide tracks, and a protected access thanks to the natural boundary of a rock and dirt wall.

With one last glance back at the mine doors, he slipped up and over the top of the hill. When one foot slid on a pile of dirt, he steadied his balance then reached for his side. The dark jacket hid the fresh rush of blood, but he could feel it seeping through the bandage. He needed more sealing powder and a clean ban-

dage. A night in a decent hotel would be good, too, but that wasn't happening.

Ignoring the thumping pain in his side, he concentrated on the water rushing through the valley about twenty feet below him. The gurgle mixed with the whistle of the wind.

He was about to head back to the mine and retrieve Cara when he saw the indent in the dirt. Half a footprint, partially covered up. He dropped down and ignored the jolt through his aching body. No, renewed energy flooded through him as he looked around. His body, sore and battered, readied for battle.

When no one stood up or starting shooting, he followed the obvious direction of the print. The first led to a second. Then he went on a few feet before spying another partial.

Too easy. Tasha hadn't identified their attackers yet, but the men had skills. This attempt at subterfuge was pure amateur time.

Fake. The word floated through his head as he stopped and concentrated on his surroundings. The need to get back to Cara pumped through him. She was his top priority.

He started to turn when something hard pressed against his skull. Not something, a gun. He knew this drill. Had lived through it several times before.

"On your knees." A Russian accent.

Glancing down, then to his side, Reid noticed the

boots and uniform. Not just Russian. Russian special forces. These guys were tough as hell but not the best in the world. They lacked the necessary bond and sufficient training, but they were not afraid to shoot. That was Reid's number one problem right now.

"Now." The guy shoved the gun against his head.

He did a mental inventory of the weapons he had on him. This guy would wise up and do a full body search soon. That meant he had seconds only. "Let's calm down. I'm just out here walking."

"Knees. Now."

The guy kept his sentences precise. They might have run through all of the English he knew, but Reid couldn't count on that. Breaking into Russian might spook the guy even more, so Reid limited his words to match his opponent.

With his hands up, he turned around to face the Russian. The man wore a helmet, and his goggles, which would have covered his identity better, were flipped up on top of his head.

Reid didn't waste any time looking him over. As expected, young. Dark hair and large build. And bigger than average. That evened the playing field a bit, but Reid didn't worry. He'd have the guy down and disarmed in no time.

"Why are you out here?" he asked, not really expecting an answer. The goal was more to throw the man off.

The Russian's eyes narrowed. "Get down."

He definitely liked repetition. "No."

The guy stared for an extra beat. That was all the time Reid needed. He smashed an elbow into his face. Blood spurted from the Russian's nose and he doubled over. Reid nailed him again. A crack to the middle of his back while a kick took out his knee.

The man dropped on a shout. He rolled on the ground.

Reid kicked his gun away as he reached for his own. "I'll ask again. Why are you out here?"

He recognized a guy on recon duty. Reid just didn't know what the hell the other man was looking for. The mine didn't appear to be operational. No tracks led in or out. Having memorized a map of the area, Reid knew every building and every hill. Yet this guy walked out here alone. No vehicle in sight.

Where the hell had he come from?

"Hey." Reid used the toe of his boot and pushed against him. The rolling around whining thing wasn't doing either of them any good. "Look at me."

In a flash, the guy shifted to his back, all signs of pain and whimpering gone. He yelled in rage as he lifted a second gun. It swung around in an arc and Reid fired. One shot, straight into the attacker's forehead. He fell back with a loud thump against the dirt. Blood dribbled out of the wound as his head tipped to one side.

Reid didn't ease up on his aim. He'd won that round and his heartbeat still thundered in his ears. The guy

was fast, but Reid proved faster. By seconds only, but those seconds mattered.

A roar of anger sounded from behind him. Reid turned in time to see a second man launch at him. Made a run and knocked into Reid full force. The blow sent them both flying. Reid landed with a bounce against the hard ground. His upper back took most of the hit but his vision blurred. A searing pain ripped through his side.

He ignored it all as he battled a man who weighed a good forty pounds more than he did. Reid punched and kicked, used every trick to keep from being pinned. But they rolled and he ended up on the bottom.

The attacker slipped a knife out of the sheath strapped to his chest. Reid moved his head, just missed being sliced by the blade. Rage had the attacker in its grip. He swung the knife, barely missing Reid a second time by slamming the end into the dirt.

Reid's gun was wedged between them. He reached around now, trying to grab the handle. The crushing weight on his chest messed up his breathing but he kept moving. When the attacker wiggled the blade out of the ground, Reid knew he had only seconds to act.

Then a gunshot boomed from above, startling him. Dirt kicked up right next to the attacker's thigh and he eased up on his hold, leaned back. Reid didn't hesitate. He grabbed the man's gun and fired into the center of his chest.

The attacker froze above him as the knife dropped

from his lifeless fingers and clanked against a rock. His body grew heavier right before he fell. A dead drop that would have landed him on top of Reid if Reid hadn't rolled to the side in time.

His gaze flicked from the smashed face now planted next to him to the woman standing above him, still holding her gun at the ready. "Cara?"

"I heard the screaming." Her voice shook but she did not move.

Reid tugged his leg out from under the attacker. It took an extra few seconds to jump to his feet.

The haze cleared from her eyes and they focused on him. "You're bleeding."

He should yell at her for taking risks and remind her about their deal for her to stay safe and inside. He didn't do either. He wrapped his arms around her and leaned his body into hers. "Thank you."

After a second her arms came up and around his waist and she mumbled into his shoulder. "You almost got yourself killed, you dumbass."

He had to smile. Only Cara would scold at a time like this.

He pulled back and looked down at her. Fought the urge to kiss her, out there in the open and still in the middle of danger. "Your diversion helped."

She snorted. "I saved you."

"Let's not get carried away." He would have won that battle. He refused to think otherwise, but the assist

certainly made it end faster and smoother. "I need to contact Tasha."

"And ask for an ambulance?"

He winced when Cara lifted his jacket to examine his now reopened wound. "Coordinates."

"Excuse me?"

"That was a scouting party of some sort. Two Russian special forces guys. There is something out here." Something people were willing to kill to hide or find, he wasn't sure which.

"Does Parker need to come and take care of these guys, too?"

Reid finished typing in the message to Tasha. He looked at the bodies and the blood. Someone would come looking for them eventually. "The hill."

"You keep saying random words."

"I'm going to roll them over the hill." When she frowned at him, he took the time to be clearer. "They will be harder to spot that way. It will buy us some time while Parker makes his way back to us to help out."

Before she could argue or come up with some scientific way to dispose of the bodies, one that would likely take too much time, he went to work. Using his feet, he rolled one then the other over the side. It felt disrespectful and wrong to him on one level, but they started it. He was just out taking a walk when they jumped him.

He turned back around to find her standing there, hands on her hips. Glaring. "What?"

"Now I patch up your side."

He didn't bother to argue. "Fine."

Her eyebrow lifted as she stepped forward. Sliding her shoulder under his armpit, she balanced some of his weight on her own.

They walked a few feet before she spoke again. "You're right about one thing."

For some reason he doubted whatever she was about to say was really a compliment. "Only one?"

"Maybe we shouldn't be outside right now."

He should have taped that admission to use later. "I'll refrain from saying 'I told you so.'"

"Smart."

They walked a few more steps, Cara taking the lead. He could get there on his own with no trouble, but being this close to her didn't suck. Having her play nurse was also pretty fucking hot.

They reached the doors to the mine and she moved ahead to face him. "You need to know one thing."

Wary now, he held back. "What?"

"I'm going to be all over you once we get in there."

"Are you scared?" That didn't make much sense. With gun blazing she'd saved his life, and had been ordering him around for the last ten minutes.

She shook her head. "No."

Something in her tone . . . it was as if the air between them changed. "No?"

"That's not what I'm talking about at all."

17

ONCE INSIDE, Cara stripped off her jacket then his. Then his insulated shirt underneath. She had him bare to the waist and still didn't know whether to kiss him or shake him for getting injured again, which she knew made no sense since she was the one who wanted to go outside. He had her mind flopping from one option to the other.

But the kiss definitely was going to happen. Kissing, touching . . . him inside her. All of it. She'd been thinking about him. Wanting and dreaming and regretting for so long.

Up until a day ago she thought she'd made the right decision when she walked away, even though that likely meant a lonely future for her. She thought about him all the time, pictured him when she closed her eyes. Remembered how safe she felt when he wrapped his strong arms around her. How she loved to watch him sleep.

Part of her assumed that eternal longing was the

price she had to pay for ever letting herself be that vulnerable. The relationship might have been quick but he owned a piece of her whether they were together or not. That love she had been so sure would fade never did.

The way he dropped everything to come find her made her ache more pronounced. He'd called out her name as he showed off that cocky walk she remembered so well. Backed up his confidence with action. Stepped in front of her and protected her again and again.

She wanted him back then. Wanted him now. Was beginning to wonder if she'd always want him.

Maybe the hormones and adrenaline mixed to steal her common sense. She didn't care. She'd seen so much horror. Lived with fear until she vibrated from the force of it.

Now she needed something for herself.

First, she had to sew him up. Make him whole . . . or as close as possible. Nothing else mattered so long as he refused to let her help him.

She rummaged through the bags, searching for what she needed. Dumped the medical supplies on his jacket on the ground then turned to him. "Lean against the wall."

"I thought you wanted to have sex."

"Health first." As gently as possible, she cleaned the wound. To keep going she ignored the way he sucked in air at her touch. The faster she worked, the better this would be.

"I'm trying to figure out if that's sexy."

The roughness of his voice signaled pain. That had her slowing down, rethinking her plans. Now wasn't the time to be selfish. "We better not."

He put his hand over hers and slowed her movements. "Are you saying that because of my side or because of something else? Because I can go right now. Don't let a little wincing stop you."

Men. "I don't want you to bleed out while my legs are wrapped around your waist."

He whistled. "That is a hell of a mental image."

She thought he'd like that one. Maybe it would take his mind off the poking as she stitched him up.

As she worked she marveled at the lack of fat on his waist and how he didn't make a sound. The sign of strength could be his way of saying he could have sex. She wasn't sure.

That meant she had to be the adult. "We'll wait."

"But you're saying it's going to happen?"

She wanted to deny it but the words refused to form in her brain. "We have a serious issue between us with danger afterburn."

"I hate when you say things like that."

"Right." She couldn't tear her gaze away. Her mind spun with the ways she could make this happen, if only for an hour. Work off extra energy, protect him, give them both a few minutes of fun. She needed all three, and getting there took some thinking and planning.

He smiled as he shook his head. "You're staring."

Her gaze toured over his scarred chest and down to his flat stomach. "You're still the most attractive man I've ever seen."

"Did you hit your head?"

Not just his body, which was *hot damn* impressive. The imperfect face with high cheekbones and a firm chin. Intelligent if a little too knowing eyes that mirrored all the pain he'd seen.

Rather than destroy him or make him distrust people, he thrived on loyalty to his team. Strong, solid, and so secretive.

He held a hand out to her and she went to him without even debating. Her fingers rested on his shoulders then slipped around his neck. When his lips touched hers, a series of tiny explosions went off inside her. His mouth pressed against hers, deepening and coaxing as she fell into his touch.

They were a mess and hurt and still in danger. They stood in a cave with a mile of old emotionally charged baggage stacked between them. There were so many reasons not to drop into this abyss a second time. So many ways this could go wrong to the point where she couldn't regain her footing again.

But the kiss raged on. Their hands roamed over each other. Her body resting against his. The mouth . . . that tongue.

After a minute of heated touches he broke the kiss

and balanced his forehead against hers. "We need to think about this."

"Because you're hurt."

"I'm capable." He shook his head and his skin brushed over hers. "Willing and able, trust me."

He might be lying but she saw the green light and jumped on it. "Then stop talking."

She kissed him again. Dragged his head down and licked her tongue along the seam between his lips. Cradled his head as her mouth slid over his.

When he broke away a second time his heavy breathing filled the air between them. "Are you going to regret this right after?"

She reached for his belt, struggled to unclasp the buckle. "Are you going to talk the whole time?"

He reached down and opened it with a simple flick of his wrist. "I'm serious."

Every choice she made impacted both of them. This self-assured man kept stopping. Not because he wanted to. No, she could feel his growing erection and the hammering of his heart under her hand. He needed this as much as she did.

That itching deep in her soul. That scratch that never fully went away.

She would make him understand.

"I've never regretted one minute with you. Never." She framed his head in her hands and stared into his eyes. "I need you to hear me this time. I mean it when I say that."

"But this is an adrenaline thing, right?"

"I don't know what it is." And that was the truth. She hadn't meant to say it and definitely didn't want to feel the doubts rise, her heart and mind refusing to merge on one thought when it came to him. "And you're killing the mood."

"Right." He winked at her. "The condom is in the outside pocket of my backpack."

Of course it was. "You still carry one."

She dropped down and grabbed the packet. Instead of standing right back up, she crouched in front of him by his feet. From this angle she could see the bulge in his pants and rough rise and fall of his chest.

He blew out a long haggard breath. "Tasha requires us to, as part of our go bag."

Cara slipped her palms up and down the outside of his legs along the material, loving the outline of every muscle. "I love her right now."

"Me, too."

She shifted to her knees and slowly lowered his zipper until his black boxer briefs peeked out. Her fingers skimmed over him, relearning every inch. Watching him grow under her palm.

"Cara." His fingers slid into her hair and held her close. "You're killing me."

She leaned forward and pressed a kiss on him. Felt the heat burn through his underwear and against her lips. In a slow striptease, she tugged his pants down. Let them drop to his knees. Reaching under the elastic,

she peeled the briefs over and off him. Shoved all the material out of her way.

He whispered her name. The husky growl was the sexiest sound she'd ever heard. It lured her in, spurred her on.

With her hand wrapped around him, she licked her tongue across his tip. Felt the hard tremor move though him. The reaction had her wanting more. She sucked, taking him just inside her mouth. After a few passes of her lips, his hips started to buck.

"Now, Cara." He reached down with the condom in his hand.

She had no idea how he got it out and ready, but when sex was the prize, men tended to perform miracles. Even with his crumbling control she wanted to string out the sensual torture. All that feminine power, enough to reduce a strong man to a shaking, begging mess. She loved this part of him. How he gave his body over to her. The trust.

She rolled the condom on, taking her time and sliding her fingers up and down as he swore under his breath. Then she climbed up his body. Touched every inch. Rubbed her body against his to create a delicious friction. Stopped to kiss his exposed skin.

When she got to his stomach, he pulled her up the rest of the way. His fingers wrapped in her hair and brought her mouth close to his.

"Do you know how much I want you?" He whispered the question against her lips.

Before she could answer, he kissed her. Holding her steady with one hand, he plundered her mouth. Over and over. Deeper and deeper.

The other traveled down to her hip . . . then lower. She felt a tug and then her pants loosened around her waist. She gasped as his hand tunneled into her underwear. That finger found her again. Flicking and circling over her until her body turned to mush and she leaned into his touch.

"Reid . . ." She tried to catch her breath but couldn't draw in enough air. "Please."

Then his finger slipped inside her. In and out until she could feel her body dance to his rhythm. She was so ready for him. So wet and willing.

His other hand snaked down her body and hooked under the back of her knee. He shoved her pants down then lifted her leg. Pulled it up and out of her pants before balancing it on his hip.

She wanted to jump on him, wrap her legs around him and take him deep inside. Only his injury stopped her. But it didn't stop him. He lifted her up until her tiptoes barely skimmed the floor.

He pressed against her then. Slipped in just enough to send her heartbeat crashing in her chest. She grabbed onto his shoulders. Dug her nails into his skin. She thought she heard his name and realized she was the one chanting it.

She shifted her body forward, pulling him in deeper.

She held him and tugged on him, silently begging for him to thrust inside. His head dropped and he pressed a heated kiss on her throat. Then another. His tongue traveled over her as his body plunged in and out of hers.

The mix of touching and tasting made her wild.

She closed her eyes and let the need wash over her. Experienced rather than thought. Held him with every ounce of strength left in her muscles as her body stiffened and clenched. And he kept moving. She tightened her legs against him, pulled everything inside her tight until her muscles shook.

He nibbled on her neck, nipping and kissing. Had her moving her head to give him greater access. When his hand slipped down and his finger pressed against her as his erection pushed one more time, her control broke. Breaths escaped her in deep pants. She closed her eyes and came. Let the pulses rumble through her.

When his back slammed hard against the stone wall, she knew he'd lost it, too. His body shook as the orgasm punched through him. He grunted as he buried his face in her hair.

The pushing and shaking continued for another minute, then her hand fell from his arm. Every muscle in her body relaxed as her bones turned to jelly. She stood there with his body anchoring her. Without his hold she would have slipped boneless to the floor.

As the minutes ticked by and their bodies cooled, she waited for the regret to set in. But it didn't happen.

If anything, she wanted to cuddle against him and steal some of his heat.

Then her mind flashed to his wound and she pulled back. Not the whole way but enough to look into his eyes. “Are you okay?”

“Pretty fucking spectacular.”

His eyes actually glowed. The satisfaction was right there to see. Not that she could blame him. Everything about that worked for her.

“Did you learn that biting move in school?” That seemed new and she liked it.

He looked around as if ready to jump back into his clothes. “Hardly.”

And there it was. The cool hit of reality. She pulled back a bit more. Put a few inches between them even though she continued to hold on to his shoulders. “That’s what I remember.”

He frowned. “Meaning?”

“I asked you a question about your past and you shut down.” This time she stepped away from him. Reached around her feet for her pants and quickly dragged them up with her underwear bunched inside. “Typical.”

He continued to lean against the wall, mostly naked. “Is that why you really left me? Because I didn’t want to play show and tell?”

“You’re being a jerk again.” She picked up his shirt and handed it to him.

He held it against his stomach but didn’t make a

move to put it on. "I don't like talking about my past because it sucked."

"You can't have a relationship with someone if—"

"We were engaged." His yell bounced off the stone walls.

"Okay, fine." Her pants shifted sideways and the zipper landed in the wrong place, so she just let them rest undone on her hips. "I can't be engaged to someone who won't talk to me. Who hides their past from me."

"What part do you want to know?" His arms dropped to his sides and his shirt hit the floor again. "How many of my foster parents hit me? Or about the one who collected the check then rationed my food? Or are you more interested in life on the street once I ran away at fifteen?"

Her heart stammered in her chest. "Fifteen?"

"I survived, Cara. That's the point. I made it through and found a career that suits me." The strain of the conversation showed on his face. Tension pulled at his mouth.

"One that puts you in constant danger." She said the words but didn't mean to take them down that road. She of all people, who had benefited from his skills over and over, understood that the world could be a crappy place. Men like him equalized the playing field. "Forget that. This isn't about your work."

"What is it about?" He stood there, totally unconcerned about his nudity. No shame and not rushing to cover up. He verbally fought back, kept pushing.

"This has always been about your past and how little you'll open up to me. How I told you I was worried about us long-term and you didn't care."

"It wasn't that I didn't care. It's that compared to all I've seen, the worries didn't . . ." He hissed. "Oh, shit."

"What?"

"Didn't seem like a big deal to me?" He winced. "Maybe I am a dick."

"You're not." But sometimes she wanted him to be so she didn't have to play the role of the bad guy.

"My parents died in a car crash and no one wanted the poor kid with the stutter." He threw his arms out to the sides "Are you happy? Does that make sense and make you more willing to take a risk on me?"

It made her furious at the system and sick for him. "That's horrible. I want to punch every single member of your family."

"The guy in front of you—the one who doesn't like crowds and is never going to be the star of the party—is a product of being left behind and unwanted." The energy seemed to whoosh out of him then. His shoulders fell and for a second pain crossed his face. "I wish I could be someone else for you."

"Don't say that." She had to touch him then. She moved to him, ran her hands over his stomach and shoulders, trying to comfort him and not knowing how. "It's not true. I don't feel that way and you saying it makes me feel like shit."

"I'm telling you what you want to know."

"I can't have kids. The cancer treatments all those years ago had unexpected side effects and that was one." The words shot out of her. She hadn't planned them and they didn't make sense in this context . . . except they kind of did. The information went to her issue about being overprotected.

"Shit . . . are you sick now?"

"No."

"Okay. Good." He nodded then stopped. "Wait, why do we use condoms?"

"They protect against other things." She eyed him up. "Remember the part about how we barely knew each other? Part of me wanting to talk more and discuss who we were—go on actual dates—months ago, was so that we could find out things like this. So we could make the decision together about what birth control, if any, we needed to use."

He nodded. "Smart."

Doubts gnawed inside her. "But you don't have anything to say about the other thing?"

"The cancer? Honestly, I don't want to think about it at all." His expression was pained. "Are you sure you're okay?"

She rushed to ease his severe frown. Skimmed a finger over it. "Really, Reid. It's long gone."

He let out a haggard breath. "Thank God."

"But the kid part." It was a test of sorts. An unfair

one that she didn't mean to give him, but the words were out and now she needed to know his reaction. After dealing with a lifetime of awkward comments and unending sympathy from family and well-meaning friends, she needed to know what he thought.

"I'm sorry. Really, that's a shitty break and I'm sorry you've had to deal with it." His eyes softened then narrowed. "Is this something that defines you in some way? Are you having trouble dealing with the news?"

It had stopped being news years ago. "Not anymore."

He took her hand and folded his over it. "You know that never would have mattered to me, right? We adopt. We have fifteen dogs. I don't care. I loved you, not your ovaries."

The words washed over her. "No sympathy."

He froze. "What?"

"No, it's a good thing." Weirdly, it was. She'd come to terms with her reality long ago.

Her mother saw the inability to give birth to grandchildren as *her* failure, as if she somehow gave Cara cancer. For Cara the inability was a fact like all the other facts in her life. It hadn't always been that way, but it was now. Enough time had passed for her to accept.

"My family has spent so much time trying to make it up to me—that I was so sick as a kid. My parents want me to have a fun career and enjoy life. They still whisper the word cancer and never discuss grandkids."

He scooped his shirt off the floor and slipped it over his head. Let it rest there. "It probably sucked to have a sick kid. I can't really imagine that."

"They treat me like I'm broken." She pulled on the hem of his shirt and helped him slip his arms through. If he did it on his own, he'd likely rip out his new stitches. And then there was the part where she liked touching him. "You didn't."

"And that pissed you off." He hesitated between each word.

She knew she was talking in circles and merging topics. But all the words had built up inside of her and now she wanted them out. "No, I'm saying I never really appreciated that until now."

He rubbed his thumb over her bottom lip. "I know you don't want to hear it, and you don't believe me, but I did love you."

Her heart went into free-fall. Zoomed past her stomach and kept going. "Past tense."

"The end was rough, Cara." His arm dropped to his side.

"Do you know why I didn't give us a chance?"

"Fear?"

In part, but if she used that word he might not understand her point. "Because I saw my life getting swallowed up in yours."

His eyes narrowed. "Okay, I'll ask you what I asked you before. Do you still?"

She had no idea what she wanted or needed anymore. Once again they'd been sucked into this huge scary situation. The exact time when she shouldn't make life-changing decisions, yet here she was.

Her brain kept misfiring. The world blurred and the right answer sat just out of reach. "What's changed?"

The life seemed to run out of him. Some of the color left his face and his shoulders fell. Bending down, he grabbed his pants. "I guess nothing."

"Reid."

He dragged the pants up but left them unzipped. "This time I'm the one who needs air."

"You know it's dangerous out there."

"I'm going to the front door of the mine and no farther." He started to turn then stopped. "And for the record, it's not that safe in here either."

Then he was gone.

18

TASHA LOOKED out the apartment room window to the city of Perm below. Niko had traveled here, which meant she'd had to follow, and drag Caleb along.

Niko came in with fanfare. Talked about donating money for research and schools. Promised the backing of oil companies working the region. It was a fine public relations display. A performance he could have delivered from home via teleconference. But he felt the need to come here, right after she visited his office. She guessed it was easier to cover his tracks from inside Russia.

That's why she hovered in the shadows. Instead of walking into a hotel where her identification would be tracked, they waited in an apartment building. A safe house used by one of her contacts. A place no one would think to look for her, or whatever name her passport said.

The question was, why congregate here? The hilly area sat on the banks of a river and was home to almost

a million people. Across the intersection sat what looked like a red brick church with fancy spires topped with gold. In the distance, rows of high-rise apartment buildings.

Sitting on the border between Europe and Asia, the city thrived thanks to the oil industry. It was a twenty hour flight from home. After having been closed off to visitors before the fall of the Soviet Union, the place still moved at a slower, otherworldly pace.

She'd been here several times during her MI6 days. Niko brought her here now. One day she might come back as a visitor and enjoy some hiking, but not today.

"I have some information." Caleb spoke from the desk he'd set up as a workstation in the corner.

He had routers and piggybacked on signals . . . she didn't even try to understand all of the equipment. If it worked to hide his identity, she supported him buying it on the black market and hauling it up here. His job was to track information without being found out or pointing to their location, two things he excelled at.

She walked over and sat on the edge of the bed behind him. "Don't tell me how you got it."

He spun the chair around to face her. "You don't want to know."

"Exactly."

He leaned back on the creaky wooden legs and stretched his feet out in front of him. "Using the coordinates of all the incidents and armed guards Reid

has encountered, along with notes and plans from the expedition, I was able to pinpoint the general area of interest and track it over time through a series of satellite images."

Since the satellites were supposed to be down, or knocked out for at least a short period of time, all of that should have been impossible. Tasha hoped his skills equaled those set out in the FBI file on him. "I sense an international incident or congressional hearing in my future."

"You have troop movement here." Caleb flipped one of his laptops around and showed her the screen. "Looks like we have troops conducting surveillance, circling and converging on this one section that stretches about twenty square miles."

"Probably guarding." No surprise there. The Russians had a lot of secrets buried in the Urals. Always had.

It was a good place to launch new programs and conduct research. Oil and gas companies moved in and out of there all the time, which added some needed income to the region and a whole new level of corruption. If she were in charge of Russian intelligence, she'd drag all of her people up there for training and then have the government hide every covert operation in the hills.

"Possibly searching for something." Caleb clicked through a series of time-lapsed photos, showing one day then the next. "These bodies aren't following an

exact path. It's more like fanning out, checking one section at a time then doubling back again."

The troop movement was minimal, as if they didn't want to draw attention. "It could be we're all in a race to find these scientists before they start talking about whatever it is they found in the field."

He frowned. "We're talking about my sister."

"Who is alive and fine." Tasha didn't add "right now" because she knew Caleb understood that much.

They had an area and movement. They needed to pinpoint a reason for all that interest. Every question led them right back to the science expedition. That made Niko her number one priority.

"Bring Cara home now." Caleb sat forward with his elbows resting on his knees. "I'm not kidding here, Tasha. She's wrapped up in something dangerous and now you have a place to look without her. Enough is enough."

He'd been repeating that refrain ever since they left DC. She'd ignored the requests because she had an agent in the field. Right there, ready to investigate. Pulling Reid out to act as a travel escort didn't make sense. They might not have that kind of time, and she had the knowledge about the team and the area. Every piece of intel pointed to keeping Reid there, which meant Cara was stuck until they figured out the endgame.

But she was Caleb's sister and hadn't asked for this. She went in with the CIA but as a scientist looking for

information. Not as an agent ready to shoot and run and hide.

Tasha sympathized . . . to a point. "I'll have Reid take a run at figuring out what has everyone's attention. If he comes up empty, I'll pull them out."

"It could be too late by then."

"They are pinned down in the middle of this thing." From the photos, it looked like the armed men on the ground were getting closer and could recheck the mine at any time. "The only way out may be to keep going and work our way through all of this until we find the answers about what everyone wants out there and are willing to kill for."

"You haven't had any trouble bringing Parker in and out."

Tasha had been waiting for that argument. "Reid made that decision at the start of this thing. That it was easier to move one person than three. But I'm sending Parker in as backup."

Caleb shook his head. "Bring everyone in. Have the entire Alliance team descend on the Urals and end this thing."

"That will guarantee a shoot-out." And she would not risk her men. They were already in there without backup or support. She couldn't depend on CIA reports because someone wanted to keep this hush-hush. That meant if a higher-up needed a scapegoat for this mission going sideways, she would catch the blame.

"Or the chaos will stop and Cara will be able to walk out without trouble." Caleb stopped looking at his hands and glared at Tasha. "But that doesn't work for you because the person behind whatever we're looking at here will scatter. Be honest, this is about the mission, not my sister."

To Tasha, those were the same thing. "It's about five dead scientists."

"Cara better not be number six."

"She won't be." Tasha vowed to make that be true.

Reid read the message from Tasha a second time and swore under his breath. The last thing he needed right now was an afternoon of recon with Cara attached to his side.

She talked about tension and aftermath like she had any idea what those terms really meant while working undercover. He'd never had trouble controlling his hormones or his needs. If a woman cut him off, he took the hint and moved on.

All of those rules and that experience faded away when dealing with Cara. She pissed him off, ripped him in half, and distracted him from the work he should be doing. He'd actually welcomed the pain from being stitched up, thinking that would keep his mind off getting her naked.

No such luck.

The sex in the mine kept replaying in his mind. Not

his smoothest work, but together they were on fire. Her breathing and the way her body clenched around his. That part of their relationship never failed them.

She insisted that's all they had. Never mind that she shared her fears and concerns. Hell, he even talked about the foster homes. Not much, but then he didn't have a single good memory, so why dissect those years? If only he could get her to understand that.

When it came to sex, she could live in the here and now. But for their lives together she needed to poke at everything that came before. So much of that part of his life was ugly and dark. She added light. Made him forget the rest . . . except when she used his past as a reason not to have a future.

She was so damn difficult. That practical brain of hers wanted to walk through every piece of the past and catalog it. She grew up with music and art and conditional acceptance. She never lived up to expectations, so she pushed even harder. But when it came to him, she didn't even bother to open the door and welcome him into the family.

He'd been her dirty little secret. That should have been his first clue that the engagement wouldn't last. Embarrassment, whatever had her turning away, ate at him.

He talked about loving her as if the feeling had disappeared. As if he didn't care anymore. What a fucking joke.

As much as he needed some space, now was not the time. Instead of obsessing about her, he focused on something he could handle—the work.

He stalked back to the main corridor of the mine but stopped before making the final curve into the open. "Are you dressed?"

Footsteps echoed back to him before she popped up just a few feet away. "We need to talk."

"No time." A legitimate excuse even though it sounded lame.

Her eyes narrowed. "Why?"

"Your brother figured out—"

"Caleb is in Russia?" Her voice flatlined as she asked the question.

"He's with Tasha." And likely working every minute. Tasha had brought him in to work with the Alliance before, for discreet projects, but Reid was pretty sure Cara didn't know that. Didn't understand that Caleb had sold his soul years ago when he got caught fishing around in top secret government programs he didn't have access to. Since then, he got called in when his particular set of skills required it.

"I can't believe he followed me here." She shook her head. Started to pace.

"We don't have time to discuss your family dynamic right now. I get that they smother you and try to make you into someone you're not." All fair complaints that, with her personality, would drive her nuts. But not the

worst upbringing. "I'm betting that's annoying, but as someone without family, I can tell you there are worse things than being loved too much."

Instead of being insulted she looked wary. Wrung her hands together as she watched him with an assessing glance. "What's happened?"

"We have a lead and we need to investigate it." All accurate information. The problem was, he still didn't know if he'd recognize the "it" in this case if he stumbled right over it.

"Outside," she said in a dry tone.

"Yes."

"And you're not balking about bringing me along?"

"No." Oh, he'd argued pretty hard on that point. Or he did until Tasha told him to get the job done and then cut off communication. She didn't always handle having her authority questioned very well.

"Man, how much did that sex scare you?"

All the words slammed together in his brain. Every argument about safety and locating the rest of Cara's team piled up on him. "What the fuck does that mean?"

"Nothing." She waved him off and turned back to her bag. Loaded it up with two guns then slipped the protective vest over her head. When she turned back around again she had a minicommando thing going on. "Let's go."

She walked right past him, not waiting to see if he followed. The mumbling under her breath was tough to

miss. Between their relationship being in shambles and the mission being nothing more than a series of guesses, his concentration wavered. That amounted to bad news. If he didn't focus, he'd get shot again . . . or worse.

He caught up to her as she reached the entrance. Without saying a word, he reached over her and pulled one of the heavy doors open. The two of them slipped through to stand in the wet grass and drizzling rain. The weather perfectly summed up what he thought of this trip so far—it was a complete mess.

Marking time to the coordinates on his watch, Reid walked them toward the last sighting of armed guards stopping a car and scanning the area. That meant being in the open as they snaked their way along the river sitting in the valley below.

They didn't get very far before she piped up. "What are we looking for?"

"I don't know." He had more information but wasn't exactly in a sharing mood. All his energy went into staying alert and watching for men to climb out from behind the boulders stacked along the path or the opposite side of the hill that led down to the water.

"That's helpful."

"Is this some sort of . . ." He stopped in his tracks and looked her up and down. "What's it called . . . defense mechanism?"

She sent him one of those you-are-right-on-the-edge eye rolls. "I don't even know how to answer that."

"Your attitude is—"

"Don't say it."

The snotty clipped answers grated on his nerves. She wanted to pick a fight. He could hear it in her tone. Still, name-calling wasn't the answer, so he refrained.

She grabbed his arm and he immediately stopped walking. He could lift her without trouble, but the whole bully thing never appealed to him. Not with people he cared about. A terrorist? Yeah, almost any maneuver had his okay then.

"For once, just tell me what's going on in your head," she said.

"You regret the sex. I'd point out that I warned you about that before we got naked." The whole idea made him want to rip the mine apart with his bare hands.

She shook. "I don't."

"Right." No way was he falling for that line. "Caleb and Tasha think we're not the only ones out here looking for something."

"Reid—"

"We're working. That's it." Having sex on a mission was enough of an aberration for him. He didn't want to miss a warning sign or plunge them into danger by dwelling on the was-it-a-mistake questions now.

She hesitated for a second before nodding. "You think the rest of my team is out here. I get that, but has something changed to push us out right now?"

"This goes beyond your team." Reid had been flip-

ping that thought over in his mind. Normally he would keep the analysis to himself until he worked it out, but she had skills. She worked through problems for a living. "What if we're dealing with more than one group here?"

"For example?"

"You were here on a job within a job. The documentary was your cover." When she nodded, he continued. "What if some of your team members were also on a second job, one that differed from yours?"

"You're asking because of the Russian commandos."

He knew she'd get it. She likely put the pieces together long before he did. "The expedition is a government-sanctioned event in support of the documentary. So, why the armed attackers?"

"The CIA believes there is something going on here that needs investigating." She made a face that suggested she was working out the factors in that impressive brain of hers. "Maybe we did stumble over something and found something we weren't supposed to find."

"Then why did they give the expedition permission to be up here at all? It's too risky." Someone was paying the bills and pulling the strings. Niko, but the CIA was involved as well. That made for two players with two agendas. The Russians added a third.

Reid wondered how many schemes they needed to unravel to figure this out. As if dealing with one group of bad guys wasn't enough.

He could almost see her mind clicking into action. Give her a puzzle and she'd work it and work it until she solved it. They could use those skills right now.

"If you wanted to hide a research lab up here—even from the government—where would you put it? Lock it away so that you needed a scientist to find it and work in it?" When she glanced around he knew she wasn't thinking complex enough. "Keep in mind the supplies you'd need. Temperatures. Space. Equipment."

"Somewhere like the mine."

"Too obvious." That would have been his first guess, too, but he'd checked the tunnels and one was flooded. Nothing lingered in there except for themselves and maybe a few rats. A fact he did not intend to point out to her.

"What about all the old hunting cabins and work camps in and out of this area?"

Another good direction, but they'd exhausted it, or at least ruled it out in light of the two-man armed scouting teams. "Tasha and Caleb checked all of them. The satellite photos show Russian special forces investigating them as well, but no evidence that points to an ongoing operation."

"A room carved into these hills." Her gaze slid over the mountain towering above them.

"Out in the open." Reid walked through the parameters out loud. "Hidden but not really. A place no one would think to look."

"But it would need to be tucked away to some degree. It sounds weird, but you'd need to be open to get materials in yet not *that* open as to be seen." She shrugged. "There, that narrows it down."

He waded through her sarcasm to her point. *Open yet not.* A place with natural cover. Obvious but not too obvious.

He turned and stared at the steep drop-off beside him. "Like in a valley."

Her eyes widened as she ventured to the edge of the hill and looked down. "Where does this lead?"

"Not sure, but we know from personal experience it's not the first place armed guards check." The perfect hiding place. He took Cara's hand. "You any good at sliding?"

She looked at the incline then at him again. "I have a feeling it would be easier to roll."

"Whatever you need to get down there."

Before she could balk, he started moving. Walked down sideways, letting his boots grab the earth and then leaning into the slides as the soles glided over pebbles and dirt. She followed behind him, keeping one hand on the ground beside her for leverage. It was a longer process than he intended but neither of them rolled into the water, so that was a plus.

At the bottom, standing on the bank, he glanced up and down the waterway. After a double-check of the coordinates from Caleb and Tasha, Reid started walk-

ing. In silence they trudged along the water's edge. The walls of the valley muffled the sound, and no person or animal crossed their trail.

When they reached the one mile point, Reid started to doubt this was the place. "Let's turn around."

She nodded, still quiet. At first he thought the silence counted as punishment of some sort. Then he noticed her eyes kept scanning. She walked and watched. Took it all in. As he looked for footprints or other signs of human activity, she focused on the earth around them. Picked up a rock here and there. Frowned at more than one of the things she saw, but he didn't know why.

After another ten minutes he was ready to declare this trip a waste of time. If something obvious stuck out then it was too obvious for him to see it. He thought about dragging Parker in here with him. Possibly getting Tasha to acquire a drone and fly low along the river to cover more ground and obtain photographic evidence.

Because flying drones wouldn't attract attention. He almost laughed at his internal joke. But nothing about the situation struck him as all that funny. "Nothing."

She shook her head as she crouched down. "Something."

"What?"

She held a rock that looked like every other rock. "This is wrong."

He wasn't even sure if he knew the right questions to ask. "I don't know how to respond to that."

She stood up with the rock in her hand. "I could throw a whole bunch of terms at you about this area back when it was covered by an ocean. Paleozoic sedimentary rocks and evidence of rift activity."

"I'm begging you to not to use any more terms like that."

"I know what we should find on the banks of the river." She held the dark gray lump out to him. "Not this."

He took it and felt the weight in his palm. What struck him was the perfect cut to the rock. It hadn't been chipped away. It looked as if it had been chiseled.

He still had no idea what that meant. "Okay."

"Limestone generally lines the riverbeds in this area." She took the rock back. "This is grabbo. It forms when magma is trapped beneath the earth's surface."

He must have had a blank look on his face because after a quick look she nodded then kept going. "It contains minerals like nickel, cobalt, gold, silver. In the case of this one, and the ones dropped here, they've been shaved down. They are too perfect in shape."

He'd never been so happy to have a geologist on his team. "Why?"

"I don't know yet, but I think your lab is here somewhere. Right here." She pocketed the rock. "And someone is using this, though I have no idea what for."

That still didn't solve the question of the actual location. They had educated guesses and some rocks that

might or might not matter. Not a lot to go on as they walked around in the light rain.

Reid looked down the length of the river and forced his mind to focus. He shut out the sounds of the water and the presence of the woman beside him. Instead of looking for what was there, he shut off and searched for what wasn't.

His gaze slipped from one side of the bank to the other. Bushes, rocks. Patches of grass. Scanned one section then moved down. He repeated the process several times, not seeing anything out of order.

His attention zipped back to the left bank about twenty feet ahead. Something stuck out. Something he couldn't quite figure out at first. He kept turning the facts over in his mind. Green and brown. Patches . . . that's it.

"Found it." He almost took off running, but stopped.

She stood beside him. "Tell me what you're looking at."

"Nothing."

"What?"

He knew the answer sounded ridiculous but it actually made sense. "A few feet up the hill on the left side. Look for the solid block of brown. No patches of grass. No tumbling rocks. When you block everything else, the patch sticks out."

She smiled. "A door."

It didn't look like anything, but he agreed with her guess. "We'll know in two seconds."

Once they walked up and stood over it, the differ-

ence between that one square of land and all the rest became more obvious. He didn't see hinges or a handle. The makers of the entrance had been smarter than that. Still, it would open. He'd bet his life on it.

"Stand back." The problem with dropping into a space was that anyone could be down there.

He felt around the area, trying to find a way in. When that didn't work he put his foot on the middle of the suspect block. Not all of his weight, just a little. He heard a shallow thumping sound.

"Metal." Cara made the observation as she dropped down and ran her hands over the space.

After a click, the door under his foot gave way and fell an inch below the rest of the land. Now Reid knew where to push. Throwing some weight behind it, he got the slim doorway open and looked down at the ladder leading to . . . somewhere. Lights attached to the wall showed the way.

Cara shifted as if she planned to step inside.

He wasn't about to let that happen. "I'll go first."

"I'm coming with you."

He didn't bother arguing because he didn't want her waiting out there without him. "Nice and slow."

He slid his body inside the hole and fit his boot to the step. A small clanking sound echoed around him every time his foot hit a new rung, but he kept moving. Hand over hand he climbed down, glancing up now and then to watch Cara hurry down behind him.

When he got within a few feet of the floor, he jumped

and lifted her to the ground with him. Water dripped down around them and the tunnel smelled dank. There weren't any sounds other than the dripping of water and no one came running, but the entire area was outlined in metal. Kind of a dead giveaway something was happening down here.

They walked for a minute then turned a corner. A steel door led to a separate room. A very different room. One lined with plastic and filled with light. Containers and what looked like freezers. Metal cases lined the walls. Tables covered in paperwork and computers on one side. Rocks and microscopes and a whole bunch of equipment he couldn't identify on the other.

A working lab.

Cara walked around the tables. She didn't touch anything but she studied rocks and more than one metal device. When she got to a stack of papers she picked one up. Then another. Looked through a microscope.

Laptops and computers lined one wall. None of them flickered with life. He didn't try to turn them on for fear that would make it too easy to track their location. Someone with expertise different from his could handle that.

"Cobalt." She said the word from the middle of the room then slumped against one of the tables.

He didn't like the look on her face. Worry mixed with an edge of excitement, but the latter flashed and then disappeared. "Tell me what you're thinking."

"I'm not sure." Her finger swept over the lines of equations on the paper. "This isn't my specialty, but I know cobalt and there are all sorts of bad things people can do with it."

"Like?"

She swallowed hard enough for him to see her throat move. "At the worst end? Build a cobalt bomb."

It took a second for the words to register in his brain. When they did, he could only think one thing: that sounded pretty fucking bad. Literally, the Doomsday Device referenced throughout history. The one that could wipe out life.

"I've read reports about the possibility, but again, like some of the other possibilities we've talked about with what could be happening around here, they all read like science fiction. There are rumors Russia has one armed and ready to go if the U.S. ever launches an attack, but no one knows if that's true." There had been dire warnings but never any evidence it was real. Talk about how in some parts of the world cobalt was much easier to obtain than other materials. Freaky, scary shit. "You think that's what we're looking at here?"

She didn't say yes or no. "It would be a nuclear weapon, but worse than the type we've known. It's actually called a salted bomb—"

"Meaning the goal is to cause radioactive fallout that would make large areas uninhabitable." Yeah, he got that part. It was something out of a terrorist handbook.

"Yes, enhanced radiation for a longer period of time." She walked around. Scanned more notes. "But I agree with you. This has always been considered theoretical, with countries pretending to have the ability and using that as a deterrent. But the general consensus is these bombs aren't being built."

He feared the right term was *weren't*. "But?"

She lifted her head and stared at him with eyes filled with fear. "From the look of this lab, someone seems very serious about trying to get the process going. And this isn't about just one. These notes reference multiple storage areas, which suggests more than one cobalt bomb."

"All this hidden in a space near the water in the mountains of Russia." The place seemed too small and insignificant to play host to that much death and destruction.

She glanced at the small kitchen station and empty coffeepot. "Where is everyone? Why wouldn't this be guarded and under watch? There's no way the Russians would risk having this be found."

Which raised the issue of a third player—not the CIA, not the Russians, possibly not even Niko. It looked like someone was playing games on Russian soil. "All good questions. Now we need to answer them."

19

THEY SLIPPED back out of the underground science bunker without any trouble. Cara half expected to pop out into the open to a sea of men holding guns. The in and out proved too easy. That sort of lab should have alarms and specialized tech protections. Having it out there, open and vulnerable, made the entire world vulnerable.

She was about to point out the need for guards when Reid started fiddling with his magical watch. She leaned over and watched him note the coordinates of the hatch. Mapped it out. Not with a huge X but so they could find it again. Then he produced a tiny camera and took a few photos. Those got uploaded to the watch next.

She guessed he was sending all of the information to Tasha. Getting all of the Alliance up to speed and ready to move in.

Good. Let her bring in her men and knock it all down. "Can we go?"

Reid glanced up at her and his gaze searched her face. Finally, he nodded. "Sure."

They took off. She almost ran but settled for a near sprint. Well, to her. Reid took it all in his long strides. Didn't look winded or worried about the pace. She never dreamed she'd be so desperate to get back to that mine, but she didn't want any part of whatever her science brethren had planned for Russia and the rest of the world.

She still couldn't grasp the enormity of what they'd found. The pure destructive firepower of a weapon like that. Setting that off would change everything. Forget about evening the playing field. It could level it.

No wonder the CIA had people on the ground and wanted tests done. Bringing in experts with specialized knowledge would have been smarter, but it was possible the CIA didn't know what it truly was hunting for. The people in power were right to panic. She'd slipped right into get-me-out-of-here mode.

After about five minutes of racing along the bank, Reid touched her arm. "You okay?"

She glanced up to find him staring, the worry obvious on his face. She wanted to comfort him. Wanted him to say something soothing to her. Her brain, the one part of her she counted on to be sensible, was a jumbled mess of need and fear.

She inhaled, trying to think of the next steps. They'd need a Hazmat team and scientists with nuclear training. Engineers. Armed guards.

They could start with the basics now and get to the more complex stuff later, including the intricate international relations issues that went along with all of this. "We need to let Tasha know. That has to be dismantled and the intel destroyed."

Reid's expression went blank. "Okay."

That fast she had a new target for the ball of anger and frustration growing inside her. "I don't like that tone."

He held up a hand. She hated when he did that. The gesture looked innocent enough, but underneath it was all bossy and commanding. He just disguised it in a reasonable request.

"Hear me out," he said in a coaxing tone.

And there it was. She didn't need to weigh her response or pick her words. "Reid, no."

"We will handle it, but not yet."

That was the totally wrong answer. He was a smart guy. From all he said down in the makeshift lab, he understood the importance of this type of finding. This was end-of-the-world stuff. Not the time to be throwing on the brakes and reevaluating options. "Please be kidding."

"There could be more sites." When she started to argue about the idea of having the world blanketed in a radioactive cloud, he showed her that hand again. "You know I'm right. You read the notes and said this could be one of many. Dismantling one won't resolve the bigger issue."

"Which is?" Reid's point about possible other sites

stuck in her mind. That was too horrible to think about, but they had to. There had to be a specialized test they could run. She'd look that up later.

"We don't know what we're dealing with here or how big it is."

"Is there something bigger than worldwide annihilation?" She was a scientist, and the horrors playing in her mind dealt with overzealous experiments and losing the line between what they *could* do and what they *should never* do. Those were ethical concerns she dealt with every day. He was about finding and fixing. Today she wanted his usual way. Locate the problem and remove it.

"We don't know who's behind this," he explained. "I can't stop some unknown 'they.' I need to know the scope, how many people. Who is in charge."

She went with the obvious because spinning this into something else didn't make sense until she ruled the clear solution out. "Russia."

"You said yourself the lab setup didn't make sense." He glanced around and up the side of the hill. "There are armed guards walking around this area. Why aren't there any in the lab or along this waterway? Something of this magnitude would be locked away, deep underground and buried under layers of security if the Russian government sanctioned it."

The arguments all made sense. She mentally clicked a box and moved to the next possibility. "You think this is some rogue player."

"Yes. Likely someone the special forces guys here are trying to find before the CIA or anyone else does."

She hated this part of the job. She knew when she signed up for the expedition she'd be playing with people who preferred mind games and mass destruction to science. She'd convinced herself she'd survived danger before and this was really about getting the necessary intel. Her job would be easy. It sure as hell hadn't turned out that way.

That would teach her to seek adventure. She'd been trying so hard for so long not to be the good little girl who enjoyed paintings and her piano that she might have flipped too far to the other side. If she was honest with herself, she'd been taking bigger and bigger risks ever since the kidnapping. Since losing Reid.

She did not want to examine the psychological reasons behind that. She had enough to deal with right now, including the very real possibility she might have been hired by a sociopath. It was a cover, but still.

"Niko. You think the foundation is really a front for . . . what?" The man had a history with Russia, but this made him out as some sort of undercover spy.

"Moving weapons. Selling them. I wish I knew." Reid shrugged. "But he has the money and connections on the ground here."

When his voice trailed off Cara knew some other thought was bouncing around in his head. "What?"

"It's just that Russian special forces is all over this.

It's as if they're trying to find what we just found." He walked a few steps up the riverbank. "If they suspect Niko at all, think his expedition is behind the bomb, then why let you guys in the country? Niko is in Russia. Why not bring him in for questioning?"

"Niko is here?"

"Did I forget to mention that?"

Another example of his inability to share, but she decided not to point that out. Not now.

"That leads us back to someone else. A third party." She did not find any comfort in having yet another person running around collecting dangerous materials. Then there was the idea that any member of her expedition could be working against them. Not just against the reason for the documentary, but in opposition to the CIA and to Reid's Alliance.

"Or Niko, and he's really damn good at pulling this off."

She was about to tell Reid that he needed to pick a theory and stick with it when she heard a steady thumping. They were a good distance away from the hatch now and making their way back up the hill. This sound came from above them.

She glanced at Reid. "What's that?"

He was already moving. He had his gun out and was pushing her toward the ground. In an instant he stiffened and clicked into action. Morphed into the lethal protector. Even his expression changed. "Down."

They both hit the dirt on their stomachs. The footsteps grew louder and she picked up the sound of gasping breaths. There was a grunt and then a body flew over the side of the hill boots first. A male body, long and wiry, launched up and into the valley. Hit the dirt and rolled.

He threw his arms to the side to stop his slide. Pebbles rained down and the rough skid filled the air with thuds and strings of whispered profanity. Being dressed in head-to-toe black with all his skin covered helped slow and then bring him to a halt. It also made him look like one of the special forces guys, only without the gun and protective helmet.

But there was something. A memory tickled in the back of her mind. The look . . . that voice. She shook her head because it didn't make sense. She was about to tell Reid she'd officially lost it when he started scrambling.

On his hands and knees, Reid hurried to the guy, flipped him over, and froze. "What the fuck?"

Blond hair and in his late thirties. Even with the cuts on his face and black eye, Cara recognized him. "Simon?"

His eyes popped open. He continued to inhale deep breaths but his gaze roamed over the landscape before settling on Reid. "Who are you?"

Reid didn't lower his gun. It pointed right at Simon's head. "You're supposed to be dead."

He was. Cara would have sworn to it. She remembered his lifeless body on the floor near Cliff back in the abandoned work camp. She shimmied her way over to the men. Confusion numbed her whole body. She couldn't get her muscles to work or her brain cells to fire.

She lifted a hand, almost touched Simon, then snatched it back. "You were on the ground. Covered in blood."

The vision still played in her head. All that loss. She'd been lucky and now she knew why. Cliff had gotten her out of there. But the others? She thought they'd lost Simon even though his body hadn't been found.

"Cara?" Simon tried to sit up.

Reid pressed a hand against his chest and flattened him against the ground again. "Stay right there."

Anger flashed across Simon's face then disappeared. He turned to Cara and the sad pleading returned to his voice. "You disappeared back at the tents."

"I was dragged away." For some reason it felt right not to tag Cliff as her hero. Not now, not to Simon. She should be happy to be alive and grateful—and she was—but none of this made sense to her. Until it did, she wasn't offering any extra information. Not saying anything that anyone could later twist around.

Reid tapped Simon's arm with the side of the gun. "How did you get out of the work camp?"

"The what?" Simon scooted on the ground, clearly trying to get away from the gun. "Listen, I was grabbed

by men with weapons that night when they attacked the tents. They took me with them and kept moving locations. They questioned me about some lab."

"And?" Reid asked in a sharp tone.

Simon's mouth dropped open. "What?"

"Why aren't you with them now?" Reid emphasized each word.

Cara knew from experience his patience was running low. She couldn't blame him. Simon stammered and balked. All fair for a guy running from armed men. It made sense . . . but for some reason it didn't.

"They killed Brad in front of me." Simon turned to her again. Shot her an intense terrified look with those dark eyes. "He started talking about cobalt and a cave and they went to work on him and I got away. I've been running ever since."

The information made sense. The special forces guys were looking for the hatch, just as Reid thought. They found Simon and Brad and those two bore the brunt of the examination. Not that Simon looked tortured. He didn't. Even the matted blood in his hair back at the prison camp was gone. It was as if he'd been washed up and sent out again.

For some reason she could not get around those facts. She wore half-clean clothes only because she'd made it back to the expedition's compound and grabbed a bag. Without that she'd have been running around in blood-soaked ripped shreds.

She glanced at Reid then back to Simon. "Where did you get the change of clothes?"

For a second his victim mask crumbled. His eyes narrowed and a red flush stained his cheeks. "What is with all these questions? We need to get out of here before they come for—"

"Shut up." Reid put a hand around Simon's neck. "If you say one word I'll shoot you."

"Who are you?" Simon whispered the question.

Cara thought it was the wrong one. "Just listen to him."

She'd been following Reid. He was the only reason she was alive. Despite the jumping in her stomach and strings of panic that kept filling her brain, she trusted him. He would get them out of here . . . somehow.

She motioned for Simon to stay down and hunkered down next to him. She held her gun in her pocket, careful not to show him she was armed. If Simon made a stupid move, she'd be ready.

A vehicle rumbled to a stop above them. She suspected it was too much to hope they wouldn't come to the ridge a second time. There were no voices. No yelling of directions or moving around.

This was a hunt, and somewhere along the line she'd become one of the prey. The stalking, preparing to launch from above. She could see it all play out in her mind and waited for the attack to start.

She glanced over and watched Reid type something

into his watch. One of these days she'd take the thing and examine it, figure out what it could do. She just hoped she'd get the chance.

Simon turned over onto his stomach and lay next to her. He looked like he wanted to say something. She shook her head to get him to stop.

The silence dragged on. No one moved. It was as if one side waited for the other to fire. Little did they know that Reid could wait forever. He'd sit, half crouched, for hours if that's what he had to do. Gun up, ready to fire.

A bang rang out above her head. She swore she could hear the bullet whiz by. She heard a ping then a splash. Still, Reid waited. He'd inched up higher and she wasn't even sure how or when. He now waited above them, more than halfway up the steep sloping side.

When a head peeked over the hill, Reid jumped up and lunged. Grabbed the attacker's pants and yanked. Dragged him right into the valley and sent him tumbling. Then he stood up and fired. Two shots and the world went silent again.

The whole thing happened in a few seconds. Each moment spooled in slow motion, but she knew it zoomed by her. Her mind went to the first man who'd come down, and she spun around, ready to fire at anything that moved at the bottom of the hill. Seeing his body and the way he landed, the odd angle of his neck and one leg, she knew she didn't have to.

Then Reid was there. He skidded down the hill,

flying on the side of one shoe. It was an amazing sight. When he got to the bottom he checked the man for a pulse and shook his head.

She wanted to ask questions but didn't know if they were clear or if more men were pouring out onto the open area above them.

"He's dead?" Simon whispered the question but it still sounded loud in the relative quiet of the cloudy day.

"Yes." Reid answered as he walked back up to where they lay in the mix of dirt and mud. "Both of them."

Simon's head fell back on the ground and he exhaled. "Thank God."

"They were after you?" Reid's eyes narrowed as he talked.

Simon didn't move. "I heard a truck and started running."

She needed to stand up. Reid held out a hand and she grabbed it, springing to her feet. That put them both in a position towering above Simon. He looked relaxed and relieved and not even a little bit upset about the idea of a dead body lying just a few feet away.

"Thank you," Simon said as he sat up.

Reid let his arm fall to his side but he didn't put the gun away. "You can make it up to me later."

Simon's eyes narrowed. "Excuse me?"

"You have some questions to answer." Cara thought that seemed obvious, but she filled him in anyway.

"Uh, yeah." Simon stood up. Didn't wince or reach

for any injuries. He stood straight, as if he'd been out on a leisurely hike. "Of course."

Reid glanced at her. "Of course."

"We're getting out of here, right? I'd like to be on a plane home as soon as possible." Simon brushed his hands on his pants. Seemed oblivious to the fact that he'd just issued an order of sorts.

Reid took a step toward him. "I'm not your travel agent."

"I don't know what you are."

"How about the guy who just saved your life?"

"Gentlemen." Cara knew if she didn't step in she'd be mopping up after a bloodbath. She leaned into Reid's side to get his attention. Also to hold him back. "We should get out of the open area and into somewhere more protected."

Simon nodded. "Onto a plane. That's what I've been saying."

"Get up there and get in the truck." This time Reid did aim the gun.

Simon looked at the weapon, then at Reid's face. "What truck?"

"The men following you were nice enough to leave us one." Reid touched his side. The move took a second and he never showed weakness. "It will make the trip back to the mine go faster."

Cara knew she needed to check his wound, but there was no way Reid would allow that to happen in front of

Simon. Reid viewed Simon as a threat. She could tell from the way he spoke and how he handled himself. He had not lowered his guard even one inch.

She knew she should stick up for her fellow team member but she couldn't. They barely knew each other . . . and she didn't trust Simon either.

Simon glanced from Reid to Cara and back again. "What mine?"

For the first time since they found the hatch, Reid grinned. It was feral and carried a threat as he regarded Simon. "I'm afraid you're not done with Russia yet."

Simon snorted. "I get a say in that."

Reid's grin only widened. "No, you don't."

20

THEY SETTLED back in the mine less than a half hour after the latest shooting. Then the talking began. Question after question. The routine went on for over an hour without providing Reid with any new information.

There were enough dead bodies on the ground. Reid didn't want one more, but he might make an exception for Simon. Nothing about the guy's story made sense.

Reid had absolutely been in situations where the truth sounded like a lie and vice versa. Simon might truly be the most unlucky man alive. All possible. None of that explained the limited injuries and fresh clothes.

He claimed he escaped from a group of Russian special forces. Trained men who, from Reid's experience over the last few days, didn't have any qualms about shooting first and verifying identity later. They might not be the top fighters in the world but they were still damned good, and tough as hell. Had to be to survive in this sort of business. Reid admired them for doing their jobs. He hated killing them for performing as they

should, especially if Simon turned out to deserve killing, but no one touched Cara without her consent. Ever.

Reid figured he'd know more about Simon and his objectives in the next few minutes. After walking through his wild tale about being driven all over the Urals and threatened while watching his coworker die—none of which added any new facts to what he'd said back on the hill—Simon asked to "stretch his legs." Reid assumed he was considering running away. Which was why he waited just around the bend of the mine tunnel on the way to the entrance doors.

He could hear Cara humming in one of the rooms. She said something to him about it being one of the songs her father composed. Reid had never met him or heard the tune before. But it never ceased to amaze him that her father was a man who wrote symphonies . . . ones that never sold.

Her mother kept the family alive on an elementary art teacher's salary. Together they hated Cara's science career and, from what he could tell, anything that didn't directly benefit the arts. Never mind that Cara excelled at everything she did. Their billionaire tech genius son Caleb was no slouch either. A royal pain in the ass, but successful under any calculation.

Maybe Cara had been right not to introduce him to them. They would have hated his lack of talent. Probably hated him. He pretended not to care about that.

Hated that he hadn't read a book in more than two

years. Been horrified that he couldn't remember ever stepping into a museum. He did knit. A habit he picked up while undercover but hadn't done for a while. He bet the skills were still in him somewhere.

But the truth was, if Cara had asked him to do any of those things—hell, he'd sit through one of her father's symphonies or even listen to a lecture about paintings or whatever—he would have. As much as he hated being weak for her, he was. Whatever she needed from him, he'd give. It's why he mentioned the parade of terrible foster families. He'd hoped that would be enough to satisfy her curiosity about his past, but he doubted it.

He leaned against the mine wall and listened. A few seconds later the scrape of a boot against the dirt floor echoed back to him. He checked his watch. Hell, it took Simon long enough to make the move. Reid wondered what he'd been doing for the last ten minutes while he skulked around the mine tunnels. There were only so many places to go. Reid knew because he'd explored each shaft until he ran into a blockage.

Now the issue of how to handle this. Nice or not.

Simon's shadow passed on the far wall, which meant he was getting close. Sneaking to the door and then . . . Reid had no idea. He was half tempted to let him get outside and follow, but the truck stood out there. Simon might be stupid enough to jump in and try to start it.

More footsteps.

Reid knew he had only seconds to decide. Appar-

ently, shooting the guy was out of the question. That wasn't his rule. Cara told him no. He couldn't even persuade her that one bullet to the thigh might get them answers faster.

Women.

Simon picked up his pace. He rounded the corner and ran smack into Reid's chest. The expression on his face, half fury and half shock, was worth the body blow.

Reid tried being nice. "Hello."

Simon just stood there.

Well, the guy had his chance to finish this with some self-respect and wasted it. One swing and Reid slammed his gun into the side of Simon's head. Used just the right amount of strength to drive him to his knees. Reid was about to take a second shot when Simon fell over on his side in the dirt.

"Huh." Reid leaned down to check his pulse. Still breathing. That was probably a good thing.

Parker walked in a few seconds later and stood across from Reid on the other side of Simon's still body. "I see we have company."

Always on time. Parker had messaged ahead to say he'd be there in ten minutes. He'd stopped to take care of their newest round of casualties and hide the bodies to lessen suspicion as much as possible, so he missed the initial questioning. Lucky him. Reid had filled him in about the lab and the theories about the conflicting

players in this game. He hadn't quite gotten to the intel on Simon yet.

Reid continued to stare at the body at his feet. "He's alive."

Nothing about that seemed to impress Parker. "Is that good?"

"I'm not sure yet." Reid looked up. "We found our missing scientist wandering around the riverbed."

Parker nodded as he pushed against Simon's arm with the toe of his boot. "Convenient."

"Right?"

"And then he tried to sneak out past you?" Parker laughed. "The dumbass."

The move did strike Reid as wildly optimistic. The poor bastard. "He has some trouble with authority."

"Apparently." Parker dropped down and checked Simon for weapons. "No ID. What does Cara say about him?"

"She doesn't know him well and won't vouch for him. They got thrown together on this expedition. She'd never heard of him until he showed up for the flight."

Parker snorted. "That's not suspicious at all."

"He's a botanist." Reid wasn't sure what that added, but Cara stated it as an important fact, so he passed it on.

"Plants, right?"

"Something like that." Reid hadn't asked what, if anything, that would have to do with a cobalt bomb. He figured they had some time while they tried to work out

how to handle the lab, their new guest, and the crap ton of moaning that was headed their way from the Russian government for being on its soil without permission. "She keeps staring at him like he's an experiment she can't figure out."

"So that makes three of us against this guy." Parker put his hands on his hips and walked around the body. Seemed to be assessing Simon while he slept.

"You just got here and you already hate him?" That seemed about right for Parker. He figured people out fast and didn't hold back.

"He's too clean for a guy who's been on the run." Parker gestured in Reid's direction. "I mean, look at you. You look like hell. You even smell."

"That's not a really big concern for me. And Cara seems fine with it." He'd already bled all over the one person he cared about on this continent. She'd sewn him up and never complained about dirt or a smell or the lack of a shower. Another reason he thought she was a keeper.

Parker snorted for the second time in a minute, which might be a record. "Well, for now. Give her time."

Reid froze. That tone meant trouble. He recognized it and knew he should walk away. Still, curiosity had him asking. "What does that mean?"

"You already used your emergency condom. Unless you had sex with Simon here, I'm thinking Cara is okay with your stench."

Reid looked around to make sure she hadn't snuck up on them—again. He felt a kicking in his gut, and not the good kind.

"When did you check my bag?" The words were out before Reid realized he'd failed to deny the comment. But why bother? Even if it was an educated guess, it was the right one. Unlike her, Reid didn't regret the sex or being together. She wasn't some secret shame he needed to tuck away and never think about again.

"I got here before your distress call about me needing to bury more bodies, then headed out again." Parker reached over with a small packet between his fingers. "Here's mine. Enjoy."

"What if you need it?" Reid asked as he snatched it out of his friend's fingers. No need pretending he wasn't hoping one would magically appear. Tasha insisted on a condom being in the go bag. He'd stupidly *only* included one.

"One of us shouldn't be thinking with his dick right now."

That came really close to the one step too far. "Careful."

Parker held up both hands. "I was just going to say the same thing to you."

A heavy sigh preceded Cara's entrance. She stood right by the bend in the wall and glanced at the condom in Reid's hand then frowned. "Wishful thinking."

Parker barked out a laugh. "I really like her."

"At least you two tried to whisper this time." She walked around the body, following the same path Parker had taken and stopping beside him. "He's alive, right?"

"Yes," Parker said.

Reid wasn't quite ready to let her dramatic entrance go. The rush of his heartbeat at the sound of her voice would take a while to slow. "You have a habit of sneaking up on people."

"Unless I want a dunk in the pool, there's not a lot of places to hide in here." She'd changed since being outside. Wore a dry thermal pullover. Looked like she might have brushed her hair. The wild concern still showed in her eyes but her body no longer buzzed with unspent energy.

He took that all as a good sign. As a scientist she understood the ramifications of finding that lab. Rather than wither, she came out fighting.

He loved that about her. Standing there, looking at that round face and thinking about all they'd been through together, he knew he felt more here than loving *things* about her. He loved her. All of her. Even the frustrating, stubborn bossy parts. Loved her to the point that this time he would fight for her. Run the risk of losing all over again, no matter what that would cost him.

He felt the sudden need to sit down.

"Pool?" Parker pointed at Simon. "We could throw him in and be done with him."

"The water could be contaminated." Cara sounded very serious as she pointed the fact out.

Parker's eyebrow lifted. "So?"

Reid's mind scattered. All of a sudden he didn't want to deal with death or Simon's stories. He needed a minute with her. She talked about how they got sucked into this danger vortex and it spun their feelings out of control. He didn't buy it.

"We need to get rid of the truck." The words just popped out of him. He knew he'd missed something in the conversation or context because both Parker and Cara stared at him.

Parker cleared his throat, clearly covering a smile. "Is that my job, too?"

"We'll do it." He pointed to Cara. "The two of us. Together."

Great. Now he sounded like a bumbling teenager. Much more of this and he'd start fidgeting. That would just be fucking fantastic.

Cara frowned. "What?"

"Oh, really?" Parker asked at the same time.

Reid rushed to think of a reasonable excuse for walking out on an interrogation. He usually stuck around to ask the questions. Probably had something to do with his control issues and fear of missing something. "Me staying around here isn't going to get us any intel out of Simon. He doesn't like me very much."

"You did threaten to shoot him." Cara took a turn

trying to move Simon with her foot. "And it looks like you knocked him out."

"Both were justified." No matter what happened with Cara, Reid knew that much was true. Simon should be tied to a chair and forced to spit out whatever information he had. They had enough unknown variables without adding him to the mix.

Unknown variables . . . now he was thinking like her.

Parker shrugged. "Probably."

"We'll get out of here for a few minutes and you can question him." Reid spoke to Parker but didn't look at him. He could imagine the grin and that was enough. "Simon might trip up."

Cara looked from one man to the other. "If not?"

"Parker will shoot him."

Her face fell. "You're kidding."

"Is he?" Parker asked in an amused voice. "Because we should clarify the parameters here."

None of this was getting him where he needed to go, so Reid just conceded. "I am joking."

He probably would have said anything at that moment. The need hit him hard and out of nowhere. He was not the type to risk her safety by driving all over the Russian countryside in search of a safe place for a booty call.

"Then let's go back to the part where you two leave." Parker crossed his arms in front of him. "How is that going to work, exactly?"

"Should I stay?" Cara asked.

"Good question." Parker would not stop smiling. "Reid, should she?"

A few more minutes of this and he might hit something. Reid bit back the frustration roaring inside him and tried to keep his voice steady. "I promised Caleb I wouldn't leave you, so you're with me."

"That's what this is about? A promise to her brother?" Parker asked.

Yeah, two seconds from punching. "You want to say something about my plan?"

Parker shook his head. "Nope."

Cara treated them both to a long drawn-out sigh. The kind that said she was sick of male nonsense. "What's happening?"

Lucky for her, so was he. Reid looked at Parker. "Is it raining now?" When Parker shook his head, Reid turned back to Cara. "You're going to get to ride in a Russian truck."

She winced. "Lucky me."

"We'll see if you think so when you get back." Parker winked at her then bent down and started dragging the body toward the other part of the mine.

Tasha sat on the oversized bed with the oversized pillows, in the oversized hotel suite. The place struck her as overkill.

She bounced up and down on the mattress. Just a

little but enough to test it. Not bad. There weren't exactly luxury accommodations in this part of the Urals. Cozy houses, good apartments, and hiking cabins. Not five-star properties, but that didn't stop Niko from staying for a while.

As soon as she thought about him she heard the lock. The door swung open and Niko walked in carrying a tablet and reading something on it. He was three steps inside with the door closing behind him before he jerked to a stop and looked up.

Rather than make a scene, he dropped the tablet on the desk and walked over to the bar sitting under the mirror. Made a show of pouring a drink then finishing it. Even took off his jacket and gently folded it over one of the leather chairs in the sitting area.

He turned around to face her and sighed. His gaze went first to the gun. Then it traveled all over her.

She'd plunge into a scalding hot bath later.

"I'm beginning to think you have an unhealthy attachment to me." He walked over to the bedroom area, dragging the desk chair behind him. "Should we warn your fiancé?"

She refused to get derailed. Of course he knew about her personal life. The Alliance was top secret and need-to-know only, but they'd had a run-in before. People whispered when they shouldn't, especially if enough money changed hands.

"You're definitely not my type."

His head tilted to the side as he sat down in front of her. "You don't like rich?"

"I'm anti-asshole." Which was why she had checked the room twice, barred all other entrances, and paid off the housekeeper to warn her when Niko got on the elevator. And why she was not putting the gun down.

Some of the amusement left his face. "You have two seconds before I call security."

If hotel security could stop her, that would be the signal it was time to retire. "Call."

Niko sighed as he leaned back in his chair. "What do you want?"

"Cobalt."

"What?"

She had to give him credit. The knitted brow and dropped mouth—the confusion looked real. "That's why you're here, right? Use the expedition to find the cobalt so you can build your bombs."

"You've officially lost your mind." Niko shook his head. "I almost feel sorry for Ward."

The voice matched the blank reaction. She'd been trained to pick up cues of deceit. Increased blinking, selective wording, repeating the questions to stall for time, throat clearing. Those were just the beginning, and none of them were present. It could mean the man lacked a conscience, and she didn't discount that possibility. It could also mean whatever sins he committed did not include this one.

She pushed a little more, watching for any nervous tic or fidgeting. "Did you think you could bomb Russia back into power?"

"I have no idea what you're talking about."

So smooth. He didn't ask a follow-up question because he barely seemed interested in the topic. "My people are combing through every inch of your life right now."

He brushed a hand over his pants. "There's nothing to find."

The move matched his comment, which she knew was wrong. When someone tried to mess with her records, the computer system back at the office went wild. Their tech expert watched over all of the identities, real and not, that each Alliance member used. The wealth of information passed through . . . she didn't even know what. She just knew someone tried to make it look as if she'd been accepting illegal payments. Tried and failed.

"Mysterious payments." She'd started with the withdrawals they found buried, but connected the dots back to companies within companies that were owned by him. "It seems you didn't just fund an expedition here. You've been paying for equipment and intel."

"I can only assume by this conversation that you're setting me up again."

And now for the *other* payments. "Well, since you tried to phony up some deposits to me that traced back to Chechen rebels, it would serve you right."

Niko shifted. Crossed one leg over the other. After a few seconds he did it in the opposite direction.

She took that as confirmation.

"I'm a businessman."

He liked to fall back on that explanation. As if it meant anything to her. "So you keep saying."

"I am trying to reestablish communication with the expedition, then I'm pulling my people out. After that I will talk to some of my friends and let them know the Alliance is illegally operating in Russia. Maybe implicate the CIA. Generally cause you enough trouble that you'll lose your precious team." He folded his hands together on his lap. "And if you've been funneling money to the Chechens, you could have some trouble."

"The scientists are dead. Almost all of them." She hated that part, but that blame started with the man in front of her. He put them in danger. He told lies and used them for his personal agenda, whatever that might be.

He sat up straighter and the chair creaked beneath him. "That's not possible."

"Your plans to build a cobalt bomb are done." It didn't matter whose plan it was. She would end it.

"Why would I want to bomb Russia? I am determined to restore its greatness. To move out corrupt leaders, something you should be trying to do." He leaned forward, his voice growing louder with each word. "Starting a war gets me nothing. That would likely keep these incompetent men in power even longer."

The argument made some sense. That sucked, because if he wasn't at the bottom of the secret lab, it meant there was another player on the ground. One she hadn't identified yet. One who could be stalking Reid and Parker even now.

She stood up. "Where's Mickey? Isn't he supposed to be watching over you at all times?"

"I have other guards."

"I got in here without trouble." She stood, dragged her finger along the dresser as she walked by. Fingered the closed file. Stopped in front of the stack of clothes on the end of the bed. She'd looked through everything when she first got here. This was her way of letting him know that in her mind there was nothing left to see.

"Let me worry about my staffing issues." Niko spun around in his chair as his gaze followed her around the room. "What's your next move here, Tasha?"

She headed for the door, keeping him in her view at all times. This was not a man a smart woman turned her back on. Besides, there was no need to extend her time there and invite trouble.

After a quick check out the peephole to make sure it was clear, she slipped her gloved hand over the door handle. "I suspect you'll follow me and find out."

"I don't trust you."

Since she needed to check in with her men and watch Niko, the easiest thing to do was convince him

to follow her. She was betting the temptation would prove too great for him to sit around and wait in a hotel room.

She glanced at him one more time. “Then we’re even.”

21

CARA WAITED as they drove around in circles, slowed down, sped up . . . hid behind a boulder. As far as subterfuge went, Reid was not playing around. The man was a master. He had her half dizzy with motion sickness by the time he slid into an empty space behind a falling down cabin.

She expected him to go in, guns blazing. Instead he sat there with the truck idling. The engine hummed in the background until it vibrated inside of her.

From this position she could see through the building to the front. The caved-in roof had water spilling into what should have been the inside rooms. One window had been taken out and leaned against the wall. A hole by the back door gave her a view of what looked like a stack of pots and pans.

No way was anyone in there. No one had been for a long time. The place didn't offer shelter but was large enough to cast a shadow over the small truck. At least for now that would work. She just had to hope

that eventually someone in the Russian special forces would notice patrols kept going out and never coming back. Seemed like an obvious issue to her.

But none of that explained why they still sat there.

For a second she wondered if the plan had been to get her out of the mine while Parker tortured Simon. The second the idea flashed through her, she blocked it out again. She didn't want to know how the Alliance gathered intel or what they did to people who lied to them. She'd never sleep again if she knew that piece of the puzzle.

Still, she couldn't imagine Reid hurting someone just for the thrill of it. He was not that kind of guy, and he would not let someone else do it in his place. But that left a pretty big gulf between causing pain for no reason and extracting legitimate and necessary information. If she'd never been kidnapped, she likely would have had one take on the issue. But as a survivor of a terrifying crime, the line between right and wrong blurred for her a bit.

She could imagine it did for Reid as well. Not that he'd ever tell her.

With a sigh, she leaned her head against the seat behind her and looked over at him. Even his profile spoke to his strength. From here she could see the outline of his jaw. That sexy neck.

Her gaze traveled lower, to his hands. She loved his hands. Long lean fingers and the ever-present black

watch on his wrist. The calluses on his palms spoke to the amount of physical labor he performed, the strenuous workouts he put himself through. She'd seen one or two. The tire flipping made her lower back ache just to watch it.

But what he could do with those hands. From the way he toured his fingertips over her, to the gentle touch of his palm to the side of her face. Tough yet careful. Always so controlled in his use of force and show of strength.

He turned the truck off and turned in his seat, just a bit. Enough to face her. "What do you want to know?"

Her brain sputtered. Jumping from the thoughts running through her head to his comment left her spinning. "What?"

"I keep trying to figure out what the one thing is that I could say that would make this right."

The cobalt. Russian. Simon. The list of what the "this" could mean was pretty long. "Reid, I don't understand—"

"That's how it works, right?" He stretched an arm along the back of their seats. "You need me to tell you about my past before you can trust me. I'm not sure what part you need to hear. Just tell me and I'll say it."

Understanding dawned and her heartbeat took off in a gallop. This odd mix of anxiety, hope, and doom hovered over her. Followed by a swift kick of guilt. This is what she'd reduced him to. This man, all in control and

barking orders, wanted her to come up with one question that would let them move forward.

If only it were that simple.

If only everything that happened between them before hadn't brought them to this emotional place.

She scooted over, just a bit closer to him, and put a hand on his thigh right above his knee. "First of all, I do trust you."

"With what?"

She didn't understand the question. "Trust is . . . you know what I mean. The word has a logical definition."

He had her stumbling over her words and doubting her hearing. The man could strip away all of her defense mechanisms in two seconds flat.

"It's not really one thing." He didn't sound angry. He looked at her as if he genuinely expected her to have a rational answer. "Do you trust me to keep you safe? Trust me not to physically hurt you? Trust me not to cheat on you? Which is it? Am I failing in one of those categories or is it something else?"

"I trust you in all of those ways." For her, trust was a much bigger concept. This all-encompassing thing that included her mind and body.

"Do you trust me to tell you the truth? Because sometimes I can't. Not all of it." He slipped his fingers into her hair. Wrapped a strand around his thumb. "That's part of the job."

"I get that and I'm fine with it." She didn't have a

choice on that score, but she meant it. She wasn't naïve. "I would imagine Tasha doesn't take security breaches very well."

"She'd cut off my balls." He shrugged. "But I'd deserve it. My job isn't really about me. I have to remember that every time I walk out the door."

Cara got that. She understood how clearances worked. Knew that sometimes sharing every bit of information could cause more damage. Like everything else in life, it was a weighing process.

But her need to really know him wasn't a gray line. "It's not as if I want you to list a few things from your past so I can check them off before I'll invite you into the house."

"Okay."

She knew from his tone that he still didn't get what she wanted. "The communication needs to be authentic in how we talk to each other. Like when I told you about having kids—"

"That issue only matters to me if it matters to you. There are options. With my past, I'm the last person in the world who would think family is only about biology."

God, she loved him for that. He took the news in stride. Made it about what she needed and not what he would lose. He might not understand all of her points, but some things he intrinsically understood better than almost anyone else she knew.

And she needed him to get this, too. "My point is, at that time in the conversation it made sense to share something with you. It created an extra level of intimacy between us."

He frowned. Looked almost amused by her comment. "I thought we had the intimacy part of our relationship down pretty well."

He could be such a dude sometimes. "I'm not just talking about sex."

He had the smarts to wince. "Of course not."

"I want to know about you. Who you are and what you believe. I need to know we are in this together." *Were* . . . She should have said *were,* but couldn't make herself go back and fix the sentence.

He nodded. "So you can make sure I'm a good risk."

"No." She didn't even know where that came from. "So I can *know* you on a level that connects us."

"What if I can't figure out how to give it to you?" He cleared his throat. "Give it again, I mean."

That shot landed. She doubted he meant to throw it but the words knocked into her with the force of a punch. The reality was, she'd turned that question over and over in her mind. The problem with their relationship stemmed from both of them. He phrased every question in terms of what he could do for her, but really she had so many limitations. She fell back on work. She panicked when people got so protective that she felt suffocated.

She didn't really trust the idea of getting swept up and so attached to someone else that she couldn't see straight. It wasn't logical to her. Yet it happened. The man who whipped her life around and yanked it apart sat a few feet away, running his fingers over her neck. Making her shiver like he always did.

"What if I can't be enough for you?" Giving voice to the question cost her something. She hated being vulnerable and asking him for what she wanted or needed. She plowed ahead and made plans. This thing with him blew all of those learned behaviors apart. "Don't you worry about that?"

His head snapped back. "That's ridiculous."

Not to her. That was the great fear. That he'd wake up one day and realize she was living her life wrong and try to shove her in a different box or make her into someone else. She'd experienced that sensation her entire life. It made her shut down and push away. Hell, she'd done it to him already.

"I messed up." There, she finally admitted it out loud to someone other than herself.

"What?"

She stared at the truck's ceiling for a second as she gathered the courage to take responsibility for the mistakes she'd made with him. Own up to her part of this, and not just blame the situation and hormones and whatever else made it easier for her to walk away and stay away.

"The tracker wasn't your best move but I didn't hand back the ring and leave because of that." She touched the empty space now. Remembered how she used to twirl it around on her finger.

"You left because I wouldn't talk to you."

"I left because I was afraid that the rush we felt would be temporary. I wanted out before it walloped me." The sensations had been so strong and so new. She'd been afraid because it was safer to go back to lukewarm dates and sex that led nowhere. She believed that didn't cost her anything . . . now she knew better. "Before you moved on."

"Cara." The soothing tone made her melt. "I proposed to you because I loved you."

There was that past tense again. She swallowed hard to remove the lump in her throat. "I know."

The back of his fingers danced over her cheek. "Still do."

She didn't dare believe it. "Really?"

He laughed. "Yes. Love, full on and still happening."

A zing of light and happiness tore through her. "I don't know why."

He laughed. "Some days I've wondered about that myself."

The honesty. She loved that about him, too. "I'm not sure where we are now or if we've just flipped back into this cycle where it's thrilling and energetic but not real."

"Only you worried about that being an issue between us." He exhaled. "I know I've dismissed that concern in the past, but we can work through it. You just have to be willing to try."

She didn't understand how he could be so sure. For a long time she thought that meant he wasn't that engaged in the relationship. That the ring and the talk about sharing apartments and lives was just this shallow thing for him. A way for him to feel normal when everything else in his life was absolutely not.

Now she saw that she took her fears and projected them onto him. She heaped every negative on the situation and could not believe he meant anything he said. She really did wonder why he ever loved her.

She leaned forward, closing the distance between them. One minute she sat on her side of the bench seat. The next she slid over, almost onto his lap. "You're a good man."

"Prove it."

Her mouth hovered over his. "Any chance you brought that extra condom out here with you?"

"As soon as Parker gave it to me, I stuck it in my pocket. I have it now."

She didn't want to know what conversation led to that exchange. But the conversation back in the mine now made more sense.

She tried to forget Parker's grin right before they left. "Well, get it."

"Have we settled the issues between us?" He wrapped an arm around her neck and dragged her in even closer.

One of her legs slid over his. With every touch concentrated, talking grew harder. "I'm not sure it's a light switch we can just flip on and off."

She'd finally apologized and the relief soared inside her at having unlocked some of that guilt. Right behind that came a very different feeling. One that required him to lose the pants.

"I am sitting in the middle of Russia, being hunted by at least one group of armed men." His hand slipped up and under her jacket. "And all I can think about is stripping you naked."

"Are you saying I wreck your concentration?" Man, she hoped that's what he was saying because that was pretty damn sexy. A guy like him getting all riled up? Yeah, she'd love that.

"I'm saying I break all the rules for you."

Even better. That might have been the hottest thing she'd ever heard. "Kiss me."

His lips crashed over hers. Heat sparked between them like it always did. His mouth slipped to her cheek then down her neck. Every touch sent need spiking through her.

He pressed a hand between her legs. Pushed until she gasped. Rubbed his fingers back and forth. The friction of her pants and his hand had her squirming

to get closer. When the sound of the zipper screeched through the truck, she almost laughed in relief. She needed his fingers on her, inside of her.

The material shifted around her. The tugging and yanking—in a few pulls he had her pants down to the top of her thighs. His fingers skimmed under the elastic band of her underwear. She heard a rip but didn't care.

"Tear them off." She gave the order between kisses. Held his head and kept his hot mouth locked to hers.

The inside of the truck flipped around on her. For a second she lost her balance. Then she was sitting on his lap, straddling his legs. He had his zipper down and the condom on. She didn't know where he found the time or the extra hand and she didn't care. He was ready and that meant they could do this now.

She lifted up on her knees, rising just above him. His fingers slipped up her thighs and into her heat. She couldn't handle the foreplay. She wanted it all. Now.

Taking his erection in her hand, she guided his tip inside her. She lowered her weight and let him plunge inside her. Slow at first, giving her body time to adjust. Then the rhythm took hold. She plunged and retreated. Looked down and watched his body disappear into hers.

He pushed her hair back and held it there. "You are so fucking sexy."

Every time her body fell, he lifted his hips and pushed in deeper. The truck rocked and squeaked. Ev-

erything about this, about him, felt right. Their bodies fit together, matched in need.

He grabbed the bottom of her jacket in his fist and held the edge up, just off her stomach. Then it was his turn to watch. With each push, his mouth opened. The awe was right there on his face. The hunger. All for her.

Energy pulsed through her. Every muscle inside her screamed for release. She wanted to ride him, enjoy the sensation of controlling the thrusts, but the waves of pleasure already crashed over her.

When he held her hips steady and lifted his body, slipping inside her—in and out—she almost lost her mind. Her thighs trembled and the tightening inside her cried out for release. She wanted to hold back the orgasm and revel in this moment. Enjoy every precious second.

Her chest pounded and her body started to buck. She remembered the talk about intimacy and for just a second wondered if this was enough. If this moment, being so tied to him and his pleasure, could last.

That was her last thought before she came.

22

"We have incoming." Parker stared at his watch as he delivered the warning.

Now that they'd been back in the mine for twenty minutes and needed to concentrate, Reid figured this would be a good time to stop watching every move Cara made. Safety needed to be the number one concern. They had one wild card in the building with them—Simon.

While Reid and Cara were in the truck, Parker had questioned Simon, who didn't break. Didn't really say anything. He came off as a smart guy who was smart at one thing—his job. Socially awkward and a bit of a blowhard. He also tended to say things that didn't make sense. Reid couldn't tell if he was a mastermind or someone who needed a handler.

Reid looked over Parker's shoulder. "Do we have an ID?"

"I can't really tell eye color from a dot on my watch." Parker ended the sarcastic comment by giving Reid the finger.

"You need a better watch." An alarm system would also be good. All they had to go on right now was the GPS and some other functions on the watch. The beeping of the watch alarm had to do with proximity. They used it when hunting predators. Reid feared that might fit now.

Cara walked into the mine entrance with Simon right behind her. She ignored him and looked from Reid to Parker. "What's happening?"

The small vibration in her voice suggested either frustration with Simon or worry. She had a sense for danger, so it was likely the latter. After their turn in the truck, all the talking and sex, he wanted more. But it looked like dealing with a new wave of armed guards took priority.

"Someone is coming." That's all he said. He figured she could fill in the blanks. It wasn't as if they had confirmation of anything anyway.

Cara being Cara, she didn't let the conversation drop there. "Russian special forces?"

"What?" Simon shoved his way past her to stand in front of Parker. "They're here?"

Parker rarely rattled and he didn't this time either. "Possibly."

"We need to move." Simon walked around in circles. His nervous energy bounced off the walls.

Maybe the part about being hunted by special forces did have some validity. But they were left with the reality of being trapped in a mine. "And go where?"

"Outside."

"The person or people heading our way are outside." Parker sounded like he wanted to add "dumbass" or some other comment to the end of his sentence but he refrained.

"Isn't there a second entrance?" Simon kept walking around. He looked two seconds away from bouncing into walls. "Didn't you plan for that contingency?"

"We didn't build this place," Reid said, pointing out the obvious.

"Okay, let's calm down," she said. Simon looked like he wanted to argue with her, but he stayed quiet. She took a few deep breaths before continuing. "Do we know how many are out there?"

"No." Reid had to admit that would make life easier. Having one come through the door was no big deal. Hell, the way he and Parker shot, ten could come through. But if the special forces guys realized they were missing a bunch of friends, a whole crew could be about to descend on them.

Simon snorted. "That's helpful."

"Let me hit him." Parker looked at Reid. Practically begged. "Just once."

"The door is locked, right? I mean, he or they or whatever can't just come in."

"You need to calm down," Parker said.

"These guys killed Brad right in front of me." Simon pointed at his temple. "Shot him in the head, and that

was after they beat the crap out of him." He glared at each of them and stopped on Cara. "Do you get what I'm saying?"

"Panic isn't going to help," she said in a rational voice.

Simon answered back in a voice that inched higher with every word. "Easy for you to say."

She frowned. "What does that mean?"

"They'll protect you." Simon threw his arms wide in a gesture that included the entrance tunnel hallway and openings to tunnels farther back.

He wasn't wrong, but Reid had still reached the end of his patience. He had a good store of it, but he was fucking done. "That's enough."

The banging started a second later. Two thumps then another two. If it was some sort of signal, Reid didn't recognize it. From Parker's confused expression he didn't either.

Then another sound reached them. A muffled voice. Reid couldn't make out the words. The whole thing could be a trick to lure them in closer then shoot through the door. It was old but still metal. The person on the other side would need a hell of a weapon, but Reid wasn't taking a chance.

The voice grew louder. Shouting. Saying something.

"Anyone getting that?" Parker asked.

A name. Cara's name.

Simon glared at her. "Who is that?"

She shook her head. "I have no idea."

"Sound familiar at all?"

"How do I tell?"

Reid searched his mind, tried to think of a way special forces would know her identity. They could have a list of scientists on the expedition. Or . . . he looked at Simon. "Did you tell them her name?"

Simon's forehead wrinkled and he shook his head. "No."

"Could it be Caleb?" Parker asked.

Simon threw up his hands. "Who the hell is Caleb?"

"It's someone who doesn't have a way to contact us." The unstated answer was "not one of us." Reid knew that much was true.

But standing there wasn't fixing this. Whoever was out there knew her name, which likely meant they would not move until they saw her. Him, her, they—the person had Reid's full attention now. Much more banging and the person could draw attention or break the doors they needed between them and the outside world.

He motioned for her to get back and then yanked Simon out of the way. "Stay back here."

Parker nodded as the two of them approached the doors. Inched forward without making a sound. They pressed against the opposite side of the main tunnel. Neither of them stood in the middle, where they would have been an easy target. Once they were in position, Reid called out, "Who's there?"

"Mickey Stoltz."

The name sounded familiar because he'd studied the expedition files. It appeared on a few pages. This guy made the arrangements. He had some security title with the foundation but as far as Reid could tell he'd failed to provide anything to the scientists.

The bigger question was how he got there and why. Tasha was following Niko, and Mickey should be pasted to their sides. She'd reported not seeing him for more than a day. Now Reid knew why. Mickey made a side trip to their neighborhood.

This just got interesting.

Reid nodded to Parker to open the door. When he did, Mickey stood there with no weapon and no discernible backup. Just one man out in the middle of the Ural Mountains.

Yeah, that made sense.

Mickey's smile fell when he looked at the guns pointed at him. "Wait a second."

"Hands up." Parker gave the order and the man immediately complied.

"I am here on behalf of Niko Murin." Mickey took one step. Then another. "I work for the foundation."

"You're a long way from your plush DC offices." Reid didn't have much time for the foundation or any business that sent innocents out to dangerous areas unprotected. This guy, with his fancy credentials, should have known better.

Mickey nodded. "We have a missing science expedition."

"Do we look like scientists?" Parker asked.

"Hardly." Mickey lowered his hands. "You look like you work for Tasha."

The guy acted like saying her name gave him a free pass. Reid didn't like it. "And?"

"She's with Niko right now. They've decided to work together. They sent me out ahead to scout for you and the expedition." Mickey reached into his pocket and Parker took aim. "Wait!"

"Don't be stupid."

"I was going to show you the message on my phone."

Since he'd checked in with Tasha ten minutes ago and she described being with Niko as a form of slow torture, Reid doubted everyone was as chummy as Mickey pretended.

"Mickey!" Simon yelled the man's name from one of the tunnel rooms farther back.

"I knew I should have shot him." Parker said it, as Reid was thinking it.

A smile spread over Mickey's face as he shifted around, clearly trying to look past the bed in the tunnel where Simon's voice had come from. "You found them."

"So your work here is done." Reid wanted this guy gone. Something about the calm demeanor and monotone voice had his senses firing.

Simon broke free then and stopped in the arched tunnel. "You're here."

"Where is everyone else?" Mickey kept looking around.

"Gone. I mean, I know Brad is." Simon swallowed a few times before continuing. "He was with me and they shot him."

Mickey frowned. "They who?"

"Men with guns."

When Mickey scanned the mine again, Reid explained. "Other men with guns. Not us."

Not that he wanted that intel out. Simon only talked about Brad, but the rest of them were gone. For now, Reid planned to keep that bit of news quiet.

"I'm here." Cara slipped out from behind Simon.

"Lock the door." Reid nodded to Parker before looking at everyone else. "Let's step back into the larger room."

Still jumpy, Simon took a step toward the doors. "We should leave."

Mickey stopped him with hand on his shoulder. "Soon."

The tone worked with Mickey's demeanor to keep Reid on edge. He felt a move coming, big and unpredictable. The kind where people got hurt. So long as Cara stayed safe and they got some answers, Reid was fine with whatever came next. He just wished he could get a better handle on Mickey.

He worked for a guy with a big ego. That had to be tough for a man with Mickey's past. He enjoyed being in charge. But in this game he didn't have the money and the power. Reid thought there was a pretty good chance he'd overreached and tried to get some of both.

Mickey looked around the mine as he walked farther in. He peeked first into the shaft with the cart blocking the way then into the room with the pool of water. He wasn't exactly casing the place but seemed to be indexing every crack and pebble.

As he walked by Cara's bag, he hesitated. Not for long. It barely lasted the time of a blink. Reid saw because he was watching for it. He couldn't make out everything sitting on the dark bag. Personal items and her wet coat. A few . . . rocks. What had she called them? Grabbo, grabbon? Reid didn't remember and it didn't matter. The only piece of intel that meant anything dealt with the cobalt, and those rocks were a source.

Mickey stopped next to Simon. They stood at the entrance to the room with the pool, near the lip before the water started. Seeing them together set off an alarm bell in Reid's brain. The odds of two guys randomly walking around the Russian countryside, this close to the hidden lab, had to be slim. And Reid didn't believe in coincidences.

"What are you supposed to do once you find the missing scientists?" Reid asked.

Mickey didn't hesitate in his response. "Handle them."

Reid's hand went to his gun. "Is that supposed to be funny?"

"Being honest." Mickey took his gun out of his pocket. "I hear you Alliance guys prefer that."

Cara must have clued in because she went from listening to glaring. Her gaze bounced down to Mickey's gun then back to his face. "What's happening?"

"Don't play dumb, Cara." Mickey motioned for her to come closer. "It's over."

She didn't move. If anything, she inched closer to Reid. Just like he wanted. "Leave her out of this."

"Oh, she's in it." Mickey laughed. "What, you didn't think she was really out here to investigate a decades-old case, did you?"

Simon looked around. The fact that he was in trouble finally seemed to dawn on him. His gaze traveled from person to person but he didn't move. Looked like he was frozen to the spot. Since that spot happened to be next to a wild card with a gun, he'd chosen a bad place to stand.

"Simon's your man." Reid became less and less convinced of that by the second. That was the piece that fit. Mickey needed a man on the ground. Whether he was working alone or with Niko, they'd been in DC. Someone else set up the lab and would perform the actual work.

That led Reid right back to Simon. He'd shown up at the wrong time. His story didn't make sense. Even now

he looked confused but didn't seem to have the sense to be scared.

"This guy?" Mickey hitched a thumb in Simon's general direction.

Simon frowned. "Where did you get a gun?"

"It's just stupid to be out here unarmed." Mickey looked over at Parker. "Right?"

"You should put yours down now." Parker closed in. He stood between everyone and the front doors. His size and shot would make it hard for anyone to pass.

Reid depended on that. He looked over, thinking to grab Cara, but she was a few steps too many away from him. He needed her to move.

"Not going to happen." Mickey took out a second weapon. "The guns stay with me."

No matter how many weapons he had on him he could still only fire two at a time. That put him at a disadvantage. Apparently he missed the part where he was outmatched.

"Do you want to die?" Reid asked.

Mickey glanced over at Cara. "It's time for us to shut this down, honey."

Her mouth twisted into a frown. "Stop acting like we're working together."

Reid refused to believe that. Not her. Not with this guy. "Nice try."

"What, you think I needed a botanist for my plans?" Mickey's grin turned feral. "A geologist knows about cobalt."

"What are you talking about?" Simon grabbed for Mickey's arm.

Mickey pushed him away. "This guy means nothing to me."

Reid could see they were headed right for maximum chaos. Once bullets started ricocheting in here they were all in trouble. "Okay, everyone calm down."

Mickey pointed the gun at Simon. "He's useless to me."

Simon took another step back. "Come on, man."

"See?" Mickey fired. Hit Simon in the center of his chest. A red splotch was already forming on his shirt as he plunged backward into the water.

Reid started toward Mickey, hoping to get there before he could get the shot off. But Reid was too late. The gun fired and he lunged for Simon, thinking to save him from what would likely be a deadly plunge into the pool.

He almost got there. Made it right to the edge before Mickey grabbed him. The former Stasi guard had the advantage while Reid was focused on Simon and knocked the gun out of his hand. When the pieces stopped moving, Reid was on his knees next to Mickey . . . with a gun pointed at his forehead.

Mickey looked up at Parker and Cara. "Now, let's talk about my lab."

23

TASHA SLIPPED inside the mine without anyone shooting her. That was a triumph of sorts. So was getting Niko to stay quiet. He complained the entire bumpy ride over. When she reminded him that he chose to join her, he threatened to have her thrown in a top secret Russian prison in the arctic region of the Urals.

If he was trying to convince her he was innocent, he was failing miserably.

They rounded the corner and she shoved Niko back against the wall. Had to put a hand over his mouth to keep him quiet. Then they listened. As Mickey suggested he was working on something other than Niko's grand plan, Niko's eyes narrowed. By the time they got to the lab, Niko shook with fury.

It looked like they found their rogue player: Mickey, with a very big gun and Reid kneeling at his feet. The last part didn't bother Tasha that much. Reid knew how to get out of a situation like this. If Mickey had been smart he'd have made a run at Cara. Her safety would have given him much greater leverage over her men.

Time to make an entrance.

She grabbed Niko by the collar and dragged him in with her. Being stunned and in a full fit of fury, he was easy to throw around. She had to remind herself that he was a potential target today. Her job was to protect him, even if it killed her.

"I guess we know why the security at the campsite sucked."

"Tasha." Mickey pressed the gun tighter against Reid's head. "Perfect. Everyone is here. Even my boss."

"What are you doing?" Niko asked the question as he ventured one step too close to Mickey before Tasha pulled him back.

"What you should have done but you were too busy worrying about restoring power to Russia." Mickey shook his head. "The system is corrupt. Don't you get it, the leaders can't be saved."

"This doesn't sound crazy at all." Reid's comment earned him a knock against the side of his head with the gun. He bent down and his hands hit the floor but he didn't fall over.

Tasha took that as a good sign. "It's time to put an end to this madness."

"I agree." Mickey gestured to Cara. "Come here."

Reid lifted his head. "Do not move."

"I will put a bullet in his skull." Mickey pressed the gun to Reid's temple.

"He won't." Reid pleaded with Cara now.

"He's former Stasi," Parker said, reminding them all

that this guy might not have a lot to lose. And that he had skills. Not to rival the Alliance, but he was a threat, and this close to Reid, a significant one.

"My partner apparently is dead." Mickey almost laughed as he said it.

The nonchalance seemed to snap Cara out of her stunned stupor. "Brad?"

"You're interchangeable and you will be easier to manage than he ever was. I won't even need to pretend that I plan on paying you."

"Not that it's your money anyway." Tasha glanced at Niko. "Now we know where those payments from your accounts were going."

"For all his supposed skills, he's an easy man to scam." Mickey shifted his weight as he grew more comfortable with the topic. "All that talk about Russia being strong again. So misguided. The last country capable of producing a bomb like mine or to run the world is the one we're standing in."

"I'm going to kill you." Niko took a step forward.

Tasha held him back. "Doubtful."

She mentally measured the distance between her and Reid. In close quarters like this, someone was almost guaranteed to get hurt. Hit Mickey, and he'd fire. Bullets would ping and bounce, and that barrel hovered right by Reid's ear. It was tough to miss at that distance.

Still, she knew Reid had a plan. He always had a plan. She just wished she knew what it was.

Cara tried to keep calm, a task that proved impossible. Her knees shook and her head spun. Seeing Reid in danger knocked every ounce of control out of her. She wanted to rush in and grab that gun. Stupid moves, but she wasn't thinking rationally. For the first time in her life she abandoned what made sense and moved on instinct.

Right now part of that depended on keeping Mickey talking. He seemed impressed with his plan. Fine, let him tell it. The longer they stalled, the more time Reid had, and the closer Parker could get to Mickey. Between the two of them, they could get off a shot. Add in Tasha and the combination should be lethal.

That made her wonder if there was another plan at work here. One she didn't know about.

Not that her instincts were all that reliable at the moment. She'd been so sure Simon was lying, that he had something to do with the cobalt bomb. The botany angle never made sense but the money part did. Simon was the guy who lived big. He threw money around, drove an expensive car. Had to live in the right part of town.

Word was, he took part in the expedition because he needed the cash, and an expedition with some level of danger like this one came with a bonus. In light of all that had happened, they should have received combat pay. If she lived through the next few minutes, she'd demand it.

But her staying alive was not her number one concern right now. She ached for Reid. Seeing him sitting there in the dirt ripped her inside out. She knew he had another gun, or he usually did. She couldn't remember where he put it when they came in from the truck.

The damn truck. Those stolen minutes had been perfect, but now she regretted them. If they had come back earlier or been more aware . . . She didn't know if Mickey crawled out from under his rock during that time, but being off-duty couldn't have been a good choice.

One more thing she needed to atone for. Right after she got combat pay she'd start working on her bigger apology. This time for everything. Reid would not die today, because she hadn't told him she loved him and that would happen. She refused to believe this would go any other way but her telling him how she felt about him. How she'd always felt and how being away from him destroyed her.

So much death. So many lives lost over what sounded like a man's greed. Not principles or because he was under threat. No, Mickey was motivated by money.

"So, you used your boss's money to hire Brad to set up the lab," she said to him.

"If it wasn't for the Russian special forces performing that midnight raid and grabbing the scientists from their tents, the lab would be operational now."

"Was the secret work camp location up north in

the Urals, the one that was blown up and started all of this, also yours?" Cara couldn't believe one man could wield that much power in a country he didn't live in, but weirder things had happened.

"My original partner, an old scientist friend from my days in Germany. He should have sided with me, but he took his intel to the Russians." Mickey shrugged. "His mistake."

Reid's eyes narrowed. "You're saying you destroyed the lab?"

"All I had to do was make sure some of other old friends knew about the disloyalty." Mickey actually winked. "They pulled off the maneuver. It worked, but it made Russian special forces pretty angry. Hence the scene at the tents and shaking down the scientists for information, thinking they had some but only Brad did."

She tried to process all that loss and deception. She also tried to imagine Brad crawling down into a makeshift lab each night and setting up the equipment. Even weirder to think about him doing all the work on his own. Brad had been smart but not a genius. He was the type who depended on assistants. Not exactly the guy she would pick as the father of the cobalt bomb.

Mickey looked at her. "Brad insisted he needed you. Frankly, I thought he had a crush, but grabbing you should have been easy enough."

She fought off a shiver. Refused to give him the satisfaction. "Should have."

The thought of being locked away with those two in that tiny lab was too horrible to imagine, but at least the plan made some sense now. Brad depended on her. Maybe that's why the CIA picked her. Maybe someone else was in on this. She almost didn't care so long as Mickey stopped pointing the gun at Reid.

"You used my expedition." Niko sounded stunned by the idea. He shook his head. "How dare you?"

It seemed like a ridiculous thing to say. Weapons were out. Poor Simon was floating in a pool of God knew what. Commandos could storm the building at any time. And Niko worried about a lack of loyalty. The way Cara saw it, that was the least of their problems.

"Don't pretend it was really about that hiking incident," Mickey said in a singsongy voice. "You lied and I lied. The only difference is I stand to make a lot of money off my lie."

"A perfect match. Greed for greed." Reid didn't even bother to mumble his comment.

The last thing they needed was for him to tip this madman over the edge. "Reid."

"Yes, Cara. Warn your boyfriend to be careful with what he says," Mickey said. "Tasha might tolerate insolence. I don't. Not after having to listen to Niko here drone on about unnecessary bullshit and follow his useless orders just so I could get closer to the money."

She hated that he acted so familiar. First he tried

to pretend she was in on his plan. Now he stood there, ignoring the fact that trained gunmen—Alliance members, no less—were aiming at him. There was no way out here. More would die, but Tasha was not going to let Mickey get by her. No question about that.

Calling him a madman was not accurate. This guy was about ego and cash. He didn't care about anyone except himself. He wasn't mad. He was dangerous, maybe evil. She had no idea how to fight either.

"Once you get out of here you still have to deal with Russian special forces." Reid sounded so calm. The man looming above him looked ready to execute him, and Reid didn't even flinch. "They will kill you rather than let you move around with that cobalt."

"They haven't been able to do much other than kill a few scientists. No, I'll slip by just fine." Mickey called out to his boss, "And Niko, you'll get your way."

Niko shook his head. "What are you talking about now?"

"You wanted me to set up Tasha and have the authorities find her in a compromising situation." He performed a small bow. "Consider it done."

"I think that's everything." That was the first thing Parker had said in a while.

It didn't make any sense to Cara. "What?"

Reid slowly lifted his head. "Yep."

Then the room broke into a free-for-all. Chaos reigned. One minute everyone stood in their positions,

not making any sudden moves. Then everyone shifted. People flew through the air.

Reid lifted his hand and a blade flashed. One swift shift and he stabbed it into Mickey's thigh. An anguished roar cut through room. Mickey lowered the gun to fire, but Reid slammed into him. Sent him flying backward. She ducked as Parker flew across the room, He knocked into her, bringing them both down and into the dirt.

She struggled under his weight. Shoved and pushed. She needed to get to Reid. Parker yelled her name as she rolled away from him. She was up and on her feet, racing to where the men fought on the floor.

The gun shook in her hands. She aimed then tried again as their bodies flipped. Legs and arms wrapped around each other. She waited for Reid to pin Mickey down or to get a clear shot, but neither happened. One arm lifted. Punches and kicks. When Reid finally rolled to the top, she took aim at the man beneath him.

Before she could fire, a gunshot blasted through the room. A chunk of the wall blew apart. She could hear crashing behind her. It all happened so fast and all she could do was stare at the weapon in her hand. Her gaze shifted from the gun to the men crawling around in front of her.

Reid clutched his shoulder. Red seeped through his fingers but he kept fighting. Another shot in the same

area where that first one had been. His arm hung lower on one side. He made a fist but his fingers didn't move that much.

Horror raced through her. She almost dropped the weapon. It slipped from her fingers as her muscles turned to mush and she tried to focus.

She was the one who'd shot him. She panicked at the thought but feared she did it. Without thinking, she must have pulled the trigger. Now Reid was vulnerable and Mickey hadn't been slowed down.

"Not you." Parker said the words as he stepped in front of her. "Mickey got him."

A gun went off again, and for a second no one moved. Parker stood there, looking around.

It took another second for Mickey's body to slump over Reid, trapping him against the hard ground. The two men just lay there, still. Blood ran over both of them, with no clear idea where it came from.

It was quiet now. All the shouting, yelling, and grunting had stopped.

"Reid." Panic rose inside of her and washed over everything. She wanted to claw her way across the floor to get him out from beneath Mickey.

Then Mickey moved and her heart stopped. He'd survived. He must have been the one who got off that last shot, and now he was rising like some sort of otherworldly creature from a horror show.

Instead, his body flipped to the side. There was a

crack as his head hit the tunnel wall. Blood ran over the uneven rocks and a new smell filled the stale air.

Relief drove her to her knees. Reid was alive. He'd shoved Mickey aside. She could see Reid now, watch his chest rise and fall. Then she noticed the pool of blood under his shoulder. It gathered, then ran down his neck.

She could barely focus, but the red stain brought her winging back to sanity. She slid across the floor to him. Behind her, Parker was talking. She didn't know if it was to her or to Reid, and she didn't care. She kept working. Ripped her jacket off and rolled it in a ball to press it against Reid's shoulder.

He panted but then his breathing slowed and his eyes drifted shut.

She wanted to scream into his face. She forced her voice to remain somewhat calm. "Reid."

"I'm okay." He nodded but didn't open his eyes. "Where's Tasha?"

A new wave of guilt pounded Cara. Until that moment she'd forgotten all about Tasha. She looked around and saw the other woman's body tangled up with Niko's. More blood stained the floor. Pretty soon a river of it would wash through here.

Cara squinted in the semidark to better see what had happened. Tasha was on top of Niko. Covering him. Protecting him.

Tasha sat up and stared down at Niko. "You get hit?"

All the color had left Niko's face. His skin had

blanched the color of his white shirt. He shook his head, seemed unable to form a sentence.

"Good." Tasha pushed on Niko's side and stood up. She did a quick check of her torso. Her gaze stopped on the dots of red on her arm. "Small hit. I'm all good."

"How?" Cara didn't realize she'd asked the question out loud until she heard it.

"Mickey's ricochet." Tasha stepped over Niko and joined the rest of them on the ground. "Speaking of which."

She put her fingers to Mickey's neck.

"Well?" Parker asked.

"Nothing." Tasha was looking down at Reid now. "How is he doing?"

"That's the third time he's been shot in three days. Or was it only two days? I can't even remember how long we've been here." Parker talked tough but his voice sounded scratchy. "But I think you need to send him for some more training. After a hospital, of course."

"Cara?" Reid's voice drifted up to her.

"I'm right here." She grabbed his hand. "Are you okay?"

"This isn't a big deal."

It looked like a bloodbath. She didn't know how he was still talking, or why. He needed rest and an ambulance. She assumed they had those in Russia. If not, Tasha could work her magic. Either way, Cara wanted Reid to get medical attention.

She glanced up at Tasha. "He needs a doctor."

"No." Reid broke into a coughing fit.

Parker laughed as he grabbed the medical kit out of Reid's bag. "Listen to your woman."

One of his eyes popped open. "Are you my woman?"

Now was not the time for this. Not with all of them watching. But it didn't matter because her mind would not change. She'd watched him walking into danger for her over and over again. This wasn't about tension or sexual attraction or even adrenaline. Maybe they hadn't really said the words again, but this was love. Pure and simple. He loved her. She loved him. And as soon as he stopped getting shot for five seconds, she'd tell him that.

"I am." She leaned down and kissed his forehead. "Now listen to your woman and get ready to see a doctor."

His eyes drifted shut. "Bossy."

She kissed him again because it actually hurt not to. "And all yours."

Reid felt his stomach flip over. He heard machines and felt something clamped to his arm. A needle poking into his vein. He slowly came awake and struggled to remember what had happened.

His headache could be a weapon. It hurt to open his eyes. When he did, he looked around and took it all in. The ceiling tiles with the tiny holes. People talking in the hallway. The antiseptic smell. He was in a medical

facility of some sort. Likely one Tasha found and paid off the entire staff to keep quiet about.

His gaze kept traveling to the chair next to his bed. He expected to find it empty or see Parker. The view was so much better.

Cara, all showered and clean and in clothes that fit her. He'd never seen a more beautiful sight. She stared out the window as she hummed a familiar tune.

Maybe he'd died.

"Cara." When she turned and smiled, he wondered if he'd been right.

She got up and leaned over him. "How are you feeling?"

"A little rough." Now, there was the understatement of the century. But looking at her helped. And she smelled good. The scent of almond overcame whatever hospital cleaning supply tried to overpower the room.

She squeezed his hand. "Apparently it's bad for a grown man to be shot three times in less than a week."

"Who knew?" He tried to shrug but even that hurt.

"Uh, everyone?"

He wanted to ask her so many questions. He knew Tasha and Parker were safe. Even that guy Niko made it out somehow. The rest—the bomb and the other scientist—no part of that story ended well. A simple check-in on Cara had turned into a nightmare. The only good news is that they stopped some very bad shit.

Tasha had control of the cobalt bomb. That made being in a hospital a little more bearable.

So did Cara. He reached up and ran his fingers through her soft hair.

"It's clean now." She smiled. "Shampoo is an amazing thing. I always took it for granted before, but no more."

God, he loved her. His need for her kicked his butt. He couldn't think about going back to his apartment without her. Coming home and not seeing her. Sleeping alone. She made him smile. Challenged him. He admired so much about her . . . and that ass. Damn.

He wanted to tell her. They needed to make plans. Maybe that was stepping ahead, since they had so much to talk about, but after everything he needed her to know. A gun to his head, all those lies Mickey told that he never believed. So much had happened in such a short time. She'd likely chalk it up to adrenaline, but it was so much more.

She kissed him again. This time soft and on the lips. "You need to go back to sleep."

"No, I—"

"We'll talk later. You need your rest." She touched some piece of equipment that beeped.

He opened his mouth and his words slurred. It had to have been a painkiller. It worked fast. He couldn't feel his tongue. Then the light in the room started to fade.

When he woke up a few hours later she still sat in

the chair. He smiled and let his eyes drift shut again. The mix of medicine and blood loss did a number on him.

The same thing early the next morning. He could smell breakfast. In the quiet, watched her read a book for a few seconds. He almost said something but then exhaustion overtook him again.

By the time some of the meds wore off the next afternoon, she was gone.

24

Cara waited until she climbed into the backseat of Caleb's rental car before she said anything. Where he even got one of those in Russia, she had no idea. All she wanted to do was scream at him.

Reid had barely been in the makeshift clinic Tasha managed to set up, and already Caleb wanted her to get on a plane and go home. She refused and he insisted—actually threw his weight around and made a "do you know who I am" type of scene—that she join him outside in the parking lot for a talk. She only went because she feared his stomping around might wake up Reid and he needed rest.

She slammed the door and glared at her brother. "What is wrong with you?"

"Excuse me?" He sounded appalled at her tone.

Good. "There is an entire group of medical professionals in there, making sure Reid is comfortable since we can't actually take him to a hospital, and you were yelling at them."

Caleb scoffed. "That's an exaggeration."

"Then you started ordering me around." She shook a finger at him. "Which is never going to happen again, unless you *want* me to punch you in public."

He'd actually summoned her from Reid's bedside for a brotherly talk. The bullying came from a place of love. She got that. Caleb wanted to ask her a billion questions and protect her. She gave in and followed him once Reid finally fell asleep and stopped opening one eye to peek up at her every two seconds. He wouldn't miss her for an hour or so, but she absolutely intended to be in that room when he woke up again.

She refused to leave him until he was up, and they'd talked through all the baggage that kept weighing them down. No more separation. Not anymore. Keeping her distance from Reid for all those months had exhausted her. She'd been so sure she was right back then. Now she knew better. Now she knew *him* better, and she wouldn't rest until he understood how much more they each needed to give.

Doubts still lingered, but being together again, through the danger and in those quiet times just between the two of them, he had done everything—everything—right. He asked for answers and listened when she gave them. He tried to explain his point of view. And when attackers came into her life again, he'd rushed to save her. Put her life before his over and over again. Broke rules and showed her how much she meant to him.

For a second time, life threw her together with him in an adrenaline stew. Energy and danger whipped around them for almost three days. It wasn't real life. It was this bizarre twisting mess that had her emotions boiling over and her confidence sliding all over the place. But the chaos could lead to something bigger. This time she'd throw all of her energy into the task.

They needed to start with the basics. She needed to ask for a second chance and finally tell him what she should have said back then and certainly should have said yesterday. She loved him. Totally and forever loved him. She'd tried to stomp it out and pretend it didn't exist, but it just grew. Now it bubbled over.

First she had to deal with an overbearing older brother. "You have a lot of explaining to do."

Caleb turned to face her in the backseat. "I was thinking the same thing about you."

"Don't do that." She refused to play this game and be his poor sick little sister. "I was here on a job. I'm a professional, have a doctorate. I do not need babysitting."

"Except by Reid." Caleb fiddled with the door handle. Not one to sit still for long, he tended to fidget and touch things and generally hover on the brink of doing something that got him in trouble. Despite that, she was the kid everyone coddled. Never mind that he'd once been arrested, not her.

"Make your point." She loved her brother, but he hovered dangerously close to being punched.

The door handle came off in his hand and he dropped it to the floor. "You almost got killed."

"Caleb—"

"It was crazy irresponsible for you to come here."

No, they were not going to approach the conversation like that. She refused to get shoved onto the defensive. She had a career she loved and she would not apologize for it. "You don't get to decide what I do with my life and which risks I take."

His eyes narrowed. "We're talking about you working for the CIA."

"Hypocritical much?"

"What?" But the truth played across his face.

"Apparently you work for the Alliance on the side. Funny how you forgot to mention that." She could bat verbal volleys back and forth all day. Could but didn't want to. She wanted to get back to Reid and continue repairing the rift between them. It took all she had to sit in that car and not run to him now. "You think I didn't figure that out?"

Caleb looked out the window. "It's not the same thing."

"It is." When he started to say something else, she cut him off. "End of discussion."

"Fine."

She waded into the one issue that might get stuck between them, but he needed to know where she stood. Needed to know that if Reid would forgive her, she wanted him in her life.

She reached over and touched Caleb's knee. "You know I love you. Even your overbearing big brother crap."

"You're not exactly easy." When she pinched him, he jerked his arm away. "Fine. I love you, too."

"I know you don't get my relationship with Reid and—"

"No." Caleb's head shot around and he stared at her. "You've got it all wrong."

The blank expression, the confusion, threw her off. "He carries a gun and goes on assignments. I get that the danger worries you."

"Sure it does, but Reid is rock solid."

"I know." So, for some reason they were having a fight over something they agreed about? She had no idea when her world shifted. The last sixteen months had been a series of emotional body blows. Now she saw nothing but hope stretched out in front of her.

Caleb frowned at her. "Okay."

"You're saying you like Reid?"

"Why do you think I called him to help find you?" Caleb plowed forward, answering his own question. "Yeah, the tracker was part of it, but I knew he'd get to you as fast as possible."

"You hoped." Maybe a part of her secretly hoped. She could admit that now.

"No, Cara. I knew." This time he traced a finger over the window before giving her eye contact again. "I've

been talking to him during the last sixteen months. Feeding him information about you that he pretended not to care about. Saw the way his eyes lit up when I mentioned your name before he rushed to hide his interest."

The truth smacked into her. "You've been matchmaking?"

Her brilliant gamer brother. Now that didn't fit at all.

"You sure as hell haven't made it easy." Caleb's voice lowered to normal levels. "But I knew he loved you."

"I hoped he did." Thinking about the possibility now sent a rush of happiness spiraling through her.

"Since you were so miserable, I figured you loved him, too. Especially since you refused to talk about him." Caleb shook his head. "You're stubborn as hell."

That was fair. "Guilty."

Running scared was not a way to handle a relationship. She might blame adrenaline and the skepticism over falling in love so fast and a host of other factors, but her fear played a huge role.

"Then why did you leave him months ago?"

Wrong man. This was not the conversation she needed to have with her brother. There was only one man who needed to hear what she had to say. "There were a lot of reasons and none of them are your business."

Caleb leaned his head back against the seat. "Is he good to you?"

Her heart softened at the question. He really was being an overprotective big brother, but in a very normal, very sweet way. "The best."

He shook his head. "I will never understand women."

"Reid says stuff like that, too." Maybe the men in her life were more alike than she wanted to admit.

Neither of them said anything for a minute. They sat in silence, staring at each other. She itched to get up and move. To leave the uncomfortable quiet.

"So, you're going to stop all this nonsense and jump back in a relationship with him?"

That question set off a churning anxiety inside of her that made her dizzy. She could shore up her confidence and march over to Reid and he could say no. He might have had enough. She couldn't really blame him if he did . . . but she would fight for him anyway.

"I'm not letting him go." She became more indignant about that the longer she sat there.

Caleb tapped his fingers against the seat cushion between them. "Why are you here with me instead of with him?"

The question drove right to that dark place inside her. "Because you said you needed to talk . . . right?"

"So?"

She didn't understand the comment. "So?"

"Don't assume he'll always be there. Don't take whatever you have for granted." Caleb reached over and squeezed her hand.

"Are you trying to teach me a lesson?"

"Maybe." He smiled at her. "Go get him. And you can consider that an order if it makes it happen faster and with less hand-wringing."

She opened the door to get out just as a truck rushed by her. She wrote it off to medical personnel switching shifts. "I might just tie him to the bed until he listens to me."

"You can get kidnapped and track down bombs but you can't keep one man in a hospital bed without restraints? That's sad, sis."

"You're as much of an idiot as he is."

Caleb leaned over the back of the seat in front of him and picked up a set of keys. He held them up. Let them jangle. "Last chance to leave with me."

She remembered the feel of Reid's fingers through her hair. The way he whispered her name right before he kissed her. How good it felt to be in his arms again. "I'm exactly where I need to be."

Caleb winked at her. "Then get out."

That sounded like a good plan to her. "We'll see you at home."

Caleb's eyebrow lifted. "We?"

"It's time Reid met Mom and Dad." The idea scared her. They might hate each other. She could get trapped in the middle, but it didn't matter. Her choice was clear now.

"Poor Reid." Caleb made a tsk-tsking sound. "I almost feel sorry for him."

Reid seriously considered ignoring the knock at the door. He'd snuck out of the medical clinic Tasha set up and headed for the hostel she took over. Tasha was out working on the lab but she'd called, demanding he return to the clinic. So had Parker. Even threatened to plunge him in a cobalt bath.

Hell, most of the Alliance checked in and told him to get his head out of his ass. Amazing how many of them used those actual words.

But he couldn't. Not after waking up alone in that bed. He'd drifted off with Cara by his side. Now and then he'd wake up and to a nurse's poking. That last time he thought he heard Caleb's voice. And now Cara was gone.

Once again, when it came time for Cara to pick someone, she didn't pick him. She ran to her brother. Walked away from them.

The realization made him homicidal. It was a shame Mickey was dead because he'd be a good target right now.

So, no. Company was a bad fucking idea. He wasn't in the mood for one of Tasha's pep talks or Parker's stories. Every part of him ached. If he moved his head too fast he almost dropped to his knees in pain. But that didn't stop him from wanting to slam things and break furniture.

They were in an information lockdown while Tasha

and both the UK and U.S. governments got the formalities and details settled about the cobalt research. One wrong move and Russia would find out it was sitting on military intel about a bomb that could change the literal makeup of power in the world. That not everything blew up in that secret location up north.

And they weren't the only problem. The CIA wanted to come in and look around. The only thing that stopped them was the number of dead bodies and the preference that Tasha handle everything in case her work backfired. Plausible deniability and all that. Of course, the CIA didn't know the lab actually existed, which helped to keep the officers away. For now.

The knock sounded again and he started counting to ten. Being alone in the room made him think about Cara. About how he'd done everything he could and still came up short.

At the third knock he ripped the door open. She stood there, wide-eyed and clean. She'd clearly showered and her hair was damp. Shiny face, full lips . . . he almost slammed the door just to get away from her.

"What?" Admittedly, that greeting was not much better.

"May I come in?"

Her husky voice licked across his balls. Even pissed off, he wanted her. Seeing her made the heaviness inside him feel lighter.

All of that was reason alone to say no. He should

have backed away. Probably should have gotten a room somewhere else. He hadn't given her the room number. He guessed Parker sneaked her that information. Or Tasha. For being so tough, she did like to play matchmaker. He had no idea why because love sucked.

After an internal debate he did what he was always going to do and stepped aside. Gave Cara room to come inside. Then he had to fight the urge to step out and leave her in there by herself.

It was all juvenile bullshit, but right now he couldn't stand to be this close to her. They'd spent more than two days rekindling . . . or so he thought. For her it was likely just another few rounds of sex. Nothing more.

He hoped the next assignment took him to China or Tahiti. Anywhere far away. A place where the noise would drown out the memory of her voice.

"You're not saying anything." She stood just inside the door and closed it behind her. She didn't venture closer. Didn't look around or engage him in mindless banter.

That was a relief in the midst of all the numbness. "I'm talked out."

She stepped away from the wall. Took a few steps forward, which sent him walking backward. He didn't want to run or to dance, but being right on top of her wasn't the answer either.

Not that the room allowed for much space. It held a double bed and a dresser. Nothing else. Just a thin trail

leading from the bed to the door. And she was standing in the middle of it.

"I still don't know why you're here." But he did. This was the second goodbye and it would shred him just like the first one did.

"Reid, listen. We need—"

"Why the hell can't you just let me love you?" The question slipped out. It had been clawing inside him, begging for release. Now it was out there.

Not on a whisper either. He basically yelled it in a voice loud enough to shake the walls. When she didn't say anything, he pushed one more time. "You are so damned difficult and all I want to do is make things good for you."

"I want that, too."

"You push me away. You find excuses." He shook his head then stopped. "You are the most stubborn . . . wait, what did you say?"

She reached out, but he held up both hands, silently pushing her away. He had to. It was a form of self-protection. No one had ever gotten to him like this. He'd spent his life closed off and alone. With her, he hoped for something else.

Desperation clawed at him. "Tell me what's going on."

"I'm sorry." Sadness welled in her eyes. "You loved me and gave me all you could and I stomped all over it. Threw it away, or tried to."

She had the right to do that. She didn't have to

love him. "That's over. It's in the past and we need to forget it."

"It's not."

He had no idea what that meant. "Cara, I can't keep doing this with you."

This time when she took a step toward him, he didn't throw up an emotional wall fast enough. When her hand flattened against his stomach, he flinched. Not because he didn't want her to touch him but because he wanted it so much.

He ached for her. Months of waiting and hoping. He'd gone after her. Tried to call, but she was off on this field assignment or that one. She kept him at a distance. Just thinking about how lost he felt ticked him off. She took his control and smashed it and now she . . . hell, he didn't know what she was doing.

He reached for her hand, thinking to push it away, but he held on. "I know you need something else. Someone else."

It physically hurt to say the words. Every syllable sliced through him. The pain in his gut grew until he thought he'd double over. If this was love, he didn't want it.

"We met during this crazy time. We met again a few days ago during another adrenaline-pumping mess."

He was starting to hate that word. "You think it was all fake or something. I get it."

She shot him a sad smile. "You don't."

"Explain it to me." One last time then he'd never have to hear this infuriating argument again. "Just say it and then go."

"I love you."

His brain was playing tricks on him. He wanted to say something but the words refused to form in his head.

She squeezed his hand. "Totally, completely, so stupid I can't see straight in love with you."

"I thought you . . ." That's all he had. Nothing else came to him.

She stepped in even closer and wrapped her arms around his neck. The move brought his chest tight against hers. "I made a terrible mistake letting you go. I had reasons and they made sense at the time, but I am asking you to forgive me. To give me another chance."

"Together?" His brain refused to work.

"This isn't going away. I expected my feelings to fade or die off but they got stronger."

"You love me." He got stuck there. It was a big point, one he didn't quite believe.

"Completely." She dropped a quick kiss on his nose. "Like, I'm miserable without you. That kind of love. The minute I saw you again I knew the feelings between us weren't about aftermath or whatever you guys call it."

"Just sex."

"No, baby." Her fingers slipped into his hair. "It's so

much more than that, and I was ready to tell you that when you escaped the clinic."

He rested his forehead against hers. Just for a second. "I couldn't be there without you."

"I wasn't gone." She kissed his cheek. "I love you and I'm not going anywhere. All I need is for you to give me a chance."

"Love." He still couldn't wrap his head around it. He'd loved her from the start, strong and clear. She hedged and he tried to make allowances, but once she left, he couldn't put it back together. Now this.

"It lingered. Never went away." She shook her head. "It actually grew stronger until it beat like this steady rhythm inside of me."

Everything he wanted sat right there, right at his fingertips. But he'd been here before. He wanted her to understand the road might not be easy. If she wanted out, this was the time. "You're not worried you're taking a risk? I ran the streets as a kid and did some bad things."

She put a finger over his lips. "You can tell me what you want to tell me about your past. None of it matters because I know and love the man in front of me."

"But—"

"There is no test you need to pass. Take the time you need."

The heaviness inside him cleared. That clenching in his gut finally eased. "You're not going to like everything you hear. Parts of my past are pretty shitty."

She smiled at that. "Believe it or not, I'm not perfect."

He froze. "I'm afraid to respond to that."

"We're both going to mess up, Reid." She kissed him then. A lingering kiss full of promise. One that started a slow burn and heated fast. "This time I want to mess up together."

"That's weirdly romantic."

She laughed, full and rich, and for the first time since she walked in sounding genuinely happy. "I do love you. All of you. You are the best man I know."

He believed her. He could feel it in the way she held him and hear it in her voice. It practically bubbled out of her. "And I love you. All of you and forever."

She pulled back and stared at him. "You get what I'm saying, right? Meet the parents. Move in together. Plan a future. I want all of it."

Surprise spun inside him. He thought she'd want to baby-step. Do her version of a science experiment on their romance. "That's a pretty big commitment."

"You're the right man for me."

The words sparked something inside him. "I'll give you everything. Protection, love—whatever you want, it's yours."

Need whipped around him and he leaned in for a kiss. Not a small one. No, he planned for this to lead somewhere.

She pulled back just before his lips touched hers. "You need to go back to the clinic."

"Oh, that's not happening."

"Let's make a deal." Her fingers skimmed over his neck and down to the top button of his shirt. "We take a little time to make up then we both go back. As soon as you get the okay to leave, we both go. Until then, we're together."

The words spun in his mind. "I can probably live with that."

She shot him a sexy little smile. "Any chance you have another condom?"

He swore. "No."

Her fingers plowed into his hair, tickled his neck. "Then we'll have to improvise."

"I'll use my tongue." He couldn't fight a smile. "I'm very good with my tongue."

A tremor ran through her. "Will I be naked?"

"Oh, you'll definitely be naked."

"Then get busy, sweet talker."

"Yes, ma'am."

25

THEY FINALLY made it back to the hatch and the secret underground lab the next day. Just thinking about that description made Cara shake her head. Somedays she felt as if she went to sleep in that tent and woke up in the middle of a wild, out of control movie.

Activity buzzed around her now as she stood by a table and watched everyone else work. Caleb hadn't left and worked with Parker to break down the equipment according to her specifications. Reid stood next to her carefully putting rocks in containers, just like she asked.

Being in charge felt good. Not that she really was. Tasha ran this show. She issued orders that had them all jumping. The main one was that she needed the lab cleared immediately and all of their butts on a private plan two hours from now.

That was fine with Cara. She was ready to leave Russia behind. Her hand brushed against Reid's and he stopped frowning at a piece of limestone long enough

to smile at her. Yeah, she was not leaving him behind. Not this time. Not ever again.

The fear of committing to him still rattled her insides. The idea of pulling her life apart and making room for him both thrilled and terrified her. She worried she wouldn't live up and be what he needed. But he believed and she would lean on that until all of the rest of that old baggage fell away.

With every new kernel of information he'd shared last night in bed, her love and respect for him grew. He headed into danger because he believed it was his calling. And he insisted she was his forever. A woman could not ask for more than that.

"I'm ready to leave Russia." Parker looked up at Tasha from his seat on the floor. "And I mean forever. I haven't enjoyed any part of my time here."

Reid wrapped an arm around Cara and brought her close against his side. The kiss in her hair lingered. "I thought it was pretty great."

Parker snorted. "Because you got the girl."

"I think he actually always had the girl," Caleb said as he wrapped up cables and disconnected every line.

"We're going with the word girl?" Cara smiled as she scolded. Couldn't help it. Despite some of the knuckle-dragging tendencies, she loved this group.

Tasha walked around the room gathering up notes and stacking them in her arms. "I find it easiest to ignore them when they're like this."

"I'll sleep better knowing you're in charge of the research and intel." And Cara meant that. Tasha ran a winning operation without sacrificing who she was. Cara thought she might be able to pick up a pointer or two on how to handle Alliance men and not lose herself in the process.

"So, what happens now?" She got that they were packing up and going, but that left a lot of unanswered questions in Cara's mind.

Parker lifted a fist into the air. "The cavalry arrives."

For some reason that answer made Cara more twitchy, not less. "You don't mean an actual cavalry, right?"

"No." Tasha folded her arms over the files pressed to her chest. "Russian diplomats and American diplomats will get together and shake their heads and insist neither knew about a rogue madman being on the ground. Eventually they'll decide the talk of a lab was a rumor, maybe planted by terrorists and meant to scare everyone."

"That's comforting." Cara decided right then she would never understand or enjoy politics. The idea that people would get in a room and actually debate whether to keep the lab running made her temperature spike.

"Someone at the CIA will also be asking questions about where all the research notes and cobalt went to since they won't be able to find any trace of anything," Caleb said as he stood up.

Now that made her feel better. "Oh, really?"

"I'm afraid that's about to go missing." Tasha pointed at the ceiling. "Then this lab will collapse."

"You can make that happen?" It was a stupid question. Tasha conjured up weapons and helicopters in a country she didn't live in. One explosion wouldn't be that hard for her. Cara thought that was probably a good thing even though it sounded bad.

Tasha shrugged. "It's my job."

"And Niko?" Cara hated to admit that she barely cared about her one-time boss.

"I saved his life and uncovered a thief in his business, so for the time being he's decided not to try to kill me." Tasha rolled her eyes. "I've decided to watch him, but it's clear he wasn't in on the cobalt plan."

"The CIA won't get ticked off about all of this?" Not that Cara cared about that either, but she did wonder. After all, she'd been sent here to do a job. She did a version of it, but the CIA might not see it that way.

Reid nodded. "Oh, definitely. There will be all kinds of pissing and moaning. But sometimes things get destroyed in the middle of a firefight."

He sounded a bit too amused by the explanation. His assurance touched off hers. "And you guys can sell that?"

Parker pointed at Tasha. "She will and no one wants to tick her off."

"Damn straight," Tasha said. "But the bottom line

is some other members of the Alliance who have been sitting the action out in Germany and are itching to get in here will make all remaining signs of this disappear. The compound, the expedition, the mine. All of it."

"In a really big bonfire."

Cara knew Parker was kidding, but still . . . "Please don't burn the cobalt."

"There are vaults for this sort of thing." Reid's fingers slipped into her hair.

She loved his touch. Actually craved it. "That's probably more than I need to know."

This time he kissed her cheek. "You're part of the team now."

"Wait a second." Parker laughed as he stood up. "Isn't one Layne sibling around here enough? We're already stuck with Caleb and his part-time computer hacking."

"I hate that term," Caleb mumbled under his breath.

Cara decided not to take the bait. Her brother had been working for the Alliance on and off and not telling her. Had been in contact with Reid while she sat at home brooding. Of all the things she needed to let go, that was at the top of the list.

Reid smiled down at her. "It's enough for me."

Throughout the last twenty-four hours he'd told her how much he loved her. How much he missed her and hated the months they'd spent apart. Every promise was right there in his eyes. Gone was the frustration and she welcomed the change.

She went into his arms then. Laid her head on his shoulder and soaked in his warmth.

Caleb put down the laptop he'd been holding. "No kissing in the bomb lab."

"Then you might want to close your eyes." Reid turned her around until they faced each other. He spoke to the people standing around him but he looked only at her. "Because I plan on kissing her a lot."

"On the job?" Parker asked.

"Wherever she'll let me."

"Come on." Caleb groaned. "I'm standing right here."

"And I'm not going anywhere." Reid said it like a vow. Delivered it right to her while his arms rested at the small of her back.

Cara only had one clarification to that promise. "Except to our house. I'm thinking we try your place."

"I like the sound of that." Reid started to lower his head.

Parker's face popped up between Cara and Reid. "Did he mention I live next door?"

For some reason she loved that idea. "I find that strangely comforting."

Reid frowned at her. "You shouldn't."

They could argue about that another time. The way she saw it she inherited the whole team when she got Reid. This time she'd propose to him. Make sure he was happy and ready and then ask. Because she knew this was right. He was her forever.

And she was ready to start her future right now. "It's time to go."

Parker hadn't moved. "And on the way I can explain to you why it's clear Yetis are real."

"Is he kidding?" she asked Reid. Because there was only so much nonsense she could take and she feared she'd reached her limit.

He shrugged. "Pretend to be asleep."

Curled up next to him. Maybe on his lap. She liked the sound of all of that. "I'd be willing to do almost anything for you."

Reid shoved Parker out of the way and kissed her. Really kissed her. Deep and full of hope. By the time she lifted her head she wanted to be on that plane.

She smiled up at him. "Take me home."

ACKNOWLEDGMENTS

Book ideas come from strange places. This one came from reading about a decades-old incident in the Ural Mountains of Russia and the death of a group of hikers. A special thank you to the book *Dead Mountain: The Untold True Story of the Dyatlov Pass Incident* by Donnie Eichar for planting the seed that led to this work of pure fiction.

A heartfelt thank you to Walt Stone for answering all of my geology questions, even the really basic ones like, "talk to me about limestone . . ." Your help was invaluable. All of the mistakes about geology are mine because you really tried to educate me.

My deepest gratitude goes to May Chen for being the amazing, enthusiastic, and thoughtful editor she is. And to everyone at Team Avon who work so hard on all of my books—thank you!

A final thank you to my agent, Laura Bradford, and my husband, James. You are the two people who make my writing life easier.

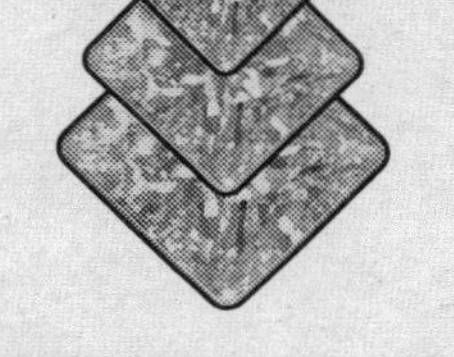

By HelenKay Dimon

Bad Boys Undercover

UNDER THE WIRE
FACING FIRE
FALLING HARD
PLAYING DIRTY
RUNNING HOT (novella)

He smiled a

Her gaze [illegible] scarred chest and down to his flat stomach. "You're still the most attractive man I've ever seen."

"Did you hit your head?"

Not just his body, which was *hot damn* impressive. The imperfect face with high cheekbones and a firm chin. Intelligent if a little too knowing eyes that mirrored all the pain he'd seen.

Rather than destroy him or make him distrust people, he thrived on loyalty to his team. Strong, solid, and so secretive.

He held a hand out to her and she went to him without even debating. Her fingers rested on his shoulders then slipped around his neck. When his lips touched hers, a series of tiny explosions went off inside her. His mouth pressed against hers, deepening and coaxing as she fell into his touch.

They were a mess and hurt and still in danger. They stood in a cave with a mile of old emotionally charged baggage stacked between them. There were so many reasons not to drop into this abyss a second time. So many ways this could go wrong to the point where she couldn't regain her footing again.

But the kiss raged on.